THE DIARY
OF
LEE HARVEY
OSWALD

A NOVEL

SIMON FOSTER

September 2020
Copyright © 2020 by Simon Foster. All rights reserved.

Dedication

For my daughters, with love.

Acknowledgments

Thanks go to my friend, Serge, for his encouragement on this and other works.

To my wife, Sandy, for her cover design, love and support — not necessarily in that order.

And to the job that often took me to Dallas, where I first realized that the only person who hasn't spoken about that tragic Friday afternoon in November 1963 is the alleged killer himself.

Report on Officer's Duties in Regards to
Oswald's Death
Detective J.R. Leavelle - #736
Sunday, 11/24/1963

Approximately 11.15 am we left the third floor
office with Oswald handcuffed to my left arm
with Detective L. C Graves holding to Oswald's
left arm, preceded to the jail elevator by
Captain Fritz, Lt. Swain, Detective L. D.
Montgomery. We reached the basement jail
office with officers in front we headed to the
automobile ramp just outside the jail office
door. We hesitated just inside the jail door
then was given the all clear sign. We walked
out and had just reached the ramp the car we
were to ride in was being backed into position
by Detective Dhority when out of the mass of
humanity comprised of all the news media,
which had surged forward to within six or seven
feet of us, came the figure of a man with a
gun in his hand. He took two quick steps and
double actioned a .38 revolver point blank at
Oswald. I jerked back on Oswald, at the same
time reaching out and grabbing Jack Ruby on
the left shoulder, shoving back and down on
him, bringing myself between Ruby and Oswald.

I could see Det. Graves had Ruby's gun hand and gun in his hands. I turned my attention to Oswald and with the help of Det. Combest we took Oswald back into the jail house and laid him down. Handcuffs were removed and the city hall doctor, Dr. Bieberdorf was summoned.

F.B.I. Record of Interview
Frederick A. Bieberdorf, Medical Student
Dallas, 12/6/63

BIEBERDORF advised that while he was with
OSWALD in the jail lobby basement until he left
him in the Emergency Room of Parkland Hospital
that OSWALD failed to make any statements
whatsoever.

Friday, Midnite

Junie befor I tell you how I cum to be sitting alone in this prison sell the eyes of the world upon me I must apolgize for any misstakes you mite find herein. Ordinarly I wood rerite endlessly use a dicshunry to correck spelling also pollish punctuashun grammer this is my usule kustom regarding importent corespondense to embassys and such. The Historic Diary of my days in Russia I revised menny times on the jurney home from Minsk the govt unfarely refoosing to pay for plane tikkets despite my erlier serviss to the cuntry leeveing me you and your Mama stranded upon a slow mooveing rust bukket the SS Maasdam. Howevver as usule I took full advantage of sed situashun consoomed an abundense of the ships stashunry completeing the diary also prepareing responses for any repporters wateing upon our arrival. The latter did not amuont to a hill of beens no press matereelised at the warf in Hobokin or wen we later flew on to Fort Wurth jus my bruther Robert wateing with a bunch of wilted roses in hand for your Mama.

It is becumming increesingly cleer that I will hav much less time to rite this missiv than my historic diary. I hav herd my kaptors tawk of transfering me to the cuonty jale over the weekend if that is the case I will shurely be serched uppon arrival so must finnish riteing this befor then misstakes be dammed. Menny former teechers hav tole me that poor riteing shows a lak of inteligense I vigorosly disagree. A lot of well red men are ignorent to the ways of the world wile conversly menny men who cood not reed nor rite there own name hav left there mark on histry. Gengis Karn was probly not much of a skolar yet regardless of wot one thinks of his exployts no one can qesshun his lasting effeck on the world. Junie you will soon see that your papa is also a man of grate deeds. I mite be self tort in my lernings but I can see solushuns to the worlds problems that other men can not resent events only serveing to prove same.

I am drivven to get the events of the past days down on paper for sevral reesons. Firstly I mite never get the chanse to explane to you wot reely happened today more importently why. The Dallas PD the FBI the secret serviss they all hav me in there cluches now who knos how that mite end. I dont wish to suond allarmist Junie but I cood disapeer in a hartbeet US agensys no better than there Russian cuonterparts in this respeck. Even befor todays events FBI agents acosted me sevral times cost me at least one good paying job. That mungrel Hasty also twise harassed your mama in her own home thretening to send her pakking bak to Russia furthermoor he sugested that I may be mently disterbed nuthing cood be further from the trooth I never wood hav acheeved wot I hav if not for the suondest of minds.

Junie these riteings shood also help you remember me shood we part ways for any length of time. As much as I hope that does not transpir it is now a distink posibilty. My own father a humbel insurense salesman died jus munths befor I was born I therefor kno wot it is to go thru life without one. To not kno my father his innamost thorts his dreems his desires left a hole in me my mother cood never fill altho she was also fuond wanting in menny other respecks. I will do evrything in my power to make shure same does not happen to you I will get these riteings to you sumhow. Wen leeving Russia I wore the pages of my Historic Diary strapped to my stummick easly eludeing the Brest authoritees sumthing simler cood work here. Perhaps I can repeet same slip it to your Mama wen she cums to visit. Then this diary will be yours forever a keepsake to cumfort you during any time we spend apart wich I freely admit may now be considrable. Shood that happen you will hav this diary also the pitcher Mama took in the bak yard at W Neely St me with my guns you can use that to recall my feetures as memrys qikly fade. Your mama never understood why I wanted that foto taken we quareled endlessly until she rellented. Of corse I knoo one day it wood cum in handy well that day has well and trooly arived. I made sevral copys of the foto at work the neks day rote on the bak of one For Junie From Papa. Thats wot this diary is also For Junie from Papa.

Rite now it is jus after midnite Friday. Five minits ago Fritz the lokal homiside captin a stokky fella set like a chargeing bull short legs wide slopeing sholders thik eyeglases perched under his Stetson marcht me bak to my sell on the 5th floor a gard flanking each sholder. A press conference has jus ended abruply Curry the polise cheef aserting I hav been charged with killing the president wen in fack I hav not. It is troo I hav been charged with killing the cop. Altho I hav not admitted same it is hardly surpriseing as menny eye witnesses saw that unfortunat chane of events howevver prooveing I shot the president will be much more diffcult.

I will be bak soon Mister Oswald Fritz sed slamming the bars shut leeveing a uniform man stashuned outside on a mettal chare barely large enuff to contane his fat behind it droops over the edges.

Sinse they ambooshed me inside the theeter I hav been held captiv at polise hedqarters in the old city hall on Sth Harwood and Mane. Between barages of qesshuns from Fritz not to menshun rigged showups I am lokked in a mettal box that smells of other mens bizness green walls steel toylet (no seet) sink with brokken hot water tap two bunk beds that fold down from the wall. The pantework is flakeing and scared with grafiti eg John was here. Vry orignal John. My sell sits on the end of a ro the rest left emty wich soots me jus fine I wood no dout suffer a constent streem of abuse were they not. On the other side of my sell beyond the steel bars sits a windo thru wich shos the dark nuthing of nite.

Appart from keeping me seprated from other prisners the authoritees are treeting me no better than a petty crimnal. One wood think that if they trooly beleeve I am gilty of there accussashuns I wood be showen a litle more respeck it is not evry day sumone manages to shoot a president. Howevver overall I am in fine shape save for a cut over my left eye a woond sustaned wen sevral polise offissers wressled me to the gruond inside the theeter. I do not like to boste Junie but it took six men to subdew me.

Who knos how long I will now spend in sells like this I cood care less in the Marines I slept in crampt dorms also did a strech or two in the brig I hav also stayed menny nites at the downtown YMCA wich wile cheep is in trooth not much better than a lokkup. If I hav to do serius time in a cage then so be it. As I menshunned there has been tawk of mooveing me to the cuonty jale aparently standerd oprating proceedure in these parts onse a person has been charged. We shall see if the moove ever happens these idiots can take forevver to orgnize anything a walk to a showup can take therty minits navigateing the press hullabaloo in the hallway an ardewus task indeed. I take evry chanse to tell the reporters barking at me like dogs that I hav not been formly charged with killing the president the way I am running rings around Fritz I probly never will.

Fritz is tawking a good game with reggards to Kennedy he is carm colekted relentless with his qesshuns howevver underneeth it all I am shure he is as big a fool as the rest of the Dallas PD. Sevral munths ago I took a potshot at Genral Walker a rite wing manniac who heds up the John Birch sosiety a man so set in his conservtiv ways he cood be the neks Hitler. Afterwerds the Dallas PD ran aruond like keestone kops there evry moove incorreck. The neks day evven tho reeding can be qite a chor for me I took grate plessure in perooseing the Dallas Morning News lerning of there missgided exployts falsly identifying the bullit as 30.06 it was 6.5mm takeing at fase vallue a witness who clamed he saw a getaway car rore off down Turtel Creek Blvd. I dont even hav a drivers lisense ha. Of corse in the grate U.S. of A one must allways drive a car it wood never occur to the cops that a man mite use his own two feet to ekscape the seen of a crime. Only a fool wood ride the bus home after makeing an attemp on a mans life well to wit one fool who they did not lay a finger on.

I hav not yet tole Fritz a wurd about the clensing or the shooting of the cop aparently his name was Tipit. So far I hav manetaned a poker fase desideing to wate untill I hav the worlds ear befor speeking. For yeers I hav tryed to sekure publisity for my cawse first fleeing to Russia then fuonding a branch of the Fair Play for Cuba commitee in New Orleens. All I hav to sho for my eforts are a few minits on TV and a farsical raydio interveiw in New Orleens the host ambooshing me acooseing me of being a communist wich is ludikrus I am of corse a Marxist. Also the Walker insident an asasinashun attemp on one of the most famus men in Dallas bearly rated a menshun in the papers the story qikly disappeering that tort me a sallutry lesson a bigger deed was reqired to take the bigger stage that I now ocoopy and from wich I will soon hold forth.

But in case that day never cums Junie for reesons outlined previus I hav devised other plans. Arriveing bak in Fritzs offise after the first showup I shook my rists as tho they aked convinsed Elmer one of my polise eskorts to remoove the cuffs for a spell. Sevral reporters had pushed there way into the room the kaos of flashing camras and shuoting for onse worked in my faver. As Fritzs men manhandelled them out the door I grabbed a notebook stuffed it down the frunt of my pants folowed same with pen. I spose a man of my ingenooity cood now use the pen as a weppon a meens of excape but I woodnt get far thru the croud in the hallway besides I hav a much better use for it.

Evry man in the Dallas PD is crazed the atenshun of the worlds press upon them they are small men cort in a hooge momment. I figgered they wood not think to serch me aggen befor takeing me to my sell as usule I figgered correck. Now I sit in the small hours faceing the korner of the sell riteing furiusly to you Junie my bak hunched agenst the eyes of the gard sitting sentree outside the door.

Thursday

I wake erly not like your mama who I kno is still sleeping suondly even tho we are miles apart. She will happly slepe the morning away howevver I hav allways been an erly riser today being no exsepshun I brissle with nervuss energy for wot tomorow mite bring.

My bedroom in the rooming house on Nth Beckly is no more of a prize than this sell messureing twelve feet by six feet max four flor to seeling windos along one side cuvered by blinds and lace curtens. An aircondishuner fills one windo seldum hav I put it into serviss in the munth sinse I mooved in the summer heet has passed fall now upon us. The room was probly not bilt as a bedroom more likly a storidge huch off of the dineing room seprated by dubbel doors. A singel bed a cubbord a side tabel with lamp are all that fit I cood tuch both walls with my arms outstrecht howevver for $8 a week inclooding refridgerater and liveing room privliges I hav no complaynts. The howse itself is vry large an expansiv livving room fansy red roof I am shure it was considdered qite grand in its day.

After reterning from my illfated trip to Mexico City sevral

munths ago too ashammed to call your mama after being refoosed entry to Cuba I stayed at the downtown YMCA on Nth Ervay. Shortlee thereafter I mooved to cheeper acomodashuns in Oak Cliff. You Junie your Mama and baby Rachel after her arrivel hav stayed with the Pains in Irving sinse Rooth Pain drove yall bak from New Orleens a few days befor I left for Mexico. I wood luv to be with yall but Oak Cliff is far closser to my job downtown also lately your mama and me hav been argewing bitterly there is a considrabel golf between us more of wich I will later explane as that has played no small part in wot has transspired.

You are of corse too yung to remember but we also livved on Elsbeth St and W Neely St in Oke Cliff pryor to mooveing to New Orleens. Elsbeth St was not to my tast a brik box with ten apartments I spent a lot of time slipping out the bak entranse to avoyd the naybors. Howevver W Neely I enjoyed considrably it bosted a small offiss ware I cood colleck my thorts of an evening also a wite timber balcunee ware I cood sit of an afternoon bounseing you on my knee or letting you play with a rattel on a blanket wile I sipped Dr Pepper. I wood hav not a care in the world unless your mama ignooring her huosehold dootys joyned us interupting my thorts. Howevver dispite sum bad memrys I always liked Oak Cliff wile its huoseing and inhabbitents are poor working class the area itself is cleen cheep and holds grate convenense for those travling downtown for there employ. In my partiklar case the book depossitry is huosed in the Sexton Bldg on the western edge of downtown bearly two miles as the cro flys from Oak Cliff a fifteen minit bus ride across the Hooston viaduck of a morning and afternoon does the trik.

Most days I partake of brekfast in the kichen if anuther roomer alreddy ocupys same then in my room percht on my bed jus a simpel cup of blak coffee wile reeding a book is all I need. My previus landlady an old cro called Mrs Bledsow on Marselis St had an ishew with storeing food in the fridge over this we parted ways on vry bad turms in fack the mizer still owes me two dollars in overpade rent. I am shure that mungrel Hasty also had moor than a litle to do with Bledsows change of hart he and anuther FBI agent came sniffing aruond aksing awkward qeusshuns about me. Wen I mooved to my currant room I took the wise precorshun of registring under the name O H Lee to thro Hasty off the trak. An old but effectiv trik I pickt it up from How To Be A Spy perhaps now I will rite my own espeenage manwell ha. Howevver this taktic of employing a fake name unfortoonately cawsed ferther bad blud between your mama and me as you will soon see.

Mrs Jonson the landlady Mrs Roberts the cleener on Nth Beckly hold no such qalms abuot keeping food in the frige or our rooms nor shood they as I hav allways run a vry tite ship. Jus aks your mama I am qite the stikler for clennlyness. In Minsk it was I who mopped the apartment flor dayly your mama too tired after werking in the farmacy all day wile pregnent howevver I was not willing to liv in unsannitry condishuns sertenly not with a baby on the way. In New Orleens I behaved simler dedicated myself to keeping our litle apartment cleen your mama wood live in a tip if left up to her I frekwently menshun same.

Normly I am not a big brekfast person consoomeing sed coffee in my room but knoing that one way or the other today will hold sumthing speshal I treet myself to eggs at Dobbs Huose a pancake joynt a few bloks away on Nth Beckly and Collorado. I sumtimes brekfast there vry ocashonly eat dinner. A fine supper of stake french frys salad and desert can be bort for $1.25 howevver that is offen more than my meeger budget will alow I stik to the cheeper brekfast opshuns only eating dinner there onse or twise of a weekend wen not vissiting you and your Mama.

Haveing bathed the nite befor as is my kustom I thro on a wite tshert brown shert gray trowsers blak shoos grab my dark blew jakket the Dallas wether has growen considerably cooler over the past few days. I slide on my wedding ring my Marine core ring also an ID braselet that hides a scar on my left rist its cawse not my finest huor but the ends justifyed the meens. I reech up to the top shelf of the cubbord feel aruond for my Smith and Wesson .38 speshal a snub nose revolver. I take it down then put it bak a desishon I wood later cum to roo howevver I do not wish to carry a pistul aruond at work all day unless absolootly nesesry. After visiting with your mama tonite I will kno one way or the other if I need it I can allways cum bak to fetch it shood I need to proteck myself folowing the clensing.

I open the nite tabel draw ware my life saveings reside. I wedge the wod of bills into my wollet without cuonting them let myself out the frunt door. It is six thirty the rooming huose dethly qite Mrs Jonson the four or five other roomers suond asleep. The men are mostly unemployed lofers who wood not work a day if there life depended on it one of them fresh out of jale after serveing time for brake and enter the others good for nuthing layabouts who expeck the world to be handed to them on a plater. Obviusly a man of my politikal leenings suports the state takeing care of those who are unabel to do so on there own dime howevver there are definitly men who take advantige of sed gennerosty. I for good reesons and thru no falt of my own hav fuond myself on unemployment beniffits most resently in New Orleens surviveing on thirty-three dollers a week forsed to report my job seeking eforts to the Lousiana Employment Comishon evry Tewsday a report that I will freely admit contaned its fare share of ficshun. I onse stated I had applyed for employ at NASA I wood make an excelent addishun to Kennedys spase rase ha. Seriusly I do fermly beleeve that a man needs to work to hav any self respeck. That is one of the strengths of the Soviet sistem evryone is ganefuly employed altho as I lerned in the raydio faktory the work is offen far from intelectully satisfying.

Troothfully tho Junie I hav not made the other roomers acqantance vry deeply. I mostly rede in my room of a nite James Bond pollitical biografys and such. Ocashonly I wotch TV in the livving room with them reruns of I Led Three Lives howevver seldum do I engage in conversashun.

The frunt door cliks qietly shut behind me I scoot across Nth Beckly dodgeing erly rush huor traffik cars blasting there horns at me for no partiklar reeson the poyntlessness of there existanse probly the primery cawse. Hed down hands in pokkets I walk two bloks north to the diner a red seement bldg set on a promnent corner with mettal raleings skurting its exteria. Dobbs House is cheep and cheerfull always busy of a morning this one being no excepshun the parking lot is jammed with cars pikkups and comershal vehikals.

I thred my way betwene the vehikals to the frunt door. Elvis sings Bossa Nova Baby on the raydio as I approche the hostess an older woman with a beehive hare do held in plase by abuot a thuosand bobby pins.

Jus the one she says not reely aksing a qesshun.

Thats rite.

Theres only one booth left she says poynts to a spot beside a man and woman who are both sitting bak stomaks bulgeing smoke billoing from there mouths and nosstrils like puff the magic dragon. I can not stand the smell of smoke it is a most disgusting habbit also a totel waste of munny as Ive tole your mama menny times. Of corse she never lissens to me on that or in fack any other scor as you will soon see. Wen we first met she was a chane smoker gradully I cut her down to one or two a day becos of the baby altho I am sertin she still sneeks them behind my bak. I hav fuond them hidden all over the plase at the Pains even in the bathroom behind the sistern.

Anything else? I say.

She shakes her hed says Nope even the cuonter is jammed up.

I almost tern aruond walk strate bak out the door howevver a man needs to eat of a morning also I do not fansy walking bak to the rooming huose to brekfast on my bed nor the thort of hedding off to work on an emty stumik.

Takeing the booth I use a menoo to wave away the smoke as best I can. Mary one of the reglar watresses walks over a woman with a plessant fase hidden behind too much makeup her perfoom also not sparingly aplyed. Frendly enuff she seldum has time for small tawk the restorant like most commershal enterprizes run with a minimim of starf little thort givven to the working men or wimmin who must bare the brunt of the labor.

Mornin hun whatll it be?

The usule pleese eggs over easy home frys coffee.

Cummin rite up she says and off she woddles.

The smokers extingish there butts imedately fire up there neks. I cleer my throte lowdly of corse they pay me no mind.

Wots this? I say a few minits later wen Mary slides a plate in frunt of me.

Brekfast cums her reply a litle too sassy for my likeing.

I can see that but these eggs are over well I ordered over easy.

Fool that Mary is she trys to convinse me I ordered over well I am haveing nun of that. I mite not as the Chuck Berry song goes reed or rite so well but I am not stoopid also I hav been to Dobbs Huose menny times allways ordered my eggs over easy shurely she must kno same by now.

I poke the eggs with my fork they hav the consistansy of a hokky puk.

I can not eat this I say.

Now a man in a booth across the isle takes his tern to cleer his throte I see he glares at me from beneeth a polisemans hat. Not wishing to attrack the atenshun of the law I dismiss Mary with a wave of my hand start in on the eggs furius at paying hard erned munny for sumthing I did not order. Howevver wen Ricky Nelson cums on the raydio singing Fools Rush In I carm down sum. I am not a grate luvver of poplar music prefering as I do the classiks but I soon find myself humming allong thinking indede they do Ricky indeed they do.

After I finnish Mary tops up my coffee. I add a splash of swete milk to cool it off gulp it down then pay the chek fifty cents with an ekstra dime for Mary. Despite my dissatisfacshun with the meel I kno that Mary probly servives on tips I am not about to deprive her kids of food jus becos she misherd my order or more likely the short order cook was hungover at the stov.

I depart Dobbs House wate ten minits at the bus stop on W Collorado a sutherly depositting a chill in my bones after the heet of the overcrouded diner. A bus pulls up the driver is lissening to a transister raydio he drums allong to Ruby Baby on the steering weel. I slip him a nikkel he releeses the brakes heds towards the Hooston St viaduck. The razed rode curvs towards downtown the skool book depossitry soon vissibell a seven story brik warehuose on Hooston and Elm made all the more promnent by that grate capitlist blite advertizeing. A yellow billbord bolted to the roof blares Hertz Rent A Car in big red letters a clok also shos time and temprature at leest serveing sum praktical purpuss. It is 7.28 the temprature 54 degrees wen I get off at Mane and Hooston aproch the depossitry along the west side of Hooston. I cross over Elm walk past the frunt entranse to the bldg wich is manely used by the offise workers I hav only enterred those doors twise the day I was intervewed and the day I started work. I vencher a half blok ferther on Hooston enter via the lodeing dok take a half duzen stares from the dok up onto the 1st flor make strate for the domino room in the north east corner of the bldg.

The domino room is fernished with formika tabels wooden benches chares cotehooks also a shower for cleening up after work perhapps one mite be hedding strate to the opra ha. The domino room is called same becos it is ware menny of the men play dominos and cards durring the lunch brake. Personly I dont indulge there is always much smokeing and swareing not to menshun waggering and who has munny to thro away like that? I preffer to spend my lunchtime more constructivly reeding and such but like menny men my fella workers do not see the valew in lerning. I usuley partake of lunch alone in the 2nd flor lunch room it is intended manely for the use of the publishing cumpny workers who are more controled in there ways and do not seem to mind the presense of an ordinry worker. Wen the wether is hospittabel I may vencher out into Deely Plaza sit by the fuontins eat a sandwitch from home cold cuts or peenut butter and jelly. If I am feeling like Rockafeller I mite buy a newspaper also a sak of potato chips but that is not offen these days with your mama and now not one but two yung muoths to feed.

Work does not start until 8am so the domino room is allways peeceful wen I arive the other men not yet pressent sum stumbel in with only secunds to spare work obviusly not a pryoritee for them. My usule kustom is to reed any newspapers left behind from the day befor Junor Jarman or Harold Norman the mane contribbutors. I reed the papers cuvver to cuvver this can take me sum time with my reeding diffcultys I also pay extra speshul attenshun to politics and world news. The only secshun I skip is sports a trew opiat for the masses altho I do like to wotch a football game of a Sunday afternoon at the Pains they hav a brand new TV set. As I tell your mama whenever she sneers at me lyeing on the liveing room flor a man needs to relacks at the end of the working week. I genrally root for the New York Giants a habbit I pikked up as a boy living in the Bronx. The Dallas Cowboys are a rich mans toy bort to the city a few yeers ago by Clint Murchoson. Tho yet to make the playoffs I sumtimes root for them as they are the underdogs agenst the estabblishment I suport them for that reeson only sertenly not out of any grate loyallty to this town.

The same as evry day this week The Dallas Morning News is

filled with histeria about the Presidents vissit. Oh the grate and wundrus leeder of the free world has daned to visit our fare city of corse the media and the masses lap it up like cats with boles of fresh creem. I skip all the hoopla only intrested in wether any changes hav been made to the parade root announsed on Tewsday. I am not surprized to see that the changes are zeero the parade still skeduled to pass down Mane and Elm rite past the depossitry windos. Like Frank Sinatra in Sudenly I will be posishuned rite abuv ware the pressident is to pass but unlike Franky boy I did not need to plan it. Not for the ferst time I feel like forses outside my kontrol are shapeing events giveing me the oportoonity I hav been wateing for sinse reterning from Russia. I had originly thort that shooting Walker was my reeson for being or perhapps Nixon anuther target I breefly considered but I now see it is sumthing much bigger that histry has in stor for me. My mother an extreemly annoying presense to be shure her demands and constent whineing offen straned our relashunship howevver in this case perhaps she was rite she always tole me from a vry yung age that I was speshul better than the other kids destinned for grate things it seems that her theery may vry well be proved correk the parade root takeing the pressident rite past my plase of employ a sollid case in poynt.

Aruond 7.45am Billy Luvlady sum other men arive filling the domino room with shuoting and smoke. I hav soon had enuff I fold the newspaper hand it off to Charly Givvens a tall qiet blak man with a wife no chillren Charly also likes to keep abrest of currant afares.

I kill ten minits in the 2nd flor lunchroom till starting time then vissit the orders desk pik up my first job of the day. The order slips are plased by the clerk in a box labeled Scott Forsman the pubblishing cumpny I mostly pull books for. I take a qik look at the slip kno that evrything I need is on the 6th floor my sharp memry cumming in vry useful on this job. I take the frate elevater in the reer of the bldg my kustom wen hedding upstares cumming down I mite use the stares that is offen qicker.

As I exit the elevater Junor Jarman a yung negro ex-navy is loyterring agenst a post takeing his own sweet time getting started. Personly I preffer to jus get strate to work the day goes fasser that way but menny a man here seems alergic to his alotted task. I pass Junor without a word I dont convers much with the other men they dont seem to understand a lot of wot I say primmarly a lack of educashun on there part.

Snip snip Junor whisspers I smirk to sho my sense of humer altho the joke is vry tired indeed. The other men offen teese me about needing a harecut thretten to hold me down do the job thereselves. I cood do with a trim espeshally the bak of my nek howevver I hav much better things to spend muney on than makeing myself look pritty. Besides I am a marryed man it does not much matter how I look your Mama will allways be by my side that much is cristal cleer between us. If she ever mooves bak to Russia wich sum days I think wood be for the best and with resent events she may not hav much choise in the matter but eether way she is my wife she will wate for me for as long as I want divorse compleetly out of the quesshun in my veiw.

Junor Charly Givvens three or four other men hav been laying new three qarter inch plywood on the side of the bldg overlooking the raleway traks for the past few days. The old floor bares the stanes of oliv oil from the previus tenent Sextons a grosery holesaler from Chicago. The oil sokes thru the bottum of the book boxes rooning the contents hense the need for replasement of the wood. Charly and his croo make a hek of a rakket all day long hammers banging saws buzzing particals of dust danseing in the lite that streems thru the windos along Hooston of a morning and Elm of an afternoon. I do my best to shut out the suond go about my bizness wich at its simplest is take an order from the box on the 1st floor clip it to my clipbord go to the upper flors four five six or seven wherevver the text books I need to fech are stored. Then I lokate the books wich can sumtimes be a chor each flor the size of half a football feeld with thik wooden suport posts blokking the vew in menny plases. After I retreeve the books I carry them bak down to the 1st flor ware the order is prosessed for shipping. I like the job well enuff hav definitly dun worse Loov-R-Pak cutting sheet mettal with sheers cums to mind the work so menyal it drove me bananas. Also my boss here Mister Trooly is a nise man and working with books all day a reel pleasure I hav a grate respeck for them the knoledge that they hold. The job pays $1.25 an huor not bad compensashun for a job a munkey cood do with sum traneing. It also does not rekwire much comunicashun with the other men as long as I perform my dootys I am left to my own devises jus the way I like it.

The past few days Charlys croo hav mooved menny boxes over to the east side of the 6th flor stakking them to the seeling in plases so they can lay the new floring on the west side. This slos my work sum as a few boxes arent ware I recall but that doesnt bother me nun the confooshun cawsed by all the mooved boxes meens that if I shift boxes aruond to soot my purpusses tomorow morning no one will be any the wizer.

I work two sollid hours stopping jus onse or twise for brakes at the water cooler. Around 10am I drop an order in to the shipping department bump into Wesly Frazer doing same. Wesly traned me as an order filler wen I first started at the depositry it was thru his sister Linny May that Rooth Pain first herd there mite be a job opening here for me.

Mornin Wesly.

Mornin Lee how you doin?

Good. Jus wundring if I cood aks a faver of you.

Sure thing Lee he says wich is how I expeck him to respond. Wesly tall skinny pock markt cheeks is the most accomodateing kid I ever cum across. Good harted grashus to a falt. If evry nineteen yr old was like him the world wood be in better shape no dout. Wen he first lerned Mama was staying at the Pains in Irving and I at the rooming huose in Oak Cliff he offered me a ride out there whennever I wanted. Wesly livs jus down the street with his sister sleeping on her cowch till he saves up enuff munny for a plase of his own. Of corse I grashusly aksepted his offer but not onse has he aksed me for muney in return. Sevral times I offered to pay purely out of polliteness Wesly wood hav nun of that saying he was makeing the trip anyway so wot did it matter if I rode along.

Cood I get a ride home with you this afternoon? I aks fuly knoing the anser.

Well it is a litle out of my way he jokes I smile allong with him. Linny Mays huose is but a half blok from the Pains wich is how Rooth herd about the job at the skool book depositry in the first plase. One afternoon folowing my return from Mexico wen I was liveing at the YMCA despretly serching for work Rooth your mama and the nayborhood wimmen folk were all sitting aruond yakking over coffee cake wen the subjeck of my unemployment came up with the baby on the way and all. No dout there was plenny of tut tutting and oh deers then Linny May menshuned how Wesly had been doing a lot of overtime lately maybe they mite need sum more peeple down at the skool book depossitry. Well that afternoon Rooth called Mr Trooly the superviser and explaned the situashun. He sed I shood cum down the vry neks morning wich was October 15. I dewly did so introduseing myself he imediatly invited me into his offise it was pakked with fileing cabnets mettal shelves piled high with boxes the windos grimey with dust from the traffik of Hooston St trying to see past the murk like looking into a durty fishbole.

I filled out an aplicashun form wile he wotched then he took it from me.

No high skool diploma he sed reeding rite off of the page in frunt of him.

No sir I left in nineth grade to act in serviss of my cuntry.

Uh huh I see that. Marines.

Yes sir I sed looking at him a diminutiv fella with glasses substanshul ears vertikal creeses running down both cheeks. He was maybe fifty five yeers old his fase showed evry one of them. He reminded me of a shop teecher I had in high skool old Mister Hayward he was missing his left thum after getting it cort in a band saw wile makeing a coffee pot stand.

Honorabell discharg? Mister Trooly sed.

24

Yes sir I sed tho not compleetly correck the militry holding one theery as to the manner of my departur me qite anuther. Upon leeveing the marines I reseeved an honorabel discharg howevver wen the guvment fuond out I had gone to Russia and in there opinun made anti US statments they changed my discharg status to dishonorbel a compleetley unfare acshun in my book as wot I did after leeveing the marines shood hold no bearing on my discharg status whatsoevver. I stated same in a letter to Gov Conlly secretry of the navy at the time explaned that me going to live in Russia was no diffrent to Ernest Hemmingway going to live in Paris of corse a fat lode of good that did me.

Junie the trooth is that teknicly I reseeved a erly hardship discharg to care for my mother she was not well at the time needing care after takeing a nasty spill at work the sevverity of wich was sertenly open to qesshun as I had aksed her to state same promiseing I wood live with her if she helped me leeve the Marines. Of corse I did nuthing of the sort leeveing for Russia the momment my discharg pappers came thru to avoyd her usule melodramatiks.

Wot kind of jobs did you perform wile in the Marines? aksed Mister Trooly.

Manely offise work sir. I worked in radar for a wile and sum other clerikal posishuns.

Within the United States?

Yes sir. Also oversees in Japan and the Philipines.

Vry good. I beleeve it is benefishal to travel the world he sed nodding sajely Jus to see how the other harf livs.

I cood not agree more sir I sed thinking of my time in Russia but of corse I cood not tell him that.

Ever had any trubble with the authoritees? he aksed.

Authoritys sir?

Polise and the like.

Oh no sir I sed any problems with the millitry polise not relevent to our discushon as far as I was conserned. I onse aksidently shot myself in the elbo wile cleening my private weppon a .22 calliber pistol wich the MPs clamed was unorthorized insted of simpathy I got fined demoted from private first class to private also copped a stint of KP for my trubble. Then later one of the offisers invollved in that cort marshell needed sorting out in a bar I had drunk jus enuff beer to deside that I was the man to do it. That erned me sevral weeks in the brig the Marines never was the same for me after that I cood not wate to get out it is jus like evry other plase one rool for the elit anuther for the rest of us. My so called supereers cood not recognize inteligense if it bit them on the behine. This of corse came as qite a shok to me I idolized the Marines from an erly age perchased the Marines handbook wen only 12 yeers old comitted it to memry also wore my bruther Johns Marines ring as a sine of respeck. Joyning up had been a life long dreem in reality it was a nitemare of corse I did not utter same to Mister Trooly.

Vry good he sed Wot do you want to do with yuorself now that you are no longer purforming activ dooty?

Aparently he was under the misstaken impreshun that I had jus left the Marines an impreshon I was in no hurry to dispell.

Well sir I am looking for an honnest days work that erns an honnest days pay. I hav a wife and chile with anuther doo any day now.

I tell you wot Lee he sed I dont hav any permnent posishuns avalable rite now but this is our busy periud with the skools jus starting bak up and Chrissmas on the way. Why dont you report bak here tomorow morning and we will put you strate to work.

Yes sir I sed and with a handshake I had tempry work at the skool book depossitry. I freely admit that a few wite lies were involved in the sekureing of sed posishun but for me lying is aceptabel if the aim is trew and nuthing cood be trewer than provideing for ones famly. Of corse I knoo wen Trooly met me he wood offer me a job not menny employers can resist a cleen cut marryed man with an unblemmished millitry record and famly of yung muoths to feed.

A famly I am now hopeing Wesly will help me get bak to in Irving.

Sure Lee Wesly says Jus like I tole you befor any time you need a ride jus holler. Then he thinks for a momment looks at the date on the order form atached to his clipbord.

But hold on he says Today aint Friday.

I kno that I say fully exspekting his quesshun I usuley ride out to Irving with him after work of a Friday afternoon reterning Monday morning after spending the weekend with you and your Mama.

How cum your heddin out to Irving on a Thursday?

Got to pik up sumthing for my room at Oke Cliff. Marina made me sum fine looking curtens and I need to pik up sum curten rods sos I can hang them.

Oh I see he says Will you be needing a ride home tomorow afternoon also?

No Im not planning to visit Marina and the kids tomorow I hav other plans.

Riteing those words rite now I see that that was the understatment of the sentury.

My ride out to Irving orgnized I hav one other task to take care of. A half huor later wen Joe and the men in the shipping dept take one of there noomerus smoke brakes I sneek in tare about three feet of browen paper off of a roll fasshon a bag from it. I tape the ends shut fold it in half sevral times it fits neetly into my pokket I slip unnotissed from the room.

The rest of the morning I focuss on filling orders. Ocashonly I find myself standing at the windos gazeing out over Deely Plaza imagineing wot tomorows parade mite bring the crouds the polise the hoopla I also asess the best angells from wich to site the motorcade. At noon I leeve the depositry for my forty five minit lunch brake stroll ruond the plaza chooing on a ham sandwitch wile stooing over the parade roote. Junie you mite think that I wood be nervus at this poynt given the magnitood of wot I kontemplate howevver I am carm a soldeir befor the battel it will all be a matter of exacooshun onse my mind is made up.

But in trooth my mind will not be made up until after I vissit with your Mama.

After I meet Wesly in the lodeing dock at qitting time we walk to his car in employee lot nummer one on Brordway and Munger four bloks from the depositrys bak entranse across the street from the raleway yards. Wesly usaly parks beside a corragatted iron shed his 1953 Chevvy pritty well kept altho one of its reer weels is missing a hubcap. At ten yeers old his car mostly gets the job dun excep the battry runs flat evry so offen cawseing Wesly to trubble Billy Luvlady for a jump start.

I myself hav never had cawse for a vehikel in fack I am jus now lerning to drive Mrs Pain teeching me in her stashun waggon of a weekend zooming around supermarkt parking lots bakking up revers parking doing rite anggel terns I do beleeve I am getting the hang of it. Howevver I also kno it will be a long time befor I can aford a car with a wife two chillren there are more importent things to spend munny on. The trip to Mexico wile well intenshoned the cawse honorabel left me pennyless bus fare hotel room meels etc eating up my saveings. I shood hav stuk to my orignal plan hijaked a plane to Cuba with your mamas asistence. This skeme I traned for each day leeping aruond the ferniture on Magazeen St strenthening my arms and legs prepareing myself for navigateing the confined spase of an airplane cabbin. You Junie were most amoosed by these antiks standing up in your crib shreeking with laffter. Howevver your mamas inabilty to speek English prooved to be the plans undoing how cood she posibly keep hostiges under kontrol if she can not speek there langwedge. Also as she will freely admit she is not comfortabel aruond firearms does not trust herself to handel a weppon the plan was doomed from the vry start.

Wesly takes Continnentel Ave out of downtown heds west on the Stemmons Freeway. The trip to Irving takes less than therty minits sumhow we dodge the wurst of rush huor pull up in frunt of the Pains on W 5th jus after 5pm. Nummer 2515 is a singel levvel ranch huose two bedrooms a garage off of the left hand side a larg frunt windo brokken up into nine smaller rektangells a big ole oke tree shades the frunt lawn. Rooth and

29

her hussband Mikel jus like your mama and I are wethering stormy times they live appart Mikal with his own apartment in Arlingtun close to ware he works. Mikel is sum kind of engineer helikopter or plane aparently clevver altho not that clevver as he is a pasifist and ware did holding hands singing Kumbya ever get anyone? I shood kno I hav tryed the peeceful root to effeck change handed out Fair Play For Cuba leeflets in New Orleens debated on the raydio orgnized demonstrashuns for TV camras all that got me was jale time as well as a spannish inqasishun from your mama qesshuning the cost of sed activitys. She cood not unnerstand why I was seeking publisity wood not even go to my aunts huose to wotch me on TV. Givven these meeger results I do fermly beleeve unlike Mikel Pain that reel change can only cum thru violense it wakes peeple up cawses them to stop and think. Both this cuntry and Russia cood do with a sollid dose of it rite now. Wile the two cuntrys oprate under difrent politikal sistems each has there negativs Russia crushing the free spirrit of man for the bennafit of the party elit the U.S. exployting the happless worker to make the rich richer. The world wood be better off without both sistems wipe the slate cleen put a totely new order in plase. Sumone jus needs to comense the clensing well the first step may happen tomorow that sumone cood be me.

On accuont of Rooth and Mikel being seprated there is room in the huose for Mama you and Rachel altho not that much with only two bedrooms on offer. Rooth has two litle kids of her own so both your mama and Rooth hav there kids sleeping in there rooms with them. Sumtimes wile wotching the football of a weekend I play horsey on the livving room flor with Rooths boy

Cristoffer he rides on my bak endlessly enjoying it imensely he misses haveing a father in his life I can sertenly simpathize with him on that scor.

Wile obviusly it wood be better to be together as one famly it is more conveenent for me to liv close to work also your mama enjoys liveing with Rooth and her Westinghuose washing masheen to kope with the constent streem of dirty dypers also a new TV set and copius sope opras to keep your mama amoosed. The huose is far better eqipped than any plase we ever rented. In retern for her kindness all Rooth aks of Mama is that she teech her Russian that is all they speek around the huose I dont mind as it helps me keep praktised in the langwege as well.

As Wesly pulls over to the kerb I can see your mama thru the gest room windo playing peek a boo with you on the bed.

I will pik you up at the usule time tomorow then Wesly says as I open the pasenger door Hav a nise nite Lee.

Thanks Wesly. You too.

I slam the car door your mama looks out the windo she is unnerstandably surprized by my pressense.

I wotch Wesly drive off towards Linny Mays then walk up the Pains drive. As your mama does not cum out to greet me I enter the frunt door hed for the bedroom ware I find Rachel sleeping in her wite crib a pink bunny with jugling balls paynted on its end. You Junie hug your favrite teddy bare on the bed smile as soon as you see me.

Hi sweet pee I say bend over to kiss your cheek also avoyd your mamas gaze the wall of silense that has stood betwene us for the past week createing an awkwerdness that no man and wife shood hav to bare.

Cho ty zdes delayesh? she says Russian for Wot are you doing heer? Your mama does not speek english so well to be fare she has pestered me constently for lessons sinse ariveing in Dallas howevver I hav not budged I also insist we speek Russian at evry oportoonity. I mite vry well end up bak in Minsk one day and do not want to loose my profishensy. Not knoing english mite make it diffikult for her to convers with peeple but it is the rite thing to do givven our currant sichooashun wich I freely admit is now evven more unserten. After sevral argooments about same I forbade her to reed rite or speke english of corse she is not happy about that howevver in my book a wife obays her hussband end of discushon.

Well thats a nise how do you do I say also in Russian. Sum peeple find takeing up a second langwedge diffcult but not me it cums vry eesly.

I remoove my jakket lay it over the rales of Rachels crib careflee so as not to disterb her.

I didnt expeck you to cum out today she says Its Thersday not Friday.

I got lonesum for my gurls I say kissing your soft litle cheek aggen. You sqeel and hug teddy titer.

Why didnt you call?

I unnerstand her confooshon I hav never visited the Pains without first calling ahed I am not one to invite myself anyware but these are extennuateing cirkumstanses I can not tell her same.

Marina I wanted to surprize you.

I grab her sholders leen in for a kiss. She terns her bak arms folded still vry angry about our latest falling out.

We hav not spokken sinse last Sunday nite wen Rooth tryed

to call me at the rooming huose on your mamas beharf and whoever ansered the fone sed no one livved there by that name. The mixup was my own stoopid folt I made the misstake of giveing Rooth the fone nummer a munth erlier wen your baby sister was ekspected. In the end Rooth had not needed it as I was in Irving at the time of Rachels arival. That weekend was my twenty forth berthday Rooth Mikel and your Mama thru me a surprize party. I was vry tuched by the cake the wine all the truble they went to dekorateing with streemers etc. Teers welled in my eyes wen they sang Happy Berthday so choked up I struggeled to blo out the candels wich numberred twenty two not twenty four but of corse I did not complayn. The rest of the evening I folowed your mama aruond like a puppy dog wotching for any sine of the babys arrivel. We lay together on the sofa wotching TV I rubbed her legs to eze her akes sum vanes had brokken in her ankels she was all swelled up like a overstuffed sossage. We wotched the moovie Sudenly ware Frank Sinatra makes an unsucessful attemp to kill the president from a high windo overlooking a raleway stashun. The story I freely admit had sum influense on ware I find myself today howevver your mama dozed rite thru it.

Then aruond nine therty your baby sister started cumming Rooth drove Mama to Parkland Hosspitel wile I stayed at home with you chillren. She rang and tole me of Rachels arivel erly the neks morning befor Wesly picked me up. After work I vissited Mama in the hosspitel with sum reluktanse feering they mite discuvver I had a job forse me to pay for a ridicoolusly expensiv hosspital bed. It is crimnal in the extreem aksess to doctors and medisin in any cuntry let allone the richest on Erth shood be a rite not a privlege. It is free in Russia one of the few good poynts about liveing there. Howevver dispite Rooth alreddy telling them about my job the hospittal stay sumhow terned out to cost me nuthing. I showered your Mama with kisses so pruod of her even tho I had hopped for a boy I wonted to call him David teech him to gro up one day be the grate leeder this cuntry needs. I dreemed same for you Junie befor you were born howevver we all kno a woman can never be president nevver mind you are perfeck jus the way you are.

My thorts hav wandered relieving plessant memrys perhaps becos befor today they were few and far betwene. Last weekend Mama aksed me not to vissit the Pains saying Rooths little girl Lyn was haveing her forth birthday party I wood only get in the way. Of corse I oblyged. Also I knoo Mikel Pain wood be in atendense and didnt much feel like argewing with him aggen his aproche to politiks vry diffrent to mine. I stayed close to the rooming huose all weekend tryed to get my lerners permit at the drivers stashun on Saterday howevver wen tole I wood not be seen untill after closeing time I promply left. I red a book in Lake Cliff Park also wotched TV did my lawndry at the washateeria across Nth Beckly. I ate dinner Saterday nite at Dobbs Huose then called your mama sevral times onse to see how she was a seccund time to find out wether you were enjoying Lyns berthday party she sed you were haveing a ball. Howevver dispite these menny calls your mama still mist me hense the fone call Sunday nite wen Rooth discuvvered no one by my name was livving at the rooming huose on N Beckly.

Of corse I did not kno anything about this so wen I called your mama on my lunch brake the neks day my usule kustom she confrunted me with wot had happened.

We tryed to call you last nite she sed ware were you?

I was at home wotching TV I replyed.

Rubbish I was standing rite there wen Rooth tryed to call you.

Nobody called me to the fone I sed Are you sure Rooth had the rite nummer?

Yes. She aksed for Lee Oswald. They sed there is no Lee Oswald here. Rooth then aksed if this was the rooming huose and they sed yes. Then she dubble chekked the nummer and the man sed that was correck so Rooth sed thank you vry much and hung up.

At first I was confoosed then reelised wot went rong.

Dang it I sed I dont live there under my reel name.

Why not?

I use the name O H Lee I sed Wen I rented the room I did not want Mrs Jonson the landlady knoing that I had livved in Russia my name has been in the press menshuning same.

It is nun of the landladys bizness ware you hav livved your mama sed.

You dont unnerstand a thing. I also dont want the FBI knoing ware I live and you must not breethe a word of this to Rooth in case that fool Hasty cums bak aggen.

Well thats wen your mama reelly hit the roof.

You are bak to your old lyeing ways she sed Wen will this ever end? You and your long tung they always get us into trubble. Here you are jus bak from trying to get to Cuba to help your frend Fidel and alreddy you are starting aggen with your foolishnes.

Your mama has qite the muoth onse she gets started by this

poynt she was reely steemed there was no stopping her.

All these comedees she shreeked furst one then anuther. And now this fictishus name. Wen you lie you end up makeing me lie. Wen will it stop?

You are being stoopid I sed You do not understand a thing. Hasty of the FBI has been out to Irving twise to quesshun you and fool that you are you hav been all nice and pollite and cooprativ with him.

Wot wood you hav me do?

Wot I tole you befor do not tawk to the man he is not to be trusted.

Well I kno that. Why do you think I rote down his nummer plate for you?

It is trew she had ritten down the nummer plate of his vehikel also the moddel make and collor at my reqeust I will giv her that.

Well I sed Im haveing nun of Hastys rubish thats why I used a fake name at the rooming huose shood he try and trak me down.

Oh you are such a geniuss Lee.

Yeah well Im smart enuff to go down to the FBI offises on Comerse St and put an end to all this harassment.

Wot do you meen?

Exackly wot I sed I went down and confrunted Hasty.

You did not.

I did too. The woman on the frunt desk tole me he was out to lunch cowerd that he is he was probly trembeling under his desk. I left a note with her telling him in no unserten terms that he shood leev me and you alone if he knos wot is good for him and that if he wanted to tawk to me he shood not approche my wife. Get this to Hasty I tole her then stormed out.

Wen your mama scoffed at my bravry I rang off telling her that I cood tawk no longer I had work to do wen in fack my lunch brake had annuther twenty minits to run. I cood stumak no more sed I wood call her bak later that nite.

Well I did call her bak later that nite Rooth ansered the fone in the midle of fixing supper I cood heer eggs or simler spitting in the pan.

Rooth is Marina there pleese?

Oh hello Lee she sed Yes jus one momment.

Marina its for you Rooth called out in Russian.

Who is it? your mama aksed in retern altho she had to kno it was me for who else wood be calling? She had met vry few peeple in Dallas sinse our arrival a fack that was to my satisfacshun I did not want her galivanting all over the plase tawking behind my bak sumthing she has been gilty of in the past.

Lee sed Rooth.

I will not cum your mama shuoted from sumware distent probly the livving room. Rooth must hav then cuvvered the fone with her hand I cood heer her mermering. I wated pashently knoing that Rooth was not the kind of woman to tell a man his own wife wood not speek to him.

Sure enuff eventuly Mama pikked up the fone. It panes me to tell you this Junie but I used sum vry harsh words indede I had been stooing all day and knoo wot the rite corse of acshun was even if your Mama didnt.

Lissen devushka I sed useing a Russian word not sutabel for chillrens ears as I sed I was steeming mad Theres sumthing you must do for me.

Oh she sed And wot is that deer hussband?

You are to take Rooths adress book and cross out my name and telefone nummer.

Why wood I do that?

Isnt it obvius? So that Hasty dusnt find it neks time he vissits.

Dont be so stoopid she replyed I cant do that. Its not my book and I hav no rite to tuch it.

Marina lissen to me.

Why? Is the big man going to use his fists on me aggen?

Marina pleese lissen.

No Lee. You lissen. Rooth is my frend she has been vry kind to me and the chillren. I will not tuch her persnal property.

Honessly Junie most times I cood unnerstand that argooment but rite then I cood hav aksed your mama to eat a peece of her favrit pie my reqest wood hav been ignoored with glee.

Marina I sed I order you to cross it out. Do you heer?

I wont do it! she shuoted.

After that there was a lot of yelling name calling bak and forth etc untill she abruply hung up.

I did not call her rite bak nor did I call her bak Tewsday Wensday or Thersday. She desserved to be punnisht for not folowing a reesonable reqest from her hussband as is her riteful dooty it is not for nuthing that the marrage vows say luv honor and obay. She of corse did not call me bak eether thus we did not speek aggen until I now arrive unannuonsed at W 5th St.

Mama poynts to lawndry piled on the bed.

There are your cleen clothes she says Go and wosh up. It is cleer she is not yet reddy to forgiv me.

I look at myself in the mirrer all swetty and grimey from

hawling books up and down stares all day definitly not the best condishun in wich to woo her. To pleese her I do as I am tole take my leve to luxuryate under a hot shower trying not to recall that there was onse a time wen your mama wood gladly run a bath for me of an evening after I reterned home from the raydio faktory. The water was ussuley too hot or too cold howevver seldum did I complane jus tryed to apreshiate her efort those times now seem well and trewly gone.

I set the shower to blasting jump under singing Shikuvskys Qeen of Spades my favrit Russian opra as I scrub myself with sope. Based on a short story by Pushkin it is about a Russian ofisser called Herman obssessed with the nummer three convinsed that it holds grate magikal powers and will be the kee to his sucsess. Wen we lived in Minsk I played the record over and over aggen driveing your mama and the naybors crazy with my singing. Now I do not hold bak belloing evry word Take hart my frend do not forget that after a carm day cums the storm I sing water streeming down my fase my probblems with your Mama forgoten for an instent.

Heer I am I say All skweeky cleen. Are you still angry with me?

Draped only in a towl I leen in to kiss her. Onse aggen your mama terns her bak then makes for the bedroom door I deside to play a game from wen we were noolyweds I wood blok the bedroom door refoose to let her pass untill she kisst me. Jus marryed this of corse wood result in grate dissplays of pashun now howevver she jus givs up cappitoolates her body limp like three week old lettuss. She lets me kiss her but I feel no better than a drunken broot in a bar makeing unwonted advanses.

39

Enuff! I shuot pulling bak to fase her You are getting spoyled staying here Marina. Tomorow I will find us an apartment in the citty ware we can all live happily together.

Shush she hisses Youll wake Rachel.

Well tomorow you are leeveing here with me I wisper.

I wont go she says shakeing her head.

Fine if you wont go I will take Junie and Rachel and leeve you behind. You mite preffer your frends to me but the chillren luv there papa more than you luv me.

Ha! she says Jus you try nersing Rachel and see how far you get. You can see wot thats like and wots more it will be less work for me.

I hav no time for more work. I am busy enuff at my job and straytning out the mess you made with Hasty.

Aggen with the FBI you foollish litle man.

Well as I tole you this foolish litle man went down there and sorted things out they will not bother you any more.

Oh yes Im sure they will lissen to you mister big man of the world with your fansy dreems and ideas.

They will if they kno wots good for them. Jus like you.

At this your mama aggen heds for the door. Previusly I may hav blokked her path we hav sertenly had fisical altercashuns in the past one time on W Neely St after the Walker shooting she turned the tabels lokked me in the bathroom. Nixon was cumming to town she was ritely afrade I wood take a potshot at him jus like I did Walker. Befor she wood let me out she made me promiss never to use my rifel agenst anyone ever aggen a conceshun I granted to win my freedum but wich I may now vry well withdraw doo to her currant resistense.

I deside to let your mama pass you and your sister are in the room you shood not witness us grappel. Also I do not kno ware Rooth is. It is one thing to rayse your voise to your wife in the cumpny of others I hav sertenly dun same wen Mama has not toed the line howevver violense is anuther matta entirely it shood be kept behind clossed doors ware ever possibel.

Mama leeves Rachel sleeping in the crib skoops you up takes you to the livving room to play with Rooths kids toys dollys and such. Then she heds out to the bak yard to chek on sum dypers drying on the line. I put on clene clothes trowsers and wite tshirt slip thru the kichen wile your mama is distrakted. The garage smels of gassoleen a can of wich Mikel keeps for the lawn mower. Spare tires a hevvy dooty wood step ladder tins of paynt sundry other ittems are piled amungst moveing boxes the plase is a totel shambles as most garages are a dumping gruond for anything that does not hav a plase inside the huose propper. The garage also has a work bench ware Mikel tinkers away on weekends who knos wot he is doing perhapps making the werlds first pasifist bomb ha.

My rifel lies ware I left it on the flor neer the garage frunt door. It is wrapt in a red blanket with rektangler patern a gift from my fello workers at the raydio factory upon your berth Junie you luved to play on it on the verander at W Neely St. Neerby stand sum carbbord boxes filled with our poseshuns that Rooth and your mama drove bak from New Orleens befor I hedded to Mexico also a few carbbord barrells the Pains kids sumtimes play with.

I leeve the rifle ware it is for the time been I am still not sure I will need it tomorow altho my mind at this poynt is fast becumming made up. In the morning I will leeve this huose with one of two things eether your mamas vow that we will onse aggen liv under the same roof or my rifle.

I wonder out to the bak yard help Mama take the dypers off the line not a word is spokken betwene us wile we work. I carry the overfloing wicka basket into the livving room onse aggen amazed at how menny derty dypers a few litle kids can genrate. Your mama and I sit on the sofa folding them the activty helps lessen the tenshon between us. Junie you are playing on the flor Rachel is still in the bedroom takeing her late afternoon nap Rooth I hav lerned is out grossery shopping your mama and I can finaly speak honessly with each other. Onse aggen I beg her to return to me.

Im tyred of liveing all alone I explane My girls are out here in Irving I am in Dallas I dont like haveing to cum all the way out here to see you.

She looks up from the dyper she is folding her blew eyes meet mine they sparkel jus as they allways hav from the vry first nite we met. Wot a site to see your mama was her hare dun up high French stile a red floing gown wite slippers slim figger all the boys at the trade unoin danse in Minsk were crazy for her. For sum reeson she chose to danse with the shy American boy afterwoods I walkt her home along the river bank wen we parted I wisspered her name the rest as they say is histry.

A few short weeks later I aksed for your mamas hand in marrage even tho I had alreddy made enqirys to the US embasy about leeveing Russia. I was vry disatisfyed with the way of life in Minsk or more presisely the lak of life nuthing to do no bowling allees vry few bars pitcher theeters etc. Mama instently acepted my propposel howevver my plans to retern home wen later eksplaned came as a grate shok to her. Previously I had tole her the US govt considderd me a traytor unnabel to ever return the first part trew but eether way I had no choise but to lie otherwise she may not hav marryed me. Over time this became qite a stikking point betwene us howevver eventully your mama saw the wisdom of reterning to the US leeveing her famly and frends behind for the chanse of a better life. I sinseerly hope that that is wot she finds no matter wot happens now.

Alka she says useing my Russian name I think it is betta if I stay here in Irving. Maybe I stay here untill Crissmas and you go on liveing alone saveing munny until then.

Its not about the muney I say Dont wurry about the munny. We will be fine.

But livving with jus you I am lonly all day wen you are at work. Here I hav Rooth to tawk to and she helps me so much with the chillren. I wood be so lonsome by myself all day with no one to tawk to.

There you go aggen prefering your frends to me.

Lee that is not trew.

I hav saved a litle sinse returning from Mexico I say I can get us an apartment and I will get you a woshing masheen one even fansyer than the Pains.

She larfs tosses bak her hare. I dont want a woshing masheen she says And I dont need you to buy one. Wot you need to buy is a car. Then wen you hav your drivers lisense it will be easyer for you to cum out here and see us.

A car? Wot do I need a car for? All that trubble with repares and getting it fixed a car is not wurth it. Bessides I can get a ride with Wesly any time I want.

I put my hand on her nee the good news is she does not take it away.

A wosshing masheen is wot you need I say An apartment and a wosshing masheen. I dont want my gurl doing all her lawndry in a tub. I nod at the pile of dypers we hav jus folded it is at leest two feet hi. Two babys are a lot of work I say With two babys you cant do evrything allone you need a masheen to help you.

She plases her hand bellow mine but not on top of it.

We will see Alka is all she says.

I leen in to kiss her. For the first time sinse I arived she does not rejeck my advanses outrite howevver nor does she move closser. I leen in ferther jus befor our lips meet a car door slams outside. Thru the windo I see Rooth walk aruond the bak of her stashun waggon rayse its reer door to start remooveing grossery sacks.

The momment lost Mama and I stand up to lend a hand Rooth is a vry slite woman not abel to carry much in the way of hevvy lodes.

After sevral trips bak and forth getting all the grosserys inside I am swetting profoosely hav bilt up qite a thurst. I poor myself a glass of water leen agenst the kichen sink drinking it. Rooth cums in holding Lyn and Cristofer by the hand.

Lee the president is cumming to town she says a smile streched across her lips they are plasstered with brite red lipstik qite a cheep look but to each there own. She was wareing same wen your mama and me first met her last Febry at a gathering of Russian imigrants. We were intradoosed by my grate frend Gorge de Morenshilt. Your mama and Rooth hit it off imediately

Rooth telling Mama she had been lerning Russian for five yeers part of a Russian pen pal program to improove relashons between east and west.

Good luck changeing US Soviet relashuns one letter at a time I had sed.

We are all jus peeple trying to liv our lives she replyed.

Rooth being a Qaker sees evryone eqall under god sumthing I do not dissagree with excep for the god part. The church is jus one big con anuther part of the state masheen desined to keep us all under controll blind to the unfareness that surruonds us. Perhapps evven wurse religon is also a blatent commershul exarsise our first crissmas in Fort Wurth your mama nagged me to buy a tree I refoosed to partisipate in such a crass munny grabbing entaprize we wood then also hav to buy pressents decorashuns onse it starts it never ends.

Ah yes I now say to Rooth acting like it is no big deel that the president is cumming to town wich in sum ways is trew Kennedy is jus anuther pollitishan traveling around the cuntry scruongeing for votes.

At this poynt your mama enters the kichen with you on her hip.

Yes the president she says in Russian It is so exsiteing he is such a hansome man.

Foolish woman she is trying to make me jellus becos Kennedy bares a strong resemblence to her old boyfrend Anatolly. We hav discusst this menny times does she reelly think I am going to fall for that old trik? Last New Yeers eve she tryed to send Anatoly luv letters I cort her red handed she adressed the envelop to him incorreckly it came rite bak to our huose. I confrunted her with a fury I am shure she has not forgoten howevver rite now I am beeyond torment her reluctanse to reunite sloly egtinguishing a flame that onse burned so brite.

I am tempted to respond in kind makeing your mama jellus wood be so easy. I hav nevver tole her or anyone this Junie but wen I first met your mama I was infatewated with anuther woman at the raydio factry. Howevver Ella sperned my advances rejected my offer of marrage so three munths later I aksed for your mamas hand. I thort marrying Mama wood take my mind off of Ella also teech her a lesson lets see how much she likes it wen I rejekt her. If I tole your mama it wood of corse destroy her our marrage seemingly bilt on a lie howevver this is not trew as I sloly fell in luv with your mama troo luv allways finds a way.

Yes I carmly agree the president sertenly is hansome.

I wood so much like to see him in person she gushes And Jackie of corse. Lee do you kno ware I mite be abel to do that? Ware and wot time cood I see them?

I hav no idea I say.

Confushon crosses her fase. Why do I not kno the detales of the presidents vissit shurely with my intrest in all things pollitical I shood kno. Howevver I dont want her thinking I hav payed the slitest bit of atenshun to his trip otherwise she mite do wot she did wen Nixon came to town lok me in the bathroom untill Kenedy has safely passed.

I walk over to your mama she cowers eva so slitely Rooth does not notiss but I sertenly do. I lift you off of her hip hoyst you up onto my sholders take off running aruond the huose a game that allways cawses you to sqeel with delite your hed barely missing the top of the doorways. I charg thru the livving room zig zag down the hall in and out of the bedrooms bak down the hallway past Mama and Rooth in the kichen out the frunt door onto the lawn with you shreeking Rooths litle Lyn not far behind all the wile your mama half shuotting half wisspering stop it or you will wake the baby.

In less than five minits there is a bunch of us playing out frunt naybors kids and the like enjoying that care free huor befor dinner. The sun beggins to set but we continoo to galavant abuot even after it disapeers belo the horizen the evening magikal the fadeing twilite lending a golden hew to all it tuches. You remane percht on my sholders as we chase butterflys try to cup them in our hands of corse they are too nimbel for us. I put you down to cach falling oak wings you sqeel with happyness wen one flutters down and I plase it in your palm. One of the naybors kids brings over his raydio flyer you clime in I pull you up and down the drive so menny times I loose count. All the chillren are haveing the time of there lives shouting jibberish at one anuther your mama cums out to see wot all the fuss is abuot.

See I say to her Livving in America our chillren will lern both english and russian.

I can see that she says bounseing Rachel on her hip she is freshly wokken from her nap. Rachel is the most beutifull litle baby strong as an ox jus like you were Junie. As I hav tole your mama menny times it is becos you are both fed on mamas milk. Bottel milk is simpley not good enuff for eether of you a vry pore substitoot indede. Mamas milk is of corse also cheeper than botle milk wich your mama clames is all that matters to me howevver that is simplee not the case it is helth not finanses that suports the case for a mother feeding a baby her own milk.

I still dont like the name Rachel I say I think we shood call the baby Marina after her beutiful mama.

Anything is betta than Fidel she says a smile forming on her lips I manag to retern same. At one stage I wanted to call the baby Fidel if it was boy. After the Mexico City fiasko howevver I qikly changed my toon the Cuban embasy in there ignorense roodly rejecting my offer of help I will nevver forgiv them for that.

Cum on Marina wot do you say?

One Marina is more than enuff for any famly she says.

Marina I say seeking her hand for the thurd time sinse ariveing home hopeing Hermans lukky nummer three works for me now Will you pleese moove bak to the city with me? I am so lonsome and miss my babys. Let me get us a nise apartment in Oak Cliff like we onse had. I will make shure we are all happly together onse more. I voise this reqest with such sinserity I am serten that this time your mama will comply.

I am sorry Lee she says shakeing her head But I think we shood stay here a litle longer untill you mend your childish ways.

I stare at the gruond unabel to meet her eyes sumthing inside me has brokken. At times like this I can eksplode a seering hot rage spewing forth my fists hardning into seement. Howevver it is not anger I feel now but disapoyntment that qikly givs way to releef her reply is confirmashun I must do wot has always been destinned. As Marx sed histry is desided in advanse there is litle I or you or anyone can do to stop it. Landing a job at the skool book depossitry the authoritees planning a roote that takes the President within feet of its windos your mamas refoossal to continoo bilding our life toggether these are all cleer sines only a fool wood ignoor.

Yes Junie your mamas rejekshun convinses me onse and for all I hav been put on this earth as part of a grander plan to chang the path of human kind make life farer for all wite blak christan jew. Communism and capitlism are both one and the same sistems desined to keep the working man down wile alowing those abuv to prossper. Who better to kno this than I one of the few men on this plannet who has livved under both sistems I allone kno them for the lies they trewly are diffrent forms of slavry only by strikeing at the hart of one can I ignite the flames of chang begin clensing the world of ineqitty.

I look up see you Junie sqatting in the litle red waggon your hed tilted bak a look of pure joy on your fase. This is the final confirmashun I need who am I to deny you and evry chile in the world a better sosiety one that treets evryone blak or wite rich or poor edukated or ignorent eqally? Hermans words from the Qeen of Spades cum to me I wood perform a heeroic deed of unherd prowess for your sake. I hav herd those words a thuosand times befor but standing on the Pains frunt lawn in the dying lite of day I understand there trew meening for the vry first time.

The Pains huose as I menshuned previus has evry modern convenense a woman cood want the kichen bostes a twin stove the latest new fangelled ice box even a electrick can opener. The kichen walls and door to the bakyard are finnished in nateral wood the cubbords a deep golden timber with blak mettal handels. From all this I dedoos that helikopter engineering pays much better than karting boxes of books up and down stares all day Mikel being the Pains sole sause of incum Rooth probly never werking a day in her life.

Most nites we three adults eat at the dineing tabel set to one side of the kichen two hi chares also needed to feed you and Rooths oldest chile Lyn. The flor is linolleum windos on two sides fase out onto the bak yard I can see the swing set in the groing dark also the side yard of the naybors huose. Anuther doorway opens out to the garage ware my rifle lyes in wate.

Your mama is not much of a cook her speshulty Russian pan fryed unyuns with potaytos a dish I like vry much but no man can eat the same meel evry nite. Rooth despite being a qaker does not seem to hav any rooles aruond her dyet she offers up a sollid meel most evenings altho I hav been knowen to tern up my nose at her vegetabull dishes insist your mama cook her speshulty. Tonite I am vry pleesed with Rooths effert lam chops carrots mash pottato green beens three skoops of vanila ice creem to finnish.

Thruout dinner your mama is more hospitabel perhaps trying to make amends for her erlyer coldness. I try to resspond in kind but if she thinks I am going to get down on bended nee beg her onse aggen to joyn me in Oke Cliff she is vry much mistakken. Three strikes and your out I calls em as I sees em.

During desert a few muothfulls of vanila ice creem left in her bowl your mama aks aggen abuot the presidents vissit.

Do you think I can see him on TV?

I dont kno I say tern to Rooth to chang the subjeck Hav you seen that FBI man lately?

No he has not cum bak.

Nor will he.

How can you be so shure?

Oh I am shure I say I used the adress you gave me from his

bizness card and went down there to tell him to stay away from you and Marina. The secretry she tole me he was on his lunch brake so I left him a note. I dont think youll be heering from him aggen.

Well thanks for doing that Lee she says But Im not sure it was alltogether nesessry.

She starts cleering plates from the tabel stakking them beside the sink. Your mama piches in to help I wipe the remanes of baby food from your cheeks lift you from your hi chare take you into the liveing room to play. Wen your mama cums into the room to nerse Rachel I deside it is bed time for you in trooth you are not vry sleepy howevver I hav nuthing ferther to say to your mama also your bedtime is my favrit time of the day we cuddel sing the weels on the bus wile I make teddy do a jig repeeting same untill you can no longer keep your litle eyes open.

I return to the livving room after puting you down find Mama has finnished nurseing Rachel. I take her from your Mamas arms bend her over my sholder berp then kradle her on the sofa until she falls asleep. Mama busys herself with tidying up the toys scatered cross the liveing room flor bilding bloks rag dolls a wooden stik on a base with diffrent colored plastik rings to slide on and off. With Rachel sleeping peecefuly I turn on the TV find a movie Sargaent York with Gary Cooper playing the world war two heero onse more. I wotch bearly paying atenshun thinking of my rifel lyeing wrapped in the blanket on the garage flor. Eventuly I can take it no longer I carry Rachel to the bedroom lay her down in the krib besside you. I grab my jakket from the end of the crib creep from the room eeze the door shut with both hands so as not to disterb you. I walk down the hall Rooth is at the kichen sink doing the dishes her bak terned towards me. Your Mama passes me in the hall with a basket of lawndry. I say nuthing wate till Rooth looks down to pull a fork from the suds then slip thru to the garage.

I am gratefull for my jakket the nite air chilling the garage. I take the papper bag that I fashunned erlier at the depositry out of my pokket unfold it lay it flat on the gruond. I careflee slide the rifle out of its rapping so as not to disterb the shape of the roled blanket to the cazul observer it still appeers to hold camping geer or such. I hinted same to Rooth wen pakking the stashun wagen in New Orleens for her to drive bak to Dallas. Of corse you were with them wile I travelled to Mexico City menny long hours spent on a bus for no reward abjeck humiliashun wateing at the other end. Still as Neetzchy onse sedd wot dusnt kill you only makes you stronger sertenly I am a sollid case in poynt.

The rifle is jus the way I left it well oilled in perfeck working order. I perchassed it by male order from Klines sporting goods in Chicago last March the day after I commensed survalance on Genral Walkers huose. Useing a coopon from American Rifelman magazeen it cost me $19.95 with tax and shiping $21.45. I recal the exak amuont as usule munny was exsepshunly tite your mama giveing me heck for wasteing it on a gun wen we cood bearly afford to eat sumtimes only bying milk for you Junie no sustenense for ourselvs. Howevver as I tole your mama it is all a qesshun of priortys sum things are far more importent than filling your stumuk I wood gladly go hungry for a thuosand days if it wood set the world to rite.

The rifle was delivvered to the same post offise box as my revolver. I rented the box in the Termnal Annex about a yeer ago as it terns out it is within spitting distanse of the skool book depossitry. Aggen I had to consider the cost invollved but I am not so stoopid as to hav weppons delivered to my home. To ferther avoyd detekshun I ordered the guns under slitey diffrent names the revolver Alik Hidell the rifle A Hidell aliasses I hav used on sevral occashons to grate affeck for exampel wen fuonding the Fare Play for Cuba comitee in New Orleens. The first name Alik I bassed on my Russian name Alka. Hidell is the last name of a fello marine I chose it becos it rymes with Fidel that amooses me no end also makes it easy to remember wich is kee to chooseing any fake name. The middel J stands for James as in Bond I preffer mine shakken not sturred ha. To asist me in this subterfooge I created fake IDs wile working at the Jaggers-Chiles-Stovell fotografic cumpny probly one of the best jobs I ever had. I was let go for suposedly not getting along with the other men shure I kept to myself last time I chekked that is not a crime. I made ads for newspapers magazeens posters a varriety of expensiv fotografic equipment was at my dissposel makeing fake IDs a peese of cake. The final produkts look jus like the reel thing never hav I been qesshuned as to there orthentisity well that is untill today more of wich I will later explane.

The rifle you wood recognize from the foto takken in the bak yard at W Neely St. I wont bore you with the teknical detales Junie suffise to say it is a Italyan surplus millitry weppon with four power side muonted telescoppic site and lether sling a sollid workhorse of a rifle nuthing fansy but in the rite hands it will get the job dun. I had awayted its arivvel like the cumming of your berth the neks afternoon I qit work on the dot of five hedded strait home slipped inside to retreeve the rifle without your mama knoing I was there. Conseeling the rifle under a long cote despite the blazeing sun I cort a bus on 6th and Beckly rode five minits to West Commerse and Beckly scurryed down the banks of the Trinnity River levee. I spent the neks huor familleriseing myself with the weppon getting a feel for its more powerful trigger acshun how to work the bolt smoothly so as to not upset the barrell alinement also callbrateing the scope to hit a small target area. Even tho I had never used this type of rifle befor it took no more than fifteen or twenty shots to get evrything alined. I hav allways been good aruond weppons a keen hunter from a yung age my bruthers and I wood shoot rabbits and sqirrels in the feelds around Ft Worth. Ferthermore obviusly I am an ex-Marine onse attaneing the stattus of sharpshooter. I trayned at Camp Pendellton CA fireing at targets five hunnerd yards away it is not sumthing evry man can do. Howevver shooting a rifel over those kinds of distanses is like lerning to ride a bike Junie you never reely forget. That ferst afternoon on the Trinity River it felt like I had nevver put a rifle down wen in fack sinse the Marines I had barely tuched one excep to hunt with shotguns in Russia a vry primitiv form of hunting in my vew I purformed poorly was the subjeck of much derishon.

Sheets of newspaper are spred out on the garage flor ware Rooth has been paynting bilding bloks for her kids. Rooth is qite the nite owl she mite retern to finnish the job at any moment I must get strate to work. Fortunatly I spent menny a swetty nite on the porch on Magazeen St disasembeling and reasembeling the rifle with a nickel I cood do same blindfolded if reqired. First

I chek that the rifle is not loded even tho I alreddy kno the anser to that I wood never leeve a gun in such a state one has to be eyether stoopid or insane to do same cleerly I am neether. I pull bak the bolt slide it foreward a litle then pull on the trigger the bolt cums free in an instent. Aggen not to bore you to deth with detales Junie howevver I am prowd of my militry lernings not evryone has my skil aruond wepponry. I remoove the cleening rod unscroo the thred from the frunt barrel loossen the scroo on the frunt barrell band slide it off. From there it is plane saleing flip the rifle over side barrell band off lift off hand gaurd flip the rifle over aggen remoove scroos in trigger gaurd asemblee lift off assemblee and then lift stok off of acshun. Hey presto one dismanteled rifle now half its orignal size makeing it easy to carry and more importently conseel.

I rummage thru the dettritiss of the garage find an old tshirt it is adoorned with the red Texaco star. Why anyone wood ware a simbol of an oil cumpny I hav no idea. Perhapps Rooth plans to dry her paynt brushes with it howevver I hav a far better use for it now. I wrap the looss parts of the rifle in the shert poosh them to the botom of the paper bag slide the barrell and akshun in after then fold the unused porshun of the bag bak over itself redoose its size to about two and a half feet.

I reech bak inside the blanket my fingers eventuly find the cartrige of 160 grane ruond nose bullits left over from my last practise seshun in New Orleens. On menny ocashons I wood steel from the huose in the last lite of day hed for the Missisippi levee on the outskurts of town neer River Rd my rifle conseeled beneeth a hevvy cote. On my last sortee befor hedding to Mexico I had fired jus two shots from the six ruond clip wen I bekame distrakted by sevral high skool kids smokeing up a storm beneeth the Hewy Long bridg. I imediatly finnished up leeveing the four ruonds in the clip that I now hold in my hand. That shood be ampel ammunishon with wich to commense the clensing I hav to hit my mark in three or four shots anyway or I will run out of time it is as simpel as that. Four is also by my ruff calkulashuns the maxmum nummer of shots I can get off in the time the motorcade will take to pass the depossitry. Howevver like Herman from the qeen of spades I am begining to feel that three is my magik nummer. Of corse the nummer of bullets at my disposel is a moot poynt I do not hav time to buy moor tomorow four bullits are wot I hav at hand that nummer must simpley suffise.

I slip the ammo in with the rifel then slide the paper sak bak inside the blanket lay it all down in the same spot on the flor. The rifle has sat there undissterbed for sevral munths shorely it can go unnotised one more nite.

I heer footsteps thru the door to the dineing area probly Rooth wipeing down the tabel and high chares howevver she cood also be cumming bak out to the garage to finish paynting the toy bloks. I bolt to the garage door twist the handel rayse it over my hed qikly duk under. As I lower it behind me I notiss the overhed lite is still on I hav forgotten to extingwish it. I dare not go bak now for feer of being cort in the garage without plawsible explanashun I lower the door leeve it burn.

I skurt Rooths car in the drive the evening still and sillent. I reenter the huose thru the frunt door manageing to avoyd any awkwerd quesshuns from Rooth or your Mama by eazeing myself into the liveing room. Gary Cooper is still playing heero but now to an emty sofa he is of corse saveing the day. I park myself to wotch howevver I can not consentrate on the akshun plans for tomorow swurl in my mind as I considder difrent sennarios.

The time is nine oclok I do not normly retire untill eleven howevver the neks day will be like no other an erly nite a wise corse of akshun. I hed out to the kichen your mama is helping Rooth finnish up. Rooth wares a apron printed with cowboy boots and lassoos aruond her middel to proteck her wite blowse.

Need any help? I aks.

No we are almost dun says your mama.

OK then I think I will hit the sak.

But its so erly says Rooth. She puts a plate on the draneing rack I wotch as bubbles slide down its fase.

I kno but I am beet. I had a hard day at work today and will hav anuther tomorow.

All rite she says terning bak to the dishes.

I dont think Ill be out this weekend.

Why not? your mama says. She keeps wurking does not evven bother to turn aruond.

Its too offen I was jus here today.

OK she muttas wether or not I vissit obviusly of litle consern to her.

Well good nite I say and with that we are dun.

I walk to the bathroom wosh the rifel oil off of my hands then brush my teeth.

In the dark bedroom you and Rachel are sleeping peecefuly in the krib breething almost in unisson not a care in the world.

Tomorow is the first step in makeing sure it stays that way.

Altho far from sleep I remoove my trowsers eaze myself betwene the cold sheets. Plans for tomorow run thru my hed like looping film I hold them up to the lite eksamine them from difrent angells see no flaws. I am wurrying needlessly the Walker shooting went off without a hitch the cops nun the wizer doo to my metikulus planning. I survayled his ressidense for menny huors noteing ware the windos are there distanse relativ to the bak fense I even mapped out my ekscape root and indentifyed a plase to stash the rifel beside sum neerby raleway traks ware I retreeved it two days later. I also took refrense fotos of the bak of his huose and reer allee filled an entire blew lose leef folder with these perparashuns pooring over them nitely in the studdy on W Neely St. Your Mama thort I was working on my Historic Diary only after the fack did I sho her my detaled planning. She was nun too pleesed of corse cood not unnerstand why I wood contemplayt such an act made me promiss never to repeet same. She also insisted that I bern the folder and its contents feerful of it being used as evidense aggenst me. I wood hav much prefered to preserv the notes as a keepsake but there was sum wisdum in her thinking I finaly conseeded burning them in a bakyard bonfire.

As an egsampel of my meticulus approche to these mishuns I will for you Junie rekreate a list of instrucshuns I left for your mama shood I be detaned folowing the Walker attemp of corse it was not needed I eckscaped scot free. I remember the poynts of the list well rerote them menny times but maybe not the exack wording as I rote it in Russian for your mama. To this day I do not kno ware the originel note is wot Mama did with it she may still hav it in her poseshon for all I kno. I sertenly hope so it may well cum in handy now.

1. Heer is the kee to the post offise box wich is lokated in the mane post offise downtown on Ervay St the street ware there is a drugstor ware you allways used to stand. The post offise is four bloks from the drugstore on same street. There you will find our malebox. I paid for the malebox last munth so you neednt wurry about it.

2. Send informmashun about wot has hapened to me to the Embassy also send newspaper clippings if theres anything abuot me in the papers. I think the Embasy will cum qikly to your aid onse they kno evrything.

3. I payd our rent on the 2nd so dont wurry about it.

4. I hav also payd for the water and gas.

5. There may be sum munny from work. They will send it to your post offise box. Go to the bank and they will cash it.

6. You can eether thro out my clotheing or giv it away. <u>Do not keep it</u>. (Junie, I did not want your mama pineing over my belongings.) As for my persnal papers (both millitry papers and pappers for the faktory) I preffer that you keep them. (This in case I needed them at a latter date.)

7. Serten of my papers are in the small blew sootcase.

8. My adress book is on the tabel in my studdy if you need it.

9. We hav frends here and the Red Cross will also help you.

10. I left you as much munny as I cood $60 on the 2nd of

the munth and you and Junie can live for two munths on $10 a week.

11. If I am alive and taken prisner the city jale is at the end of the bridg we allways used to cross wen we went to town (the vry begining of town after the bridg).

As you can see I left no stone unterned made shure that you and your mama wood be fine in the unlikly event of my kapcha.

Evrything else about the Walker shooting was also vry well thort thru. The notes the fotos the maps all invallubel if it had not been for a stinking windo frame Walker wood be a ded man the bullet takeing the slitest deflekshun at the last seccund to save his hide. The world wood be a far better plase for it Walker a tottal fascist his ideas of race thretten thuosands. Jus imagin how menny lives wood hav been saved if sum brave sole like myself had stopped Hitler befor he seemented power it wood obviusly nummer in the millons.

Howevver I hav no reeson to beleeve that tomorow my luk will be as bad as that nite there shood be nuthing to get between me and the president excep maybe a street lite or tree branch from wot I hav assertaned looking out the 6th flor windos. The shot itself shood be easy for a man of my traneing. Of corse I hav no idea hoo else mite be on the 6th flor wen the parade passes by I will jus hav to deel with that wen the time cums. All I can do is focuss on executeing my plan to the best of my abillty I am more than reddy to do same.

I set the allarm roll over fase the wall. I am still awake wen your mama enters I am not shure how much later. Deeppening my breething I pretend to be asleep I am unshore if she falls for it howevver she does not speke to me wich is my primery gole. My mind is made up I do not want any furtha tawk of reuniteing that conversashun is ded and buryed as far as I am conserned.

Your mama falls asleep fast always one for enjoying her time in the sak. Sum time later it cood be minits or huors she lays a foot over my leg a habbit she develloped during pregnency to feel closser to me in kase of emergensy. I kno she is jus trying to apologise for her erlier roodness say sorry for her rebutals but I am haveing nun of that. I shuv her leg away with my foot perhaps more harshly than intended howevver it is too late for even a hint of fisicial intimissy betwene us.

Wen I poosh her leg off of mine Mama half wakes then rolls over to fase away from me. I lissen to her drift bak to sleep her breething sloly becuming deeper I am jellous sleep for me no more than a forlawn hope.

Friday

Of a nite I allways set an alarm but my body clok usuley wakes me befor it rings I shut it off so as not to disterb your mama or you chillren. Howevver this morning I am fast asleep wen it goes off I can not for the life of me roll over to extingwish it the land of nod haveing welcummed me jus moments befor. I lye there limp as a jelyfish the clock winding down to a stop.

I sense your mama is awake befor she spekes.

Time to get up Alka.

Okay I say feeling like it is one wurd too menny.

Fante lines of yelow lite from a street lamp leek thru the veneshun blinds. I roll out of bed stumblel down the hall the bathrooms pink tiles mommentarly blind me wen I hit the lites. Haveing showered the previus evening I perform roodamentry ablooshuns splash my fase with cold water brush my teeth kome my hare. I creep bak to the bedroom dress in the half dark orangy browen long sleev shert gray trowsers. I riggle my feet into my shoos without undoing the lases consider putting on my dark blew jaket deside it mite not be cold enuff then reelize I may need it later this cood be a vry long day indede also who knos wen I

62

will neks be bak out to the Pains to colleck it.

I pik up my wollet it contanes evry sent I hav saved sinse returning from Mexico City. I plase neerly all of it almost $170 on the boorow keep $15 for myself I do not antissipate much need for cash today perhaps jus to buy lunch after that who knos. I slip my ID braselet onto my left rist put my Marine Core ring on my left ring finger ware ordinnarly I ware my weding ring. I insted plase the wedding ring a Russian gold band in the botom of a hand paynted coffee cup your mamas grandmuther gave her menny yeers ago. The ring has allways been slitely too big slipping off of my finger evry now and then sumtimes if busy at work I wood put it in my poket for safe keeping I used to hate takeing it off now I am happy to do so wot it onse repressented to me ded and beryed six feet under.

Out in the kichen I put a pan of water on to boil. Thru the windo the grass glissens in pre dawn lite rane clowds haveing arived to delivver there booty. Mist hangs low over the suburbben roofs the sky reddy to open up aggen at a momments notise.

Befor the water cums to a boil I mix it with sum Follgers in a blew plastik cup drink it down fast without bothering to add swete milk. I want to leeve during the brake between showers so as to keep the rifle dry wile I walk to Weslys. Haveing slept thru the allarm I am running a litle late my plan is to walk to Wesleys befor our reglar 7.15 meeting time. Normly he piks me up out frunt of the Pains huose but if I walk over I can get the pakage in his car befor he gets a good look at it.

I take one last gulp of coffee put the mug in the kichen sink. A few granes are stuck to the bottum I wunder if an old Chineese lady were to reed them like tee leeves wot wood they say.

Bak in the bedroom your Mama is sitting up feeding Rachel. I stand in the doorway for a few momments wotching the rize and fall of Rachels hed as your mama breeths.

Hav you buoght those shoos yet? I aks.

No I havent had time she says eyes terned from me.

You must get those shoos Mama.

I hav been at her for weeks to buy new shoos for your litle feet they grow bigger by the day. Also the hand-me-downs from the Pain chillren look vry ragged aruond the edges. Mama has been remiss in doing so she is probly jus trying to save muney but wen it cums to careing for you Junie I will heer no excooses spare no expense that is within my buonds your wellfare is of the utmost importense.

Mama I say Dont get up I will fix myself brekfast. I am of corse jokeing there is a snoflakes chanse in hell that she will get up she never fixes me brekfast befor work preferring to lye in bed. I kno she will go bak to sleep as soon as Rachel is dun feeding howevver this morning I sellabrate her lazyness she will not see me leeveing with the rifle.

I enter the room a few feet more but maintane a distanse between us.

I left sum munny on the boorow I say. I do not menshun the amuont virtuly my life saveings I do not want to aruose her suspishons let her discuvver that after I leeve put two and two together. Take it I say And buy whatever you and the girls mite want for.

Your mama does not resspond to this no dout wateing for me to walk over kiss her goodbye as I do evry morning but this is not evry morning. I do howevver kiss you Junie as you sleep in your krib befor terning for the door.

Bye bye I say.

I walk swiffly thru the still huose strate thru the kichen out to the garage. The first thing I notise is that the lite is now off. Rooth has been out here paynting more bloks late last nite sevral lye drying on sheets of newspaper the smell of paynt in the air. I notiss one paynted with the nummer three and smile to myself.

My rifel still hides in plane site rapped in its cloth cacoon. I pik up the blanket slide the paper pakage out then lay the blanket bak down on the flor as I fuond it so it appeers undisterbed.

I rayse the garage door slip beneeth lower it behind me. The outside air smells fresh after the gas fooms of the garage also washt cleen by the rane wich has stopped for the time been if lukky I will get the rifle to Weslys bone dry. The driveways sidewalks and rodes are dark from the resent downpoor water poolled in sum spots I imagin how much fun you wood hav Junie splashing about in the puddells.

I set off down W 5th St the suond of naybors riseing and shineing all aruond. Spoons clink agenst seereel boles raydios blare a man belts out Hartbrake Hotel wile showering. W 5th St is a resent houseing develllopment no more than ten yeers old its boxey huoses bilt on land cleered of all trees giveing me litle by way of cuvver from prying eyes. I jus hav to hope that no one looks out there windo sees me with the rifel altho it is hard to tell exackly wot I am carrying. I hold the pakkage close my rite hand cuppt around the bottum the bulk of it paralel to my body the top tukked up agenst my armpit like a soldeir standing at arms.

I walk briskly down the blok to Weslys a sqot singel levvel subberban huose apart from standing on a corner lot it looks like any other serruonding it. I see Weslys sister Linny May thru the kichen windo fixing sandwitches at the cuonter her hare messy from sleep her bathrobe rapped tite aruond her waste. I step onto the frunt lawn she looks up as I skoot past the windo to ware Wesly has bakked his Chevvy up beside the carport. The kichen door into the carport cliks open jus befor I open the reer pasenger door slide the pakage in. Laying the brokken down rifle flat it takes up about half the bak seet.

As I shut the car door I heer the kichen door slam whoever came out to see wot I am doing has retreeted. Serten that person is Linny May I walk to the kichen windo ware she is bak fixing sandwitches. Her hedd lowered consentrateing on the job at hand she does not notiss me stareing at her thru the windo for a good thirty secunds. She flinches wen she does but says not a word jus stares bak as if to say I kno wot your up to. You hav no idea you stoopid woman I hold her eyes with mine.

Wesly she finely calls out not terning away from me Lees here.

Cumming I heer Wesly shuot from sumware inside the huose.

The suond of his voise brakes Linny Mays gaze she reterns to her lunchun preperashuns laying balony out on slises of wite bred. Rane starts sprinkleing I wonder under the carport the drops beet there tatoo on the thin tin roof.

Wesly you want sum sandwitches? I heer Linny May say.

No thanks I will grab sumthing at work.

Wesly appeers at the kichen door dresst in a short sleev shert with wide blak stripes browen trowsers. He has jus brushed his teeth I can smell the toothpast from ware I stand.

Mornin Lee he says walking down the side of the carport Your brite and erly.

Mornin Wesly.

He duks his head to clime into the car notisses the pakkage on the bak seet.

Wots in the pakage?

Those curtin rods I tole you about yesserday.

Oh thats rite you sed you was getting sum.

I nod pleesed my story is holding up altho I hav lerned over the yeers that peeple will beleeve wot you want them to beleeve you jus need to leed them in the rite direkshun.

Wesly turns the kee in the ignishon the engine starts first go a good sine. He pumps the gas to warm up the engin ezes the car into D the geerbox responds with a clunk. He pulls out onto Westbrook Dr takes a qik left onto W 5th St I am on my way into the sity also hopefully the histry books.

The on aggen off aggen rane is now off howevver the overcast sky and low clowd matches my spirrits I suddnly reelize this cood be the last time I make the trip to Irving no more playing with you on the frunt lawn Junie no more hopping into a warm bath with you befor bedtime splashing aruond like we are both litle chillren no more lyeing on the Pains liveing room flor of a Sunday afternoon wotching football wile you play with your toys neerby and your Mama brings me snaks whennever I aks. Howevver if this is the way it has to be then this is the way it has to be. All grate men must at sum stage make a hard choise Kennedy hisself sed same in his book Proffiles In Curage I borowed same from the library. He sed evry man must do as his conscense reqires even if unpopuler only histry will trooly understand if it is rite histry can be the only judge.

With these thorts I reconsile the sacrafises I need to make in order to commense the clensing. I am at peece as we drive up the onramp of the Stemmons Fwy. Wesly murges with three lanes of trafik the other drivers all look exackly the same same clothes same harecut folowing the same path for the same purpuss. Despite wot most men think they reely are not capabel of independant thort they jus folow wot they are tole without even thinking about it. There is no better ecksample of this than rush hour thuosands of peeple all drawen in the same direckshun at the same time for the same purpuss to scratch out a meeger existense wile makeing sum capitlist pig fatter and richer.

Did you hav fun with the babys? Wesly aks brakeing into my thorts with the first words he has uttered sinse leeveing home.

Sorry?

The babys? Did you hav fun with them last nite? I kno how much you like seeing them.

Oh yes. We had a ball. I played with June on the frunt lawn befor dinner.

That sounds nise.

Wesly falls qiet aggen we lissen to KLIF-AM mostly advertiseing during rush huor hole thanksgiveing terkeys lots of wite meet! bakers bewty loshun for cleener skin! and of corse Budwiser to keep the masses sedated. In between the ads cums a news repport that President and Mrs Kennedy are doo to leeve Ft Wurth Airport for Dallas Luvfeeld at eleven oclok the reporters voise holds much exsitement regardding same howevver I am dissgusted that the president wood fly from Ft Worth to Dallas bearly a thirty minit drive. Working men such as myself can only jus aford a bus tiket let alone a car or cab ride yet our grate leeder jets the shortest of distanses. The sistem is not jus brokken it lyes shatered in peeces all aruond one only has to look for the all too obvius sines.

About five minits latter wen a misty rane redoosses visabilty Wesly fliks on the wipers. There is not enuf rane for them to oprate propperly they skweek as they slide bak and forth over the windsheeld.

Nasty ole day if this rane dont let up Wesly says.

Uh huh.

He of corse is tawking about the wether but that is not my primery consern it is the possabilty that the rane mite affeck Kennedys parade. I am not partikly wurryed that the authoritees will cansel it shurely the motorcade can proseed with a few drops of rane howevver if hevvy enuff the president mite not ride in an open top vehikel. I hav red abuot sum kind of bubbel top that the secret serviss employs in cases of inklement wether hevven forbid Jack or Jackie shood get there litle heds wet. Even if the bubbel top is not bullit proof it will still defleck any projecktiles also make aiming at the target diffikult due to refleckshons. I fret over this for sum time wundering if I will be abel to get a cleen shot away but then relax reelise the wether is out of my hands. I mite be speshul as is becumming more aparent but not for one momment do I pretend that I am sum kind of god who can controll the wether. If the powers that be pressent me with an oportoonity to act then I will act otherwize the clensing is not ment to be. Deep down inside tho I kno that sum how sum way the wether will improove nuthing will stand in my way wen that motorcade cums thru Deely Plaza. Call it histry fate wot ever sumthing much bigger is controling this day not me.

It takes no more than twenty minits to reech the trippel underpass as we cum out the other side the Hertz clok says time 7.34am temprature 52 degrees. The trafic inches uptown thru Deely Plaza sloed by polisemen erecting rope barryers along Hooston and Mane in rediness for the parrade. A bolt of exsitement serges thru me they are prepareing Deely Plaza for my grand deed.

Wesly takes a left off of Mane onto Hooston swiches off the wipers as the rane has stopped drives a blok north past the cuonty bldg stops at a red lite. The cuonty jale is on our rite the depositry on the left without moveing my hedd I look up at the corner windo on the 6th floor reelize that is ware I may shortly be changeing histry the thort does not surprize me.

A few blox ferther along Hooston Wesly pulls left into the state parking lot on the other side of the rale yards from the depossitry. Takeing his reglar spot beside a tin shed he shifts the car into park then sits revving the engin makeing sure the battry is good and charged. He is trying to avoid later aksing Billy Luvlady for a jump start Billy can be vry tuchy about peeple aksing too menny favers offen says he has better ways to spend his time.

With Wesly preocupyed chargeing the battry I seeze the oportoonity to get the rifel into the bldg avoid any unwanted qesshuns. I open the bak pasenger door slide out the paper pakage see my handywork is holding up qite nisely. Without a word I shut the door leeve Wesly to his own thorts. As I walk away I feel for Wesly a good kid who has probly never had any trubble with the law howevver wot I am about to do may blow up in his fase. But that is a small prise to pay if wot I do makes the world a better plase for all then Wesly haveing to sit thru a few tuff conversashuns with the law is neether here nor there for me. At best Wesly will go down as the fella who drove a grate man to his rondayvoo with histry at worst the powers that be will implikate him in a plot to asasinate the pressident. That of corse is not my probblem I hav bigger catfish to fry. Wen the time is rite I will make it cleer that Wesly was not knoingly invollved in any way shape or form howevver it is anyones gess wether the authoritys will beleeve me. In my experense they create there own realtys then manoofacture evidense to fit the millitry polise were sertenly adept at same.

The rale yards are muddy from the morning rane the dips and holows between the traks filled with water. Howevver the drizzel is holding off for the time been. I klasp the rifel paralel to my body obscureing its shape take long strides over the puddels with extra care not to step on any of the rale traks I kno from experiense they can be trecherus in the wet. A Missuori Pasific frate trane perhaps forty or fifty carrages sum carying livestok trundels its way out of the city west towards the Trinnity River Ft Wurth and parts beeyond. A groop of hobos sit in the open door of the last car there legs dangleing off of the edge swing in the breez like skoolkids climed atop the munky bars.

It is aprox a two hunnerd yard walk to the depositry I am pritty sure Wesly is still sitting in his car wen I reech the lodeing dok eether that or he is so far behind he has not bothered to cach up. I clime the steps from the lodeing dok up into the first floor all appeers desserted the domino room Mister Troolys offise both emty. I hurry to the stares not wishing to bump into sumone at the elevater howevver unlikely that mite be at this erly huor. Climeing the stares two at a time I am out of breth reeching the 6th floor. I thred my way between staks of boxes to the windo overlooking Hooston and Elm.

I paws to cach my breth then leen the rifle in the corner an old steem pipe obskures it perfekly. I unlach the windo overlooking Deely Plaza it stiks a litle but thumping it with the heel of my hand I manage to prize it open a foot or so. Six flors below polise scury abuot there blue unifforms distinkt agenst the green grass of the plaza and wite concreet of the sidewalk. The fools are still stringing up there rope baricades wot a waste of time a few feet of twine can not posibly proteck the president of the United States if sumone is intent on doing him harm.

Over the past few days ever sinse the silense dessended between me and your mama and I lerned of the parade root I hav scuoted the depositry for the perfeck vantige point. I hav no dout I hav chossen the best opshun. Originly I assoomed the roof wood be best to fire from howevver a waste high ledg runs all the way aruond there is no way to stand on a ledge seven flors off of the gruond and fire a rifle without falling or being sited only a madman wood attemp same. I also exploored the posibilty of scaleing the advertiseing hording but it too is exposed I wood be spotted in an instent also wood need to hang from it by one arm shoot with the other. I may as my muther has tole me menny times be speshul howevver I am not Superman or for that matter a orangatan. The 7th flor I thort held more promiss there is a small room in the suoth east corner primarily used as a werkshop and storage plus the 7th flor is far less travelled than the others. Howevver the door to the workshop has a windo anyone cood instently spot me shood they walk onto the floor also a lege running ruond the top of the 6th flor obskures the line of site to the rodeway below. The depossitrys lower floors I fuond unsootable for diffring reesons eether too hevvily travelled too menny windos open to outside observers or too menny things interfeering with the line of site tree branches street sines and such.

My chossen spot also benafits from vews in two direkshuns the first suoth strate down Hooston I will be abel to wotch the motorcade hed on as it aproches after terning rite off of Mane. The secund vew to the rite looks west I can folow the motorcade after it terns left onto Elm sloly heds towards the tripel underpass and Stemons Fwy a street lamp and sum folage all that mite blok my veiw.

I hav not yet desided wich direcshun will give me the gratest chanse of sucess howevver shooting as the car heds away from me feels rite. Frunt on cood be problemmatic sumone seeted in frunt of Kennedy cood blok my shot also secret serviss agents may be rideing on the vehikel scuoting ahed for trubble it will be best to stay hidden at that time to avoyd detecshon. On any acuont the car shood slo to a crawel wen takeing the tite left tern off of Hooston onto Elm it is more than a ninty degree tern I will hav a far eezier shot after that as the car rolls sloly down the hill the presidents hed will remane rufly the same size in my scope doo to the cars low speed. Howevver Junie I must admit I hav never seen a presidenshul motorcade the clossest I ever saw was the May Day parade in Red Sqare that howevver is a compleetly diffrent kettel of fish the full mite of the Soviet millitry on display. It is diffcult for me to kno exakly wot todays parade will bring. Posibly snipers stashoned on surruonding rooftops scuoting for asasssins perhaps even atop the depositry itself? Or secret serviss agents serching bldgs allong the root to make sure they are cleer of threts? I will of corse remane open to all posibiltys a soldeir must deel with any and all ocurenses in battel howevver there will no dout be menny unexpekted varyables beeyond my control I will jus hav to roll with the punches as Casius Clay mite say.

I leeve the rifle unasembeled do not fansy the idea of hideing an asembled rifle inside the bldg for four huors if sumone were to find it my plans wood be wurth dirt. Howevver I do kno for a fack that rifles hav been in the bldg befor not two days erlyer two rifels were in Mister Troolys offise. One of the big wig book cumpny exectivs Mister Caster was shoing off weppons he bort at lunch time a Remmington .22 a xmas pressent for his son a .30-06 Muaser to take deer hunting hisself. Howevver jus becos rifels hav been seen inside the bldg befor does not meen I can take any chanses my rifle must remane hidden until the momment is rite. As much as I am itching to get things mooveing the time for reassembeling will hav to cum as close to the presidents arrivel as posible. Better to leeve the brokken down rifle in its paper rapper that way the other men will not give it a secund glanse shood they notiss it. If they do I will tell them wot I tole Wesly it is kurtin rods for drapes luvvingly crafted by your Mama to keep the morning sun from my eyes she is allways thinking of her hussbands wellbeen ha.

With the rifle sqirreled away I now commense stakking boxes

of books to obskure the suoth east corner from the rest of the flor. The erly huor is perfeck for this task in less than fifteen minits the flor will be craweling with men Junor Jarman Charly Givvens the rest of the refloring crew pluss order fillers like Wesly going about there bisness. They wood be shure to aks qesshuns if they saw me mooveing too menny boxes aruond it is eckspected that we moove sum in the corse of our dootys but there is a limit to wot I cood get away with without aruoseing suspishon. I most sertenly do not want sumone reporting me to Mister Trooly or Mister Shelly one of the other supevisers.

As menshunned erlier Charly and his men hav alreddy made my task much easeer by pooshing piles of boxes from the west side of the flor ware the repare work is being undertakken to the east side. Now it is a simpel matter of mooveing a few of these staks until they suruond the corner windo shift a cuppel more to blok the vew from the Dal Tex bldg across Hooston there windos fase strate onto the depositry. These boxes I put direkly behind ware I will sit. To finnish I plase one stak of sevral small boxes in the corner in frunt of the rifle I will later use these to fashun a seet and brase to steddy the rifle wile aiming. The windo ledg is too lo to use as a brase I wood hav to leen out too far expose myself to govt agents who may be wotching the windos aruond the plaza not to menshun sumone in the croud may see me.

My snipers nest reddy there is nuthing more to be dun until closser to the motorcade time. I walk over to the stareway take them two at a time to the first flor practiseing a fast eckscape I will no dout need same later. The clok on the wall neer the lodeing dok says 7.55am not enuff time to reed yesterdays newspapers befor starting work no loss they will only be full of proppaganda regarding the grate ones visit. I enter the domino room Charly Givens looks up surprized that I am not alreddy in there reeding the papers. Instently I am anoyed by the rooms rawcussness it is tite with the smell of coffee egg sandwitches men smokeing they are larfing for no good reeson there gufaws so lowd they dont suond reel. There party mood is no dout doo to the impending festivtys litle did they kno that sumone may vry well rane on there parade how qikly that will chang there toon.

A few minits to go befor my offishal starting time I am itching to get to work. Being busy will make the morning pass qikker howevver I also dont want to attrak attenshun with undoo eegarness. I take the starecase bak up to the 2nd flor lunch room wich of a morning is usuley desserted sure enuff I find it emty. I take a seet neer the pop masheen sit for a spell the tik tok of the clok the only cumpny for my thorts.

I feel no nervusness Junie a grate carm has setled over me the path I am on is a just one rite and troo. Also on a praktical level I kno the shot I need to make will be relativly eesy for a man of my sharpshooting stattus. I hav zeero conserns that I will miss the target after the huors of prepparashun I hav put in I kno that rifle inside and out. The fack that the target is a liveing breething human been a man who I grately respeck I must admit ways on me sum. As I hav sed befor to Rooth Mama Goerge any persun who chooses to lissen despite Kennedys father prakticly bying him the job he is the rite man to be president at this time his work for the poor the blaks the underprivlidged to be aplawded. Also he is relativly yung with plenty of energy and suond ideas no dowt foreward thinking as is his bruther Bobby. Howevver he is but one part of a complicated eqashun no matter how much he cares he is only one man he can only affek so much chang. It is the sistem that is rotten Demokrats Republikans both the same conserned only with holding onto power keeping the poor and opressed down. Only by clensing the sistem starting with the man at the top can things begin to be made better for evryone. The passing of a man who simbalizes captallism will cawse peeple to reevalooate wot they hold deer Americans Soviets Coobans alike. If a simpel hard werking man such as myself can get so frusstrated as to shoot the president Junie shurely sumthing must be amiss.

My carm at this time of hi stress is also a result of my Marine traneing Junie I hav been skooled in the ways of killing for my cuntry. Howevver wot I am about to do is not for luv of this cuntry it is for lov of peeple of all cuntrys most of all the chillren the peeple of the future by acting now I will bild a better one for all of them.

Wen the clok hits eight I kno I can start work without attracking atenshun. I hed bak to the 1st flor pik up three orders Hermans superstishon waying on my mind. The orders clerk Eyra a fat Mexican with saggy arms who allways seems to hav the remanes of a donut or cookie stuk in the corner of her muoth rayses her eyebrows opens her trap to say sumthing then seeing the look on my fase shuts it. One wood think I hav aksed for the kees to the city rather than takken extra work sum peeple jus spend there days looking for ways to get tikked off. The stoopid cow has probly never had an orijinal thort in her life how dare she judg me.

I dash bak up to the 6th flor the harder I work the qiker the morning will pass. The men replaseing the flor bords are still in there festiv mood jokeing aruond doing as litle work as posible. I prettend not to notiss wen they wisper snip snip as I walk by.

After completeing three trips to the orders desk smileing at donut lady eech time it must be aruond ten oclok wen I am standing at the windos faceing Elm St three new orders fassened to my clipbord. Outside in the plaza the furst gathrings of a croud are becumming evvident.

Junor Jarman walks up beside me. The man must seldum shower I sware I smell him from three feet away.

Qite a crowd bilding up out there he says.

Uh huh I say then reelize he has given me an oportoonity to sow sum seeds of dout. Wots all the fuss about?

You aint herd?

Uh uh.

He looks at me like I liv under a rok. The pressdent is cumming.

Reelly? Wen?

Charly tole me the newspapers is sayin he will be speekin at a lunchun at the trade mart aruond 12.30. He will probly pass rite by here jus befor then.

Do you kno wich way he is cumming?

Rite by the book depositry accordin to Charly. Sed the parade cums down Mane then takes Elm to the Stemons.

Oh I see I say Well thanks for filling me in Junor. I am allways the last to kno.

Junor claps me on the sholder says sumthing about litle ole Lee liveing in his litle ole dreem world howevver I am alreddy walking away hedded upstares with my neks three orders.

Howeveer I dont start hunting for books wen I reech the 6th flor I keep rite on going take the stares and a ladder up to the roof.

The clok on the Hertz sine is to my left time 10.08 temp 59 howevver I am more intrested in wot the sky abuv tells me it is cleer blew the misty cluod of morning burned away by the sun. It has becum a beutiful fall day jus as I allways knoo it wood. Even the wether is in sincronizashun with my plans this is shurely the day that the world finds out jus how grate Lee Oswald is. The yeers of strugels frustrashuns rejecshuns will all be wurth it. The Rushans the Coobans will both deeply regret not welcumming me in Mexico City. The Coobans cared not one jot that I had wurked hard for there cawse establishing the New Orleens chapta of the Fare Play for Cuba comittee even printing pamflets at my own persnal expense. This made no difrense they terned me away sed that it takes four munths to prosess a visa to visit Cuba the Russians also of zero asistence wen I sort acess thru there cuntry. I must admitt Junie our conversashuns became qite heeted weppons were drawen but there lak of asistence was simpley not good enuff a pox on both there huoses.

I walk over to the edg of the roof faseing Elm a wall running aruond it reeches to my chest. I rayse myself up on my elbos peer over the edge. Below clustas of peeple gather like ants aruond a droppt sandwitch at a piknik they croud the street corners thinning out between them no dout the sidewalks will fill out more as noon approches. Penshunners famlys with litle kids others with nuthing better to fill there day wate for a parad that is more than two huors away qite content to stand in the sun with noware to go to the bathroom jus to cach a glimps of there glorius leeder. The Kennedys are treeted like king and qeen not the dooly elekted offishals that they are the United States is an ilushon of demokracy unfortunatly allmost two hunnerd millon peeple beleev that illushon. Well kings can be execooted farytales don't allways end happly ever after. The peeple down there do not kno it but they will soon hav a windo into histry they will tell there chillren grandchillren grategrandchillren that they stood in Deely Plaza on that day jus like evryone remembers ware they were wen the Japs attakked Perl Harbor. I myself was only a few yeers old howevver my mama and her kin tawked constently about that day thru out my erly yeers.

I lower myself down off of the wall take the ladder and stares bak to the 6th flor. I skurt Charly and his men naleing plywood in plase hedd towards the corner overlooking Elm ware I hav bilt the blind. After makeing shure that no one is wotching I chek on my brown paper pakage it still stands behind the pipe undissterbed.

I continoo to work hard filling orders for anuther huor. Eventully donut lady remarks on my apetite for produktivty.

My Mister Oswald she says Sumone ate there Weetys this morning.

I smile say nuthing in reply. Howevver she has served one useful perpuss reminded me that I hav eaten nuthing all day excep those few gulps of instent coffee at the Pains I hav been running on nervus energy ever sinse. I must make time to eat becos after the clensing who knos wot will happen I may be kaptured detaned for long periuds of time without food or water. I will need to be at the top of my game if subjekted to interogashun but I will find it difikult to consentrate I get heddakes without suffishent fule it happens evry time.

I fill one more set of three orders drop the books into the

shipping dept aruond 11.30am then duk thru the lodeing dok out onto Hooston ware a food truk sets up dayly. Ordinarly it is frekwented by depositry workers and offise staff but today a long line snakes down the sidewalk towards Elm the parad croud bying hotdogs cokes reeses peenut butter cups like food rashunning is in effeck and they dont want to starv. I wate impashently for my turn increeingly worryed with each passing minit that Mr Trooly will notiss my absense the last thing I need is unwanted attenshun from him.

Eventually this feeling becums so grate that I poosh my way towards the cuonter.

I am a werking man I say I do not hav time to wate.

I expeck a heeted baklash from this dissplay of roodness howevver a woman at the frunt of the line meerly steps aside says Well after you then Mister Big Werker Man.

Ignoreing her sarkasm I order a ham and cheese sandwitch a bag of Mortons pottato chips pay the man then bolt bak to work. Entring thru the lodeing dock I hedd strate for the domino room. I hav worked up qite a swet dashing to and from the food truk I take off my jakket lay it on the windo sill. I set to eating then reelize it is not twelve oclok yet it is still too erly for lunch. The risk of being seen stuffing my fase wen I shood be working propells me up the stares to the 5th floor ware I kno I can hide away. Always thinking ahedd I leev my jaket on the windo sill ware it may later confoose the authoritees as to my wareabouts at the time of the shooting.

I hide behind the stares on the 5th flor ware no one can see me devower the sandwitch cramming down fistfulls of pottato chips between bites. In five maybe ten minits the men werking on the 6th floor will take there leeve for lunch hopfully all hedd to the domino room there absense giveing me thirty minits to prepare for my gratest moment.

Around 11.45 I retern to donut lady take one last set of three orders from the box without the slitest intenshun of filling them. Deep down I kno that one way or the other these are the last orders I will ever reseeve. I sillently assend to the 6th flor peek aruond the corner befor exitting the stare case. The refloreing crew are finnishing up the mornings work sweeping up wood shaveings putting tools bak in toolboxes etc. Charly Givvens Danny Arce Bonny Ray Willams Billy Luvlady and a few others are still foolling aruond like litle kids that is one of the menny problems I hav with my fellow werkers they dont act like men at all more like chillren. The Marines was the same the solders constently gooffing off wen in fack any job wether protekting your cuntry or laying a new flor is sumthing to be takken seriusly a matter worthy of respeck.

Charly and his crew are too rapped up in there tomfoolry to notiss as I slip bak down the stares to the 5th floor. I dash over and loyter in frunt of the elevaters knoing that they will soon make there way down for lunch I want them to see me on the 5th flor in case the subjek of my whereabbouts pryor to the shooting shood later cum up.

Shure enuff in a minit both elevaters begin there dissent wooping and hollering ringing thru the shafts. The men hav split into two groops to race to the bottom sumthing they offen do. Both cars fly past Charly standing alone driveing the older elevater on the east side of the bldg Bonny Ray Willams driveing the one on the west side with the others. Charly and Bonny Ray both notiss me as they rokket by Charly even winks.

Onse there hollering fades I reassend the stares to the 6th flor. I am now all alone the flor dethly qiet a few misst tools the only sine of resent activty. In the silense I deteck a low levvel hum after a momment realise it is the crowd in Deely Plaza six floors below.

I retern to the blind am jus abuot to remove the rifell from its hideing plase wen an elevater starts clanging its way bak up the shaft it is the older one drivven by a hand pedall that bangs wen releesed. For obvius reesons I do not not wish to be cort with the rifel I put the pakkage bak behind the pipes grab my clipbord hed towards the elevaters. The car promply arrives out steps Charly Givens he glanses my way as he goes over to ware his croo are repareing the floor. He piks up his blew dennim jakket draped over sum boxes takes a pak of Lucky Strikes from the top poket he must hav left it behind in his hast to win the elevater rase.

Boy you goin downstares? he says lookin at me strange Its neer lunch time you kno.

No sir Im fixin to fill this last order befor I go down.

Well arent you the werker bee.

I shrug my sholders tell him I am jus doin my job. That is sumthing I hav always tryed to do Junie no matter wot the task. A man can only respeck hisself if he does an honnest days work for an honest days pay altho that can be diffkult to remember under sum circumstanses the coffee cumpny in New Orleens springs to mind the work durty and tedius the men about as free thinking as fense posts.

Can you do me a faver sir? I aks.

Wots that?

Will you be shure to close the elevater gate wen you get bak down stares I say knoing that the elevater will only work if the wooden grate is pulled shut. Plees send it bak up if you hav the time it will save me time wen I am dun here. Of corse I do not tell him wot dun here reely meens.

Shure thing Charly says. He puts his jaket down hops bak abord the car closes the gate the elevater clangs as he whissles If I Had a Hammer in a vry off kee manner.

I wate until the elevater reeches the bottom shure enuff Charly sends it bak up. Wen it arrives I pull the gate leeve it open. Then I call the other elevater that is newer and can be sumoned. Wen it arrives I pull its gate open now it too is stuk on the 6th flor. There shood be no more interupshuns furthermoor anyone who trys to get up here to cach me after the shooting will need to clime the stares giveing me valuabel minits to flee.

It is now 11.55 I hav lost crooshal time deeling with Charly. There is at most thirty minits left untill I need to be in posishun. I dich my clipbord wedg it between two staks of boxes neer the stares well away from my snipers nest. I scoot bak over to the blind take the rifel from behind the pipes frantikly begin undoing the tape holding the pakage together. I rip the top off pull out the two parts of the rifel the stok and the barrell then upend the hole pakage until the peeces wrapt in the tshirt from Rooths garage tumbel out folowed by the cartridg contaneing the four bullits.

I put the cartrige on the flor beside the boxes plase the tshirt beside it unwrap the tshirt untill it is lade flat on the floor the peeses exposed reddy to be reasembeled. I pull a dime from my poket qickly go about putting the rifle bak togetther reverseing the steps I took to brake it down last nite. Junie as I hav sed I am vry experensed in the ways of wepponry I cood do this with my eyes shut wich is jus as well my hands they trembel slitely at the magnitood of wot I am about to attemp I am not ashammed to admit same.

I am slideing the side barrell band bak on wen I heer sounds. Much to my dissmay it is footsteps also hevvy breething getting closser by the seccund. Sumone has climed the stares all the way to the 6th flor my roose of takeing the elevaters out of akshun of no deterense.

Thru a gap between the boxes I see a memba of Charlys croo Bonny Ray Willems a yung blak fella about twenty yeers old. He walks towards the windos faseing the plaza his lunchbag in his rite hand parks hisself not twenty feet away on a two weeler hand truk we use for shifting large qantitys of boxes. He looks aruond as if expecting to see sum of his fello workers shrugs his sholders starts in on his food. He pulls a sandwitch from a browen paper bag it looks like chiken takes a bite then swigs from a coke that he probly perchassed from the pop masheen in the 2nd flor lunch room. Neks he tares open a bag of Freetos munches a muoth full then reterns to attakking the sandwitch.

I am a jakrabit cort in a cars brites. If Bonny Ray plans to wotch the entyre parrade from that windo it will be imposibel to acomplish my gole. After a moments hessitashun I deside to continoo reasembling the rifle if he does not moove on by the time I am finnished I will hav to figger out anuther sollushun.

In minits I hav the rifle bak in one peece the bolt slides home with a satisfying clik. I chek to see if Bonny Ray has notised the suond howevver he is so busy gawking out the windo his hare cood cach on fire he wood be nun the wiser. I slide the bolt bak lode the first bullit return the bolt home. The scope may need readjustment haveing shifted sum durring dissasembly but a superier rifelman such as myself can compenssate for any deviashun detected after the first shot. In adishon the short distanse at play here perhapps a hunnerd feet or less meens any slite discreppency shood not make much diffrense howevver if it does I will be more than reddy to deel with it.

The rifle now prepared I lye it flat between sevral boxes in the korner. I sneek anuther look at Bonny Ray he has taken a peece of meet out of the sandwitch chiken on the bone he naws at it getting evry last morsell. I wotch as he finnishes then puts the stript bone and the emty freeto pakk inside the paper bag dranes his last muothfull of coke. He belches leens foreward to onse more look out the windo at the plaza below.

I hav allways liked Bonny Ray I dont kno him so well but from wot I hav observed he is a good kid he does not giv me as much lip as the others. He lives not far from Oak Clif with a yung wife who is eckspecting that is sumthing I can relate to as Rachel was doo wen I commensed work here. Howevver I also kno that if Bonny Ray is all that stands between me and compleeteing my task I will take care of him. With four bullits in the rifel three needed to commense the clensing that leeves one left over. If Bonny Ray is still sitting by that windo wen the parad passes by I will use the 4th bullet on him shood he try to get in my way. By the time he reeches me from ware he is sitting

I will hav alreddy delt with the pressident it shood only take ten secunds to fire off three ruonds then I can tern my atenshun to Bonny Ray. Sertenly I cood remoove him from the eqashun first then take out Kennedy howevver the suond of the shot may allert the secret serviss cawse the motorcade to flee down Elm it is best to leeve Bonny Ray till last. I sinserely hope that Bonny Ray leeves the 6th flor befor the bullets start flying howevver I must be mently preparred to deel with him if that is not the case.

Bonny Ray has still not mooved he is leening foreward posed like a pore imitashun of that statchew the thinker. I silently plase two boxes in frunt of the windo stak one on top of the other to form a brase for the rifel. I press inwerds on both sides of the top box forming a creese for the barrell to rest in. Then I plase anuther box in frunt of them so that wen I neel down rest the rifel on top of the two boxes the one in frunt suports its barrell at a downwood angell thru the windo. I do not wurry about leeveing fingerprints behind after all I work at the depossitry opening and closeing boxes all day long it is to be eckspected that my prints wood be fuond thereon in fack it wood be more suspishus if they were not. I moove the box I hav been sitting on closser to the windo test the plasement of the rifle ajust the relativ posishun of the boxes a few times until the setup feels rite. In the Mareens my favorit shooting posishuns were sqotting or sitting down they help steddy the weppon make for better ame that is how I attaned the rank of sharpshooter no meen feet indeed.

Bonny Ray cleers his throte balls up his lunch bag. He drops it neer a pile of wood shaveings plases the pop bottel beside it. He stands up streches then for sum reeson perhapps a six sense spins ruond in my direckshun. My refleckses as sharp as a tak I pull my hed bak unshure if he has spotted me. I stay stil as a muose my hart raseing as his footsteps get closser. I reech for the rifle but he stops. I hold my breth for wot feels like eternaty then his footsteps start up aggen now groing qiter. I let sevral secunds pass then peer thru the gap he is hedding towards the stares. He bypasses the elevattors pleeseing me grately I wood hav to call wichever one he uses bak up to the 6th flor risking ferther exposure. He disapeers down the stares probly to find ware the rest of his croo are wotching the parad from oblivius to jus how close he came to meeting his maker.

I take a few deep breths to relacks then take one last look at my set up chek evrything is in order. The time is 12.15 Kennedy skeduled to pass at 12.25. I consider wateing out the ten remaneing minits rite here howevver if I get cort overlooking the parad with rifle in hand it will be all over I will be aprehended without acomplishing a thing. Saffer to leeve the floor for a few minits make shure my pritty fase is seen elseware pryor to the shooting hopfuly create sum kind of smoke screne for later wen the polise start aksing qesshuns. In the meentime if anyone shood find the rifle it will be unatended with no way to link it to me.

As I stand up to leeve shuoting erups from down below sum kind of commoshun happning neer Hooston and Mane. The croud parts makeing room for sumthing it is hard to tell eksactly wot untill I see a man thrashing aruond on the gruond even from this distanse it is a most disterbing site indede. Sevral polise offer asistence wile others cops remane in posishun faseing into the street wot fools they shood be faseing into the crowd ware any truble will cum from there akshuns defy comon sense jus one more ecksample of the ineptitood of the Dallas polise.

I turn from the windo take the stares cazully to the 2nd floor lunch room. It is as usule desserted. I take the tshirt that the gun parts were rapped in it is now streeked with oil I shuv it into the bottom of a trashcan pile a copy of the Dallas Morning News in after it. I wonder out of the lunch room into the publishers offise the desks are emty the hole floor outside awateing the grate presdents arival. I return to the lunch room sit at the bench clossest to the door one of the sekretrys I beleev her name is Carolin I hav aksed her for change for the pop masheen sevral times passes by takes the stares down to the first flor that leed out to Deely Plaza. I wate a minit then folow her leed take the same stares down howevver insted of leeveing the frunt of the bldg I hed towards the reer.

Junor Jarman and anuther colored fella are in the domino room nattering away over fryed chiken I do not interup them howevver sit a spell make sure they see me good and propper. Wen they leeve to wotch the parade the lodeing dok clok says 12.21 I hav but minits to spare.

Unabbel to use the elevaters I scurry bak up to the 6th flor take a few deep breths to carm my breething then take my plase beside the corner windo. Even tho the parad is out of site hidden by the cuonty bldg I can hear it the suond of cheering hollering the low throtted rumbel of escort motorsycles cums from Mane St flowing ever closser like an incumming tide. My hart beets ten to the duzzen as I pik up the rifel howevver my hands are rok steddy. This is wen a man finds out exakly wot he is made of Junie I reelise I am made of vry strong stuff indeed a revellashun that cums as no grate surprize.

As the throngs at the top of the plaza glimps the parade

cumming down Mane there noize swells. Judgeing from the crazed reakshun the convoy can not be far away now they are waveing screeming shuotting a litle girl in a brite red dress maybe five yeers old holding her muthers hand jumps up and down on the spot trying to get a better vew. It is utta madness sevral men hang from street lamps attemping to do same.

I lift the rifle slip its lether sling over my sholder. I preffer to shoot this way the sling holds the rifle tite to my body makes me feel at one with the weppon wen I moove it folows like we are wed. I neel down faceing sqare on to the boxes I hav set up. As I rest the barrell of the rifle on a box I heer the crowd gro more fevered. I grip the bolt push it up pull it bak to chek the first bullet is still in plase push the bolt bak foreward pull it down. The bullet is in the fireing chamber reddy to go.

From my erlier studys of the root I kno the limosine will appeer after terning rite off of Mane. As I alreddy menshunned takeing aim from frunt on is not the best shot I will stay better hidden if I aim down Elm. Howevver staying inside the windo I poynt the rifle up Mane site the corner thru the skope I want to get a feel for Kennedy in my sites.

Secunds pass like huors then the first part of the parad appeers obviusly magnefied in my sites to a hi degree. Two motorsycle cops doing a good job of balanseing their hevvy bikes at low speed reving their engins to frightten any stray onlookkers bak onto the kurb. Then the leed car cums into vew a long blak convertable much to my releef the roof has not been instaled. Inside the polise cheef maybe the mayor ride in frunt secret serviss agents ride in bak. Thru the magnificashun of the skope I can see they are all smileing no dout releeved that the parad is almost over evrything has gone off without a hich ha.

Wot with the motorsycles revving there engines and the croud going bannanas the noise is deffening now ekkoing ruond the plaza bounseing off the bldgs. The hood of the presidenshul vehical apeers a few car lengths behind its pantework gleeming two flags on eether side fluttering in the breez.

I kno from my extensiv reserch that the car is a blew Linkin Continentel howevver I hav sumhow forgoten that it has three ros of seets not two. The driver of corse sits in the frunt row beside him a man in a soot presoomably a secret serviss agent. Guvner Connly and his wife ocoopy the middel row Jack and Jackie ride in the reer the president on the pasenger side I am shure he likes to be neer the sidewalk ware he can soke up the addulashun. Jackie waves at the masses Junie there is no other wurd to deskribe her but raddyant dressed in pink with maching hat that she holds down with one hand to protekt agenst the wind she looks as beutiful as any of the fotos I hav seen in the magazeens your Mama wastes munny on. The president looks vry pleesed with hisself pushes his hare bak off of his tanned fase I hav seen him do this menny times wen speeking on TV perhapps a nervus habbit howevver today a necesity the wind swurling thru Deely Plaza due to the bldgs that suround it.

The croud laps it up like the Kenedys hav cum to personly vissit them in there litle suburben homes. JFK and Jacky in turn get exsited by the crouds reacshun feeding off of there energy I see the presdent say sumthing to the furst lady she smiles bak. If there is one thing pollitishans luv Russians Americans or Coobans it is atenshun they krave it like a drug well lets see who gets the most attenshun onse the clensing has commensed.

To my grate surprize no secret serviss agents ride on the sidebords of Kennedys car this pleeses me grately one less obstakle to shoot aruond. I keep my sites traned on JFK as the car procedes down Mane towards me. I center his fase in the crosshares I cood take him out rite now howevver Connlys head is bobbing about in frunt of him createing a distrakshun the guvnor chukkles at sumthing his wife says. I take my eye from the sites chek the cars behind Kennedys the first is filled with secret serviss men standing on the running bords the neks one carrys LBJ and Lady Bird folowed by other cars carrying varius lokal diggnitrys. I am shure there are also cars and busses for camramen and press but they hav still not ruonded the corner from Mane onto Hooston. Not one of the secret serviss men rayses their eyes abuv street level not one of them scans the windos or bldgs for trubble the end of the parad is at hand they think they are home scot free hav let there gard down well I hav sum vry bad news for them.

The leed motorcycle takes the tite left tern off of Hooston onto Elm looking strate down I can see the top of his shiney wite hellmet. Jus as I preddicted the motorcade slos to a krawl to negoshiate the sharp bend I cood walk faster than the leed car the presidenshul vehikel brakes to match its speed.

It is now or nevver.

I swivvel to redireck the rifel down Elm. My rite hand slips into the crook between the stok and trigger gard to steddy the barrell on the box in frunt of me. I reech out with my left hand to gide the rifle downward thru the windo.

Wen I lower my eye to the sites the kaos melts away. I heer nuthing see nuthing excep the small sircle of lite thru the skope.

Kennedys car finnishes the tern onto Elm disapeers behind a street lamp reappeers under the follage of a big oak tree. Its leeves and branches will soon obscure him I must act now. My hart puonds like a jakhammer ripping up ole road adrennalin pumps thru my vanes thorts swurl thru my hed this is the chanse I hav been wateing for my hole life the chanse to lern the anser to the qesshun I hav constently aksed myself am I the man I hav allways claymed to be sumone cappabel of afecting grate change given the oportoonity or am I meerly a prettender sumone no better than the billons of sheep baaing there way thru a poyntless existance? Am I wurthy of the chanse histry has aforded me? I sinserely hope so howevver even I do not kno the anser Junie for one only lerns that at the momment of trooth. Like the qarterback on the twenty yard line forth down one chanse left to win the champeenship can he pull off the winning play for his teem? Only wen he finds hisself in that situashun will he trooly kno.

I push all these thorts asside consentrate on the task at hand. This shot is not as simpel as the one I took at Genral Walker for starters the target is mooveing. Howevver it is brord daylite and Kennedys hed fills the crosshares like a watermelun sitting on the kichen bench the four times magnaficashun makes him appeer jus feet away. I breeth out slip my finger inside the trigger gard evry moovement feels like slo moshun as I gradully increese pressur on the trigger with my finger and fokus on absorbing the rekoil this will enabel me to manetane my pose qikly relode for the neks shot evry seccund cuonts.

From all my time spent aruond weppons I kno that there must be an almitey boom wen the rifle fires howevver I heer no bang smell no gunpowder feel no recoyl it is like I am rapped in cotton wool totly absorbed in the job hisstory has aksed me to purform. Thru the skope I see sevral leeves flutter from the oke tree the sites are slitely misalined cawseing the bullet to hit the overhanging tree take a defelekshun ricoshay off into the plaza and kill an innosent bystander for all I kno. I trewly hope that is not the case howevver menny grate acshuns play out with colatral damage if that is the case so be it histry will probly judge them a heero for the small part they hav played.

The driver of Kennedys car does the exack oposite of wot I thort he wood do rather than speed up after the first shot he slos down unshure of wot is happning. This gives me valubel extra secunds but I obviusly dont hav time to realine the scope. Without looking away from the sites I lift the bolt pull it bak to ejeck the spent cartridg it clatters to the floor. I push the bolt foreward and down to relode. My crosshares qikly find Kennedy as the car reappeers from behind the tree they settel on the bak of his hed. I make a quik mentel ajustment shift aim slitely to the left of ware the sites plase him to compansate for the skopes misalinement.

I fire a secund time. Kennedys reacshun is imediat. His arms fly up aruond his throte I hav hit my target altho lower than intended. I fite bak a riseing urge to selebrate the job only half dun. I carmly ejek the spent cartridg slide the third bullit into the chamber lucky nummer three loks in plase with a sollid clik.

The presidenshul vehikel is now rolling down the hill getting ferther away with evry secund I must fire befor it reeches the cuvver of the tripel underpass. Howevver I dont panik I am now in the zone I hav felt this sensashun menny times befor in the

Marines Junie there is nuthing in the world but me and my weppon I kno I will not miss.

I aim slitely higher and left onse aggen to ajust for the misdirekshun of the previus two shots. My finger gentley titens on the center of the trigger it seems to take an huor for the presure to bild suffishently wen the rifle finaly does fire it surprizes even me. Kennedys hed explodes in a mist of red. Tishoo and bone fly evry wich way the rite side of his head cums away like the skin of a berst baloon. I am no doktor but at that momment I kno that John F Kennedy is ded no one can survive a hedd shot like that. I hav killed the presdent of the United States I reelise the thort not as shokking to me as it shood be I hav long nown that one day I wood purform an act of monoomentel proporshuns. I allways knoo I had it in me Junie as did my muther jus aks her she will tell you she has long beleeved same.

Kennedy slumps sideways to his left falling onto the seet besside Jacky. I am shure it is an involluntry akshun on his part not a conshus efort to hide from his atakker his brane can not posibly be funkshuning. Screems not from exsitement now but abjek teror emenate aruond the plaza. Jacky scared out of her mind crawels onto the trunk of the vehikle a dark sooted secret serviss man runs up alongside pushes her bak in the car she is reluktent to go. Who can blame the poor woman her hussband is lyeing there ded harf his hedd missing also she does not kno if there are more bullets cumming perhaps she is neks in the fireing line. I want to call out tell her that she is safe that she is not the target and never was but of corse that is imposibel.

The motorsycles suond like masheen guns as the convoy

ackselerates down Elm towards the tripel underpass takeing evassiv acshun but too late the horse has well and trooly bolted. The secret serviss agent on the trunk of Kennedys car hangs on for deer life the other vehikles do there best to keep up altho they probly hav no idea wot is hapning. I shood get out of here get as far away as posibel shurely sumone has seen me fire from up here but I stand up linga for one glorius momment absorb the feeling of fulfilling my lifes dreem. It does not matter wot hapens to me now I dont care if they cach me even kill me rite this minit. All the pane the self dout the internel struggels hav been lifted. All the ridicool I endured thruout my life at skool in New York my clothes never good enuff my acksent too strange or in the Marines ware the so called men called me Oswaldsky Oswaldskovich Ozzie Rabbit Mrs Oswald thru me in the shower with my clothes on also the rejeckshun from the Russians and Cubans in Mexico City who cood not see my valew to there cawse all of that meens nuthing now. Even the tornts from your own Mama acooseing me of dreeming too big of being no more than a litle man makeing up fansiful stories it has all disapeered in the split secund the thurd bullet took to rip apart Kennedys hed. I hav now showen the douters how vry rong they were. I recall the wurds of Frank Sinatra in the moovie I watched just a few short weeks ago wen you hav a gun you are a sort of god without a gun you nevver wood hav even spat at me you never wood hav notissed me but becos of the gun you will remember me as long as you liv those words sertenly ring troo rite now.

I wotch as spektaters flee the unknowen teror raneing down from abuv. Sum hed towards the tripel underpass sum the raleway tracks others lye flat on the grass protecking there chillren from god knos wot. Thats rite I think bow down befor me you fools you trooly are in the presense of grateness.

I am not shure how long I stand at that windo savering the froots of my labor. Probly less than a minit but evry secund is wurth an huor rite now. I can alreddy feel the cops closeing in I carry the wate of the gilty man evryone will kno wot I hav dun with jus one look at my fase.

With a few deep breths I regane focus. Servival instinks kik in I get an overwelmming urge to run I dont care ware jus anyware as fast as I can. If I am brootally honnest Junie with hindsite I did not think thru this part of my plan vry well more focusst on pulling off the feet of the sentury than ensureing my own well been afterwards. Howevver now that I hav acomplished my mishon I vry much want to ekscape if only to see you aggen I kno it will not be an eesy task. Wile the Dallas polise erned zeero respeck conserning there ackshuns folloing the Walker shooting this is a compleetly diffrent kettel of fish the president shot in brawd daylite thuossands of peeple wotching the secret serviss FBI will now also be invollved frantik to find the gilty kulprit and delivver them to the nashun. Ekscapeing will be the chalenge of my life.

I leeve the three emty shell caseings ware they fell if I poket them and the cops later find them on my persson not even I cood convinseingly explane away there pressense. I slip thru the gap in the blind bent low the rifel slung across my sholder scoot dyagonly across the flor past ware Charly and the others are undertakeing repares how inconsekwenshal that task now seems. I swerv aruond staks of book cartons until I reech the corner ware the elevaters and stares reside. There I spot a gap between two stax of boxes the perfek hideing plase for the rifle. I drop my partner in crime it slides to the flor hidden from veiw one must stand direkly over the gap between the boxes to see it. I then reelize it is not far from ware I erlier hid my clipbord well if they are fuond at the same time so be it I can not stop to scuot the floor for a better hideing place and sertenly can not leeve the bldg with a rifel moments after the president has been shot that wood be serten suiside. Best to dump it as I did after the Walker shooting perhaps retreeve it later. Who knos I may need to shoot my way out of the bldg deppending on wot awates downstares. For the furst time but not the last I sinserely regret leeveing my pistul at the rooming huose yesserday morning.

The elevaters are still ware I left them I ignoor there open doors opt for the stares insted not wishing to bring atenshun to myself with there abundent clanging. In momments this desishun will proove to be vry wise.

I hed down the stares like I hav a millon times befor but this time push down on the bannaster use it for leverag to leep the steps two three sumtimes four at a time. Wen I reech the 3rd flor I heer lowd voises from below.

Are these the stares up? a mans voise aks he is on the 1st flor if I hav to gess.

Yes sir cums a voise in reply I kno it to be Mister Troolys.

Can we take these all the way to the top?

Looks like we will hav to says Trooly I cant seem to sumon the elevater.

Wile they tawk I continew creeping down the stares. I slip onto the 2nd flor jus as they start up in my direckshun. I push open the lunch room door duk inside to ekscape out into the 2nd flor offises ware I kno I can take stares down to the lobby then sneek strate out the frunt door to freedum. Who knos wot will be wateing for me in Deely Plaza but sinse I hav herd persewers at the bak of the bldg it apeers as tho I hav litle choise but to leeve thru the frunt.

I am about harfway across the lunch room wen I heer the door behind me creek on its hinges.

You! Stop! barks the same voise I heard aksing quesshuns of Mister Trooly. He has spotted me thru a glass windo in the door there is litle choise but to do as I am tole.

Turn around! Fase me!

Yes sir.

I turn to him reel slo see that the voise belongs to a motorsycle cop from the parade. He is standing a few feet inside the lunch room door his wite hellmet still strapped in plase. He must hav reelised the shots came from the depossitry and hedded strate here. For all I kno he saw me shooting from the windo if that is the case then it is all over red rover I am a gonner. He has his drawn pistul traned sqarely on my stummick. I almost rayse my hands but that wood be a shure admishun of gilt I keep them ankered by my sides.

Mister Trooly appeers over the cops sholder frowening probly wundering why a cop is holding a gun on one of his order fillers. Trooly is swetting like he is the man being held at gunpoynt even tho it is not hot in the lunch room the publishers offises always well air condishunned hevven forbid the offise workers shood brake a swet.

Cum here! the cop yells.

At this poynt I shood be shakken to the core but I am ice cool sum higher power holding me toggether. My mind qikly sorts thru the opshuns. Shood the cop try to subdoo me I do not see menny ways out. He is much bigger and stronger plus wile I work for Mister Trewly I am serten that wen push cums to shuv he will side with the law wich meens I wood need to beet off two of them. I realis aggen wot a fool I was to leeve my pistul at Nth Beckly it wood shurely cum in handy rite about now.

I walk over stop a few feet in frunt of the cop. I see that his is a boys fase on a mans body his cheeks barely need shaveing the edges of a crew cut sho beneeth the sides of his hellmet. He looks like one of those good ole boys who flunked evry class in high skool excep shop made varssity in football or basball. He is standing strate sholders bak cleerly he enjoys the power a cops unifform afords him.

Do you kno this man? he growels to Trooly not takeing his eyes off of me Does he work here?

I look at Trooly my fate in the hands of this man who hired me only weeks ago. The cop is all geed up if Trooly says sumthing that even remotely rayses his suspishuns then who knos wot mite happen he will jus as likly shoot me ded on the spot. I wood die in a pool of my own blud rite neks to a pop masheen. Realiseing that my jurney to clense the world of a brokken capitlist sistem may end at the foot of the grate god Coke almost makes me smile I deside that if thats the way it is then I will put up the fite of my life.

Trewly serches my fase for who knos wot I remane dedpan let him draw his own conclooshuns.

Yes Trooly finaly says He works here.

The cop sneers trying to deside wot to do he can spend more time interrogateing me but if he does that he risks letting whoever mite be upstares eskape. After a moment he desides I am not who he is after without anuther werd turns aruond hedds for the door folowed by Trooly. Bad move Mister Poliseman you were momments away from being a heero now you will probly go down in histry as the man who let the pressidents killer slip thru your pudgey fingers. After I am long gone they will link the rifel to me then the world will kno the greevus errer of your ways.

The two of them dash out the door continoo up the stares I forse myself not to hurry I do not want to ferther aruose there suspishons. Acting all natchral I fish a nikkel from my poket slip it in the Coke masheen. I preffer Dr Pepper but that masheen is in the dommino room Coke will jus hav to do. A bottel rattels into the tray I pop the top off of it useing the masheens opener take a sip like I am jus wetting my wissle on any other lunch brake.

I carmly continoo my jurney thru the lunch room out into the offises of the publishing cumpny. No sooner hav I set foot on the worn browen carpet than I see Mrs Reed. I am not shure wot job she does posibly supavises secretrys for one of the publishers but from wot I can tell she is a nise lady a little too christan for my likeing but well intenshuned enuff. She is walking towards me from the frunt of the bldg mitey flustered all out of breth her fase gloing pink her eyes mooveing about so wildly I am afrade she mite hav a seezure. She is tugging at her cote and scarf like she can not get them off qik enuff.

Oh the president has been shot! she says.

Reelly? I mumbel not brakeing stride not wishing to get into a long conversashun for obvius reesons.

Maybe they didnt hit him she continoos.

Maybe I say knoing full well that that anser cood not be ferther from the trooth.

Coke in hand I keep walking past the abandunned secretry desks to the stares that will take me out of the bldg. I wate for Mrs Reed to call me bak aks for help but she nevver does probly dismissing me as a lowly worker not capabel of asisting in such a calammity litle does she realise I am the cawse.

I take the stares one at a time not wishing to berst from the bldg like a gilty man fleeing the seen of a crime. The outta wall of the starewell is glass brik to give the bldg a fansy appeerense from the plaza thru them I can see wavey images of peeple running in all direkshuns. I step off the stares into the lobby menny of my felow workers are standing neer the door. Billy Luvlady for one Wesly for anuther they are all crouded aruond the entranse unshure wot to do. I push past them my hed down the kaos of Deely Plaza working in my faver no one notises litle old Lee slip past why wood they the presdent has jus been gunned down rite befor there vry eyes.

Jus as I think I hav made a cleen getaway a yung man with a flat top harecut soot and tie puts his hand out to stop me at the foot of the frunt steps. He reeches into his pokket pulls out ID. It is all over now I think he is secret serviss and has cort me ded to rites onse aggen I long for my pistol he wood not take me allive if it were in my hands rite now.

Wheres the neerest fone? he shuots.

Wot? I can scarsely beleeve my ears.

Wheres the neerest fone?

I poynt to the depossitry mumbel That way then keep mooveing I cannot get away from him fast enuff.

Thanks he shuots over his sholder then buonds up the frunt steps.

Stunned I can not fathum how I hav ekscaped the cluches of a polise offiser and a secret serviss agent within minits of shooting the president. Both organisashuns are eether hopelesly inept or the unseen hand of histry is on my side my instinks tell me it is both.

I stand on the corner of Elm and Hooston faseing the plaza. Adults and chillren alike are waleing the kids hanging onto there parents legs for deer life unshure how to reakt to a world that has gone mad. Sirens blare from all direkshuns evry polise ofisser in Dallas dessending on this lokashun. I want to blok my ears close my eyes and shut out the world those three bullits hav opened the gates of hell.

I am still reeling wen two cop cars arive there doors fly open befor they screech to a holt. A half duzen men in soots jump out. I look over to the raleway traks for a way to ekscape but it is swarming with cops and members of the publik serching the top of the tripel underpass and a neerby grassy area. I considder joyning them jus anuther conserned citzin doing his civic dooty serching for the culprit of this heenus crime howevver I kno that wood only be a tempry solushun I need to get as far away from Deely Plaza as hoomanly posible.

The trafic has stalled in all direcshuns cops holding it up to let thru other polise cars offishul vehikels etc. Pedestreens hav taken over the streets most walk in a daze unshure of ware to go or wot to do. I push past a groop of yung colored folk weeping and hugging I reelise with sum degree of allarm that I hav destroyed there grate wite hope. I want to stop tell them that this is the first step in a grate jurney towards fareness for evryone of corse I can do no such thing.

The close calls with the motorsycle cop and secret serviss agent hav made me reelise that abuv all else I must retreev my pistol from the rooming huose on Nth Beckly. Oak Cliff lyes in a westerly direckshun and I am on the western edg of downtown so it shood be an eesy task howevver I kno the area towards Oke Cliff well I will stand out like a sore thum there is not a sidewalk to be seen anyware jus mane rodes and the open spases of the Trinnity River fludplane. It wood allso take the better part of an huor to walk there. Caching a bus my usul mode of transport seems a smarter alterntive after all I rode a bus home after the Walker shooting I see no reeson not to repete same.

I cross over Hooston walk east past the Dal Teck bldg dump the coke in a trash can the bottel allmost full I never did like the tast of that stuff. I continoo uptown on Elm reech my usule bus stop at the corner of Market there are no busses in site the rodes a tangel of trapped masheenry. But two bus roots run out to Oke Cliff the Beckly and Marsallis lines one of them will shurely tern up soon.

Keeping my hed down I walk east sevral bloks heering snaches of conversashun as peeple try to make sens of the insanity that seruonds them.

I herd he was shot.

Jacky too says anuther.

His hed was blowen cleer off.

No it was jus a flesh woond.

I woodnt be surprized if that Martin Loother King fella was involved says an old wite fella He tawks bout no violense but I dont beleeve him.

Hes a dam comunist says the fellas wife they ortta take em all out and hang em.

Dam strate I allmost say linching has long been one anser to Americas probblems. Wot fools you are here I hav dun this grate deed for you I can only hope that you posess the inteligense to seez the oportoonity I hav presented you with howevver if your coments are anything to go by I am afrade you do not.

A half duzzen bloks ferther up Elm I spot a Marsallis bus stuk in traffik between Griffin and Feeld ironikly not far from ware I now sit riteing these words in a sell. Its root will take me bak in the direckshun of Deely Plaza howevver I figger it is safer to be on a bus than wandring streets crawling with cops.

The bus side advertizes Doktors nasel spray promiseing qik releef I sinseerly hope the bus afords me same. I rush over puond on its door the nummer on its side 433 the dubble threes a vry good sine. Sure enuff altho the bus is between stops the driver oblyges opens the doors with a woosh. I pay the nikel fare slump into a seet towards the bak.

After a minit I relacks sum look aruond the bus who shood I see but Mrs Bledsow the ole crow who still owes me two dollers from my aborted stay in her rooming huose on Marsallis. She is sitting direckly behind the driver bak strate all prim and propper cluching her handbag in her lap with both hands pretending she has not seen me howevver I kno she has becos she never looks in my direkshun. As much as I wood like to hav it out with her rite there and then it is not the time nor the plase it will only result in drawing unwanted attenshun to myself.

The traffik is still jammed up it is like our weels are stuk in qik dry seement. The bus soon heets up inside dispite the few pasengers I open my windo to let in fresh air qikly close it aggen sirens attaking my ears. It feels like the cops are serching for me and only me my gilty conshense is not jus tawking to me it is yelling like a mad man.

The trafik gets so bad that the driver in frunt of us turns off his engin opens the door to his Chevvy steps out into the middel of Elm St. He rayzes his hand to his forehed as he sites west down Elm servaying the see of traffik streched out befor him. Then he scraches his hed walks over to the bus cleerly he wants to tawk to the driver. For a momment my hart flutters this man cood be plane clothes FBI or simler howevver wen he tawks I reelise I hav nuthing to wurry abuot.

Jus herd on the raydio the presidents been shot he says after the bus drivver opens the door.

Oh no gasps Mrs Bledsow she cluches her handbag titer to her brest.

The fella shrugs his sholders. Must be why the traffiks all messt up he says all matter of fack like a president gets shot evry day. He terns ruond climes bak into his car restarts the engin.

Now the drivers starts gasbagging abuot the shooting.

Theyll cach whoever did it soon enuff he says.

I shurely hope so says Bledsow I dont want anyone cumming after me.

Why wood they bother I think barely contaneing my tung like most peeple on this plannet you wood be a waste of a bullit.

There chatter soon runs out of steem they becum lost in there own litle thorts. Wen the bus crawels a few feet then abruply stops an old biddy behine me can take it no longer. She stands up woddles down the isle to the driver sevral Neeman Markus bags in tow. She is wareing a skarf dotted with casseeno chips to hold her hare in plase probly did not hav time to fix it this morning sunglases with thik blak frames a wrinkeled short sleev wite frok. Her legs are like a chikens all pale and scrawny her wrinkeled nek and saggy chin do litle to dispell the comparson.

How much longer will it be driver? she says.

You herd the man maam. The Presidents been shot. Its anyones gess as to how long this will take to cleer up.

I hav a one oclok trane to catch at Unon Stashun she says like its his falt she may miss it.

The driver looks at his wotch. Well you got less than twenty minits maam I trooly dont think you will make it.

Poppycok she says bringing a smile to my fase shes a fysty old bird all rite shes got gumpshun. Poppycok she says aggen I can make it there in less time on foot.

I rekkon you may be rite says the driver It is only abuot a half duzzen bloks.

She puts down her bags holds out her hand. Giv me a transsfer.

He givs her the transsfer opens the door she piks up her shopping bags steps off onto the sidewalk. She is instently absorbbed by the croud it mooves ruond her like qiksand.

Good day to you too maam says the driver even tho he knos she can not posibly heer him.

As the doors close I reelise that the old biddy has a good poynt. Walking will be much qikker we hav traveled less than one blok sinse I borded the bus. I stand up do the same as the old biddy but with nun of the carry on so as to not attrack attenshun. I carmly aks the driver for a transfer he hands it to me I jump off the bus neer the cnr of Lamar and Elm.

I shelter in a doreway to colleck my thorts a bum sleeping neerby reeking of booze. I hav wasted ten valoobel minits on that bus giveing who knos how menny polise the chanse to converg on downtown. The need to ekscape the area reech Oak Cliff and retreeve my pistol gros more pressing with each passing minit. To my way of thinking I hav three opshuns:

(1) Walk to Oak Cliff. Howevver as I hav alreddy outlined Junie that will take far too long cood also proove dangrus I am unarmed and hav alreddy been stopped by polise and secret serviss for all I kno there is a bullatin blareing my descripshun from one end of Dallas to the other rite now.

(2) Cach annuther bus. This will yeeld the same result as the ferst I will get stuk in trafik the Beckly and Marsallis line buses all follo the same root thru Deely Plaza. Doing the rong thing over aggen is the vry definishun of insannity that I am definitly not.

(3) Cach a cab. This is sumthing that I hav never dun befor it has nevver felt rite to me to hav a werking man drive me abuot like I am better than him. Howevver unfortunatly I do not see any other way aruond it a cab it will hav to be.

Becos I hav never cort a cab I hav no idea ware to start obviusly in all this vehiklar madness one will not drive down the strete stop rite at my feet whisk me away to safty. Howevver the Grayhuond stashun is but two bloks suoth on Commerse and Lamar hopeflee I am abel to find a taxi there amungst all the comoshun. The Grayhuond termnal is also out of the way as far as Deely Plaza is conserned perhapps traffik kaos has not yet envelloped it.

The two blok walk to the bus termnal begins as a largly uneventful affare most peeple too cort up in there own feelings of greef to pay me much mind. Howevver there teers and waleing also the noise and heet from the stalled cars soon take there toll I gro more on edg with evry step find it increesingly diffcult to think strate. It takes all my powers of consentrashun to fokus on the task at hand wich is simpel yet sumhow diffkult plase one foot in frunt of the other untill I reech my destinashun.

A half blok from the termnal I relacks sum wen I spot a Chekker cab parkt at a stand rite outside the deppo. I qiken my stride reech the car leen over to tawk to the driver thru the pasenger side windo. A wite 33 is paynted on the hood neer the windscreen I can still pitcher same it gladdens my hart for jus like the nummer on the bus the threes are a sine that this cab will be my ride out of hell.

May I hav this cab? I say to the driver.

I rekkon you can he says Get in.

Thank you sir.

I clime into the frunt seet the drivers eyes widen he expecks me to sit in bak. Howevver I feel no compulshon to get shoffered aruond like lord muk. I mite be speshul as I hav jus prooven howevver I am also a werking man jus like the driver no better no wurse than him. I may deserv speshul treetment after my resent acts howevver that does not meen I need to acept same altho if I make it to Russia or Cuba I may sing a difrent toon.

His chubby cleen shavven fase grins at me over a plad shirt wite tshirt underneeth his left elbo leening casully out the windo.

Ware to? he aks.

I am jus about to open my muoth poynt him in the direcshun of Oke Cliff wen an elderlee lady dresst all in blak wareing thik glasses there lensses like the bottum of soda botles hobbels over to my side of the cab a walking stik provideing sum asistence. She stiks her hed in the windo I cach a whif of moth balls.

Driver for the life of me I can not find a taxi. Can you call one for me pleese?

Yes maam he replys.

Well Junie as much as I am in need of transportashun at this poynt in time in fack I hav never needed it more in my life I am not the kind of man who will sit by and ignoor an old lady a cripelled one at that pleeding for help.

I will let you hav this one I tell her eezing my door open. There are plenty of others I say even tho we both kno that is not the case in this traffik it mite be an huor or more befor anuther cums along.

No she says fermly The driver can call me one.

I bak off haveing dented her pride she does not want speshul treetment I admir her for that.

The driver piks up his raydio to call anuther cab wen she says Oh dont bother I think I see one cumming and jus like that off she limps.

The driver looks in his reervew mirrer shrugs his sholders.

Ware to fella?

Five hunnerd blok of Nth Beckly thank you sir.

Good enuff.

He cranks a wite lever on the meter clokwise resets the fare puts the car in geer pulls out into the traffik on Lamar wich thank the lord is floing faster than Elm. He turns rite at the neks set of lites onto Jakson folows that to Osstin ware he takes a left. As we enter Osstin two polise cars fly past on the other side of the rode hedding towards Deely Plaza there sirens blare.

Wot the hell? the driver says.

I look at the dashbord there is a hole ware the raydio shood be. He has no idea wot has hapened I stay silent I sertenly do not want to be the one to enliten him.

I wunder wot the hell all the upror is he says.

He continoos to try and get me to tawk out of curiossty lonliness or jus plane small tawk I do not kno. Howevver I pretend not to heer him meerly gaze out the windo at the world rushing by. I do not want to get into wot mite or mite not hav hapened as I do not want to help anyone make sense of the crazyness the longer evrything remanes confoosed the better it will be for me. I also refoose to get drawen into conversashun becos I kno that at sum poynt the polise FBI or CIA perhaps all three will interogate any cab drivers who were on dooty in the visinity of Deely Plaza at the time of the shooting. I do not want to say anything that will cawse the driver to remember me or my subsqent moovements. I keep my hed terned towards the pasenger windo feel his eyes studying me but do not turn to fase him or do anything that will aford him a better look.

This fella shorely knos his way ruond the bak streets tho we zoom thru downtown zig zagging past warehuoses offise blgs parking lots etc. He takes Osstin one blok turns rite onto Wood then onto Hooston. The trafik is all jammed up hedding into Deely Plaza but thankflee it is mooveing freely in the other direckshun. We pass by Uniun Stashun I remember the old biddy with chiken legs hawling her Neeman Markus bags off of the bus I wunder if she will make her one oclock trane I find myself hopeing so for her gumpshun deservs sum reward.

Soon enuff we are hertling across the Hooston St viaduck above the Trinnity River. I look down onto the fludplane the Trinnity not reely a river more like a flat vallee that fills with water maybe onse evry ten yeers the rest of the time it dont amuont to a hill of beens. Its grass cuvvered levees were bilt menny yeers ago to proteck the city from fludding as I gaze down on them now I remember going there the day after reseeving my rifle shooting sum ruonds alineing the sites famileriseing myself with its akshun etc. I thort at the time I wood perform a grate deed with that rifel howevver I am not sure even I thort that wood meen killing the president. Now that rifel lies on the 6th flor of the depositry hidden between boxes I wunder how long it will take the authoritees to find it trase it bak to me. Abandunning it there I kno they will eventuly trak down its owner but I figger that will take sum time. Howevver the run ins with the motorsycle cop in the lunchroom then the secret serviss agent outside make me reelise that things are mooveing much qikker than they did after my atempted shooting of Genral Walker. I may hav underestimatted the reakshun of the authoritees now that I hav made it out of the bldg agenst all expectashuns I will need a serius plan of akshun if I am to ferther ekscape. The first step get to my room on Nth Beckly retreeve my pistol then considder my neks moove.

By now we hav crosst the river hedding west along Nth Zang jus a few minits from the rooming house. Lake Cliff Park is on our left we spent menny a happy huor there Junie you your mama and I offen takeing pikniks of a late afternoon spredding out a blankt in the shade of a syprus I mite reed you a book poosh you on the swings by you and mama ice creems. Sumtimes I fished in the lake sumthing I lerned to do as a boy in New Orleens. I seldum cort anything big enuff to eat howevver you wood sqeel with delite wen I pulled a goldfish to the surfiss its skales flashing in the sun as it riggled on the hook. If it was too small to keep you wood wotch enrapturred as I took it off of the hook thru it bak in to let it swim away you wood clap lowdly as it wated a few seccunds befor darting beneeth the surfiss. One time I cort sevral large fish we took them home for dinner. Your mama made fish soop but I was unabel to enter the kichen wile she did so the suond of the fish thrashing aruond in the bukket perhapps aware of the boiling water that awated them too much for me to bare. I smile to myself as I remember this reelise that is wot I am now jus a big ole golefish trying to get off of the hook befor the polise reel me in put me in hot water how the tabels hav terned the hunter has becum the hunted ha ha ha.

The driver has been silent thinking his own thorts I am farely serten he has stopped wotching me with suspishun. He puts on his left tern signell stops to let traffik pass at Zang and Nth Beckly. The rooming huose is jus aruond the korner we will pass it soon enuff but I make no menshun of same. I sit qiet as tho the area meens nuthing to me in actule fack my eyes are alive skanning the street for sines of servailense. Seeing no polise cars or suspishus vehikals in the vissinty I relax sumwhat altho I kno that the polise cood hav beeten me to the punch takken up posishun in neerby huoses or inside the rooming huose itself they wood hav had to be vry swift howevver a good operativ accuonts for all possibilitys.

SIMON FOSTER

A brake in the traffik sees the driver turn left onto Nth Beckly. The rooming huose passes on our left I remane silent looking thru the pasenger windo to my rite give no hint of my intended destinashun. I let the driver continoo anuther three or four bloks past 5th St 6th St until we are approcheing W Neely the street ware I onse convinsed your mama to take the bak yard foto of me with my weppons how distent that memry now seems.

This will do fine rite here I say.

Yes sir.

The side of the rode is lined with parkt cars he continoos past them pulls up on the corner of W Neely and Nth Beckly.

The meeter reeds 95 sents I take out a doller bill.

Keep the chang I tell him.

Thank you sir.

I open the door step out on the sidewalk close it behine me. I wate for the cab to pull away from the kerb howevver the driver is wateing to see wich way I go eether to keep from hitting me or becos he is still suspishus and wants to keep an eye on me. I step in frunt of the car chek left and rite for traffik this is no time to get run over then cross to the other side of the street. The rooming huose is a five minit walk bak in the direckshun we hav jus cum from playing dum I stand on the corner as if getting my bareings in realty I am wateing for the cab to leeve so the driver does not see wich way I proseed.

Eventuly he dawdels off the cab disapeers over a rise to the suoth. I harf walk harf run towards the rooming huose my sense of urgensy groing with evry step. My mind is set on one thing and one thing only retreeveing my pistul. Onse I hav that in my poseshun I will feel saffer abel to defend myself shood the need arise altho I sertenly hope it does not one killing more than enuff for me.

On the korner of Nth Beckly and E 5th I sneek behind an oke tree servale my plase of abode a half blok distent. Wotching from the shaddows I make shure there are no sines of polise or other agensys. Disspite the aparent absense of same I debate wether to proseed. I stand at the crossrodes but deep dowen I kno that without my pistol I hav much less chanse of ekscapeing and seeing you aggen. Takeing a deep breth I hed for the huose.

I skoot from behind the tree qikly cuvver the distanse to the huose stride boldlee up the frunt path. The door has three rectangels of glass set diagonly into it I peer thru the middel one serching for anything untoward I see and heer no moovement.

I turn the door nob berst into the liveing room. Mrs Roberts the huosekeeper is bent over the TV set furiusly ajusting the antena trying to fix the pitcher the screne filled with sno the suond hissing with statik. At any other time the site mite be comikal Mrs Roberts a short vry hevvy set woman with barely contaned cleevage a permnant wave in her dark hare and catseye glasses that hav slid down the bridg of her nose. She is the last person you wood aks to fix the pitcher on a TV set she cleerly has no idea wot she is doing.

I slam the frunt door head strate for my room.

Oh you are in a hurry she says to my bak.

I dont respond howevver her words are a positiv sine if any authoritees had been aksing after me shurely she wood be acting qite diffrently all nervus and aflutter.

Crossing the liveing room I pull open the dubbell doors to my bedroom slam them behind me retreev my pistol and hollster from the top shelf of the cubbord. Wen I put on the hollster it feels cumbersum I take it off toss it on the flor. I chek the pistul is stil fully loded tuk it into the wasteband of my pants. This creates qite a bulg I grab my lite gray jakket from the closset to disgise it my only other jaket the blew one still lyeing on the windosill in the domino room proof that I was eating lunch at the time of the shooting createing an alibbi not so complikated if you plan ahed.

The jakket wile unesessary the day haveing warmed up considdrably not only cuvvers the pistol but my clotheing as well. This will help if a descripshun of me has been issewed a distink posibilty givven my erlier run ins with the cop and the secret serviss agent. Any erlier descripshun will not make menshun of a gray jaket wareing it shood thro peeple off the sent.

Neks I scoop up all my bullets nine in totel pore them into my trowser poket. I make one last chek of the room for anything else I mite need well aware this cood be my last vissit to the rooming huose I want to make serten I dont leeve anything importent behind. Howevver the room is so small most of my valubels are stored in the Pains garage. Here I jus keep sum litrature copys of the Millitent the Worker communist rags that I subskribe to despit my lak of munny I feel it is importent to allways support the workers cawse. Ocasshunly my letters to the editer appeer in there pages no dout those will now be more hevly scrootinized. I also hav a few maps one of Dallas marked with my job seeking efferts bus roots to intervews etc anuther map of the motorcade root also one of Moscow it servs to remind me of my oversees adventurs. There are also sum flash cards for lerning Russian toyletrys gluvs old shoos a raydio sevral cheep camras fotografy being a partiklar habbit of mine. Howevver I leeve that all behind the effemera of life now useless to me. I must travel lite if I am to ekscape besides the only thing I need is rite here in my wollet the foto of you deer Junie cradeled in your mamas arms that is all I need to keep me going.

I crak open the bedroom door. Mrs Roberts has sumhow wresseled the TV set into submishon the pitcher no longer jumping abuot the sound cleer as a bell. She sits on the soffa eating a egg sallad sandwitch wile Wolter Cronkite sits in his New York stoodio updateing the world of the qote unqote terribel situashon in Dallas. I can only imagin wot Mrs Roberts wood say if she knoo that the man responsibel for sed terible situashon is standing jus feet away. I consider aksing her wot is going on hav they cort anyone are they looking for anyone in partiklar etc but I do not want to aruose her suspishons unesesarly also do not hav time to waste on idol chatter who knos how soon the polise will be knokking on the door.

I zip my jakket to better hide the pistol walk fast thru the livving room Mrs Roberts too engrossed in her sandwitch and Mr Cronkites wurds to pay me much mind. Befor opening the frunt door I aggen peer thru the middel pane of glass. Seeing nuthing of a suspishus natur I slip out the door cross Nth Beckly hopeing against hope that a bus is cumming to take me ferther into Oak Cliff. After paying for the taxi ride I hav approx thirteen dollers to my name jus enuff for a one way tiket to Mexico City fleeing the cuntry now my primery gole. I dont dare retern downtown to the Grayhound termnal it is too close to the shooting also shurely by now the polise are scourring bus and trane termnals I am lukky to hav ekscaped in the first plase.

Howevver by my calculashuns a Beckly line bus to Jeffersen Boolavard will alow me to cach a 55 or 30 bus on Marsallis and Jeferson eether of wich will take me to Lancaster Rd near the VA hospitel ware I shood be abel to cach a Grayhuond heded suoth then with other connecshuns make it all the way to the border in Laredo. Of corse I do not hav my passport with me it is in the Pains garage a definit oversite on my part I will hav to work out anuther meens of entry onse I get there perhapps sneek across the border sumhow the fake IDs I allways carry in my wollet shood proove invalubel. Onse in Mexico City I will hed strate to the Cooban embasy tell the consul I am the man who shot John Kennedy unlike last time they cannot posibly refoose me entree to their cuntry for I hav dun a grate deed in the name of freedom for all men. I shood not be surprized if they wellcum me with open arms Castro hisself givs me a medal perhapps even a grand parade.

But ferst things ferst I need to get on that bus at Marsalis and Jeferson figger out the rest later. In my poket is the trannsfer from my erlier ill fated bus ride it will save me paying anuther fare. I do not regret leeveing munny for your shoos this morning Junie but now that I hav ekscaped the depositry and set my sites on Mexico City evry sent cuonts.

As I wate at the bus stop each passing minit feels like an huor then I reelize that all the busses must still be snarled in downtown traffik. Feeling extreemly conspikuos standing oposit my rooming huose I make a snap decishun to flee on foot I will be saffer folowing bak streets to the bus stop on Jeferson Boolavard than standing aruond like a sitting duk.

I walk briskley scaning the streets for any sine of trubble cross over Beckly to E 5th St hed east towards the corner of Lake Cliff Park. It is lunchtime of a Friday the park stands emty no piknikers on red chek blankits no kids playing wiffell ball no fishamen standing idoly by the lake wateing for the necks bite. Jus me doing my best not to be seen. I stay close to the sidewalk a few feet inside the propperty line use trees as my cuvver in case a car shood drive by. This teckniq I lerned from one of my favorit TV shos I Led Three Lives about an ad man poseing as a communist who reports his findings bak to the FBI. Sum your mama inclooded thort the sho stoopid howevver it is not as far feched as it suonds who better to be a dubble agent than sumone at the senter of the capitlist masheen. The ad man is of corse allways on gard agenst being discuvvered so the sho is grate refrense matereel for anyone wishing to lern the art of avoydence same can be sed for the book How To Be A Spy despit my diffculty with words I hav red it cuvver to cuvver more times than I can recal.

At the corner of the park I turn rite onto N Crawferd I kno from experense this is the qikest way to Marsallis and Jeferson. The streets in this part of Oak Cliff are confoozing do not folow any logikel patern like for excksampel the Manhatten grid. Only sumone with extensiv lokel nolledge and a razer sharp memry wood kno that this is the fastest way to my destinashun without staying on a mane rode for any length of time.

I folow N Crawferd sevral bloks past rundown woodden huoses rusty cars up on sinder bloks chikens cok a doodel doing from bak yards. I see no one on the streets this nayborhood is dirt poor its inhabitents out erning munny to pay for rent food clotheing etc. At this time of day I wood be more likly to get spotted in a snooty suberb like Hiland Park ware Gen Walker livs they probly sit aruond on there shaded porches all day sipping mint jewlips looking for the meerest hint of trubble so they can call the polise. No such probblem in Oke Cliff peeple too busy jus tryin to servive in a sosiatee that doesnt kno or care one jot about them.

I stay on N Crawfurd for maybe a half duzzen bloks until I hit a mane road E Davis. I turn left folow that for only one blok to limmit my exposhur even so sevral cars pass by also a lawndry truck I hide behind a telefone pole to ekscape detecshun. I then turn rite folow N Patton past the Oak Clif Christen Cherch. Junie it must be cleer to you by now that I am not a religus man folowing the werd of a so called god has cawsed menny ills howevver this partiklar church reely is sumthing to see. Towring colums line its entranse the cherch ocupys an entyre city blok it is simpley a plessure to walk by its grandur ignoreing of corse its prinsippal purpuss. One can eesly imagin why peeple in yeers gone by fell for the religus sell one vissit to a bldg like that wood be enuff to make them beleeve that there reely is a better life wateing for them in the grate beeyond. If only it were so Junie howevver I am far too much of a sinic to beleeve same.

From the corner of E 9th St I see Adamson Feeld ware the lokal high skool teem plays. Past that sits the high skool itself a sollid red brik bldg the US flag flys out frunt. If I am rite about Kennedys demise wich I shurely am then that flag will shortly be lowered to half staf. Seeing the skool rekindels unplessant memrys not becos I attended same but becos skool was vry tuff for me partikly in New York the other kids teesed me endlesly about my acksent also my worn out cloths my pore spelling and faleing grades. This bullying got so bad I soon stopped going to skool alltogether instedd rideing the subway for huors vissiting the Bronx zoo New York publik libry ware I lerned all abuot communism and marxism. In fack it was outside the libry that a lady gave me a pamflet conserning the Rosenberg case a compleet travvesty of justise two innosent peeple tryed and execooted jus for being reggistered communists that one peece of papper shoed me for the first time the unfareness of the world. The knoledge I lerned inside and outside that libry also later at the libry in New Orleens set off a lite bulb that burns brite to this day I did not need any classroom for that.

As you can see Junie I filled my days away from skool vry construktivly. But of corse my trewancy got me a hole helping of trubble from the authoritees speshul heerings psyckiatric evalluashuns threts to send me to a home for dissterbed boys eventully these all contribooted to me and mother leeveing New York. The authoritees grilled me sed I was not normel my reeding and riteing substanderd howevver Mother wood not heer a word of that she did not mind one bit that I skippt skool she allways knoo that I did not need a formel edukashun I was moor than cappabel of teeching myself all I needed to kno to get on in this world. She allways sed I wood lern more from books than teechers that I did not need the cumpny of badly raysed kids who had nuthing better to do than teeze sumone who was a litle diffrent. My mother she was rong about menny things allways thinking she new best howevver on this partiklar score she was rite for skools reely are jus a form of brane woshing they tell you wot to think also wen and how much to think it. Well I am too smart to fall for that I sinserely hope you are too Junie pleese promiss me one thing allways keep an open mind make your own desishuns be your own person dont you ever let anyone tell you otherwis.

I continoo suoth on Patton this part of the street has no huoses jus a furnatur workshop anuther bizness undertakeing vehikel repares. The rest of the blok is vaccant overgrowen lots with weeds but not much else by way of vegetashun wich meens less plases for me to hide. Feeling expozed I brake into a short run reech E 10th a narro street with rundown wetherbord huoses lineing both sides thankfly menny trees popullate there frunt yards. I feel a wate lift from my sholders E 10th leeds rite to Denver then Marsallis I can almost smell freedum in a few minits I will be on my way to Mexico onse aggen eloodeing the authoritees by bus jus as I did folowing the Walker shooting.

At the corner of Patton and E 10th I slo to a brisk walk cross over to the other side of the strete take a short hop up onto the sidewalk. A Chekker cab sits parkt neer the corner the driver eating a meetball heero he has probly pulled off of Jeferson Boolevard onto Paton to eat his lunch in peece. A newspaper lyes spred on the pasenger seet beside him he is bent over looking down at it one hand resting on the steering weel the other holding the heero. Red sause runs down his rist he does not notiss as I make my way up E 10th.

Jus past the corner house I heer a car cumming up the street behind me. The cab drivver with his messy heero has distrakted me it is too late to dart off behind a tree. I manetane my speed and direcshun do not fallter as I wate for the car to pass. Gravvel crunches under its frunt tires as it slos and pulls closer to the kerb but I do not tern aruond or sho undoo consern jus a reglar citzen out and abuot takeing care of bizness.

Then I cach a blak hood out of the korner of my eye. Thats wen my hart skips a beet for evryone knos Dallas patrollmen drive blak Fords. I keep walking try to prettend this is not reely happning howevver as the car sloly overtakes me my werst feers are reelized the frunt pasenger door draws level the werds Dallas Polise paynted on it in larg wite letters the nummer 10 below it.

The car stops bounses on its springs. Then the cop leens over to speek thru the pasenger vent windo. I continoo walking prettend I hav not notissed his presense Marsallis and Jeferson are so close I can allmost tast freedum.

Can I hav a werd with you fella?

The small windo muffels his soft spokken rekwest his voise sugests cuntry ways.

Did you heer me fella? he says this time with a litle more edg.

My first instink is to run but if I do that he will kno for shure that sumthing is up he will give chase also raydio for help in minits I will hav harf the Dallas polise forse breething down my nek. Better to bluf my way thru this then continoo on my way. Perhaps it is jus a rootine stop with no connekshun to the presidents shooting. I bumped into that cop in the lunch room barely a half huor ago this cop is two maybe three miles away how cood he posibly kno wot I look like?

I tern to fase him. The car inches foreward then stops aggen. The cop is still leening over to tawk thru the side windo. I leen my arms on the roof bend down to tawk to him.

Wot seems to be the problem offisser?

My eyes meet his they are dedpan. Then he brakes eye contak looks out thru the windsheeld. This is wen I kno he has made me. No dout about it says a voise inside. He has herd a descripshun of the asassin knos exackly who I am the deed I hav dun. Anuther voise cuonters that theres no way he can kno I shot the president unfortoonatly the ferst voise is by far the most convinseing. I hav been in the pressence of hostile authoritees the world over interragated by offishuls in the US Jappan Russia Mexico sum of there manners vry seveer indeed. Thru this I hav developped a keen sense for knoing wen they are on to sumthing this fella most definitly knos the score.

Going anyware in partiklar? he aks still unabel to look me in the eye the unsetled feeling in my stummik grows.

The bus stop.

Ware you takeing the bus?

Work.

He looks out thru the windsheeld aggen he is qite a hansome man thik neck larg adams appleel a cleff in his chin he cood be Kurk Duglas in Spartakus. He looks familer perhaps I hav seen him around the nayborhood menny cops are knowen to eat at Dobbs Huose of a morning.

Kinda late in the day to be hedding to work, aint it?

Shift work.

Wot kinda shift work?

Faktory. We make loovers I add hopeing some detales will asswage his suspishons. It is not exackly a lie I onse held a job in Fort Wurth makeing same.

He studys me for a long momment then says Stay rite ware you are fella.

Then the iddiot does wot I absolootly do not want him to do. He opens the drivers side door eazes hisself out of the car. Across the roof I see him stand up he is tall not fat not skinnee jus the rite bild for his hight. First thing he does is straten his hat so that it is jus so then takes a step foreward towards the frunt of the car.

I hav only secunds to deside the best corse of akshun. If he gets much closser to me with his weppon drawen the momment will be lost. I will eether be cort any dreem of being with you and Mama aggen evapporateing into thin air or I will be shot posibly killt reeching for my weppon as he will hav the jump on me. Rite now I hold the elament of surprize but it wont last long I must use it to my advantidge wile I can.

I can still see him cleer as day standing across the hood from me as he reeches the frunt of the cop car. I take a step foreward. Onse aggen he is not looking at me eether too timmid or more likely playing sum kind of mind game. Whatever the reeson I kno it is a misstake this is the momment I must seeze it. I wip out my pistol fire three times. The bullits strike him in the chest in rappid sukseshun spinning him clokwise. As he twists away from me he unsnaps the strap on his hollster fumbels for his gun. I seese fireing three shots is more than enuff if I hav not killt him I hav at the vry leest stopped him in his traks. Three is also the nummer of shots I fired at Kennedy I am possitiv my lukky nummer will also work here.

This is why I am shokked wen for sum unknowen reeson that I still can not fathum I fire a 4th shot. This bullit caches the left side of his hed honnestly Junie it is not ware I was aiming but as he falls his hed drops to the levvel of his chest. I sware Junie I did not aim for his hed it is all a matta of fisiks the downwerd moshun of his body cawseing the bullet to strike him in same. He hits the gruond with a dull thump a sack of wheet dumped off of the bak of a truk. He falls on his left side his weppon still hollstered beneeth him. His hat rolls into the middel of the street settels upside down on its lid. Four shots and jus like that I hav killt an innosent man a poor cop probly not erning much more than minnimim wage jus a fella doing his job like millons of other men. Probly has a wife kids parrents frends who all luv him. Let me say Junie that killing an innosent man was never part of my plan but wot was I to do? As you can see it was eether me or him of corse I made the same decishun anyone wood make in that situashon. I take sum consolashun in the knoledge that he did not kno wot hit him the last shot to the hed wood hav instently seesed his evry thort not a teribel way to go if one has to be shot rather than dyeing a long drawen out deth from a stumick woond or such.

I snap bak to reality the shooting a bad dreem from wich I hav jus awokken. I heer anuther engin idolling look up see a yelow pikup parked a few huoses away. A skinny fased Mexican stares at me from behind the weel he does not look eeger to engage I can assure him the feeling is qite mutule.

A hi piched shreek cums from the other direkshun a woman standing on 10th St across Patton is going bananas she has seen the hole dam thing. I move towards her in shok at the speed with wich events hav eskalated all thorts of reeching Mexico now forgotten my primeree consern to sumhow flee the seen of the crime. Reeching the frunt yard of the huose on the corner I emty the spent cartriges from the pistul into my hand as I run. Beleeve me Junie I am in no rush to shoot anyone else it is meerly forse of habbit that drives me to do same we are traned as Marines to relode as qikly as possible in case we need to reengage with the enemy.

I am closser to the screeming woman now she is still shuoting looking at me like I am sum kind of monster.

He shot him! He is ded! Help! Sumone call the polise! she screems over and over like a stuk rekord all the wile poynting her finger at me like I am the devil hisself.

I stop walking glare at her. She is about forty yeers old blak hare set in a permnent wave she is wareing a britely colored puffy blowse with one of those big stoopid bows at the coller also a nee length blak skert. She is histerical wich is compleetly undastandabel she can hardly hav been eckspecting to see a cop gunned down wen she left home that day but there is not much I can do abuot that. I hav two bullets left in the chamber it wood take but one to shut her up for good and on a moor praktical levell elimanate one eyewitness. Wot I am thinking also dawens on her she ceeses her screeching closes her trap clenches her eyes shut. She puts her hands over her fase like she is abuot to meet her maker but is in no hurry to see wot he looks like.

Despite the obvius benaffits I can not say that I ever seriusly considered killing the woman Junie two murders in one day plenty enuff for me. Besides there are other eyewitneses the Mexican in the pikup for one probly also the cab driver I cood be here all afternoon takeing care of them. I compleetly abandun the idea wen the door to the corner huose opens and two wimmin stik there heds out to see wot all the fuss is about. I am standing on there lawn I turn to fase them the situashun so bazar I can not help but smile they of corse see nuthing amooseing about a cop lying ded on there doorstep. They wotch me in horror as I toss the emty cartriges onto there lawn relode four bullits leeveing six in the chamber five in my pokket a good

Marine allways knos his cuont.

By this poynt Junie I must admitt that I am not reely thinking strate. I hav no idea ware I am hedded I jus kno that I need to get as far away from 10th and Patton as posibel. I trot across the frunt yard cheking for persooers then cross over Patton hed towards Jeferson. Reverting to my millitry traneing I run in the raysed pistol posishun the gun in my rite hand my elbo bent the pistol poynted strate up in the air. I pass the taxi ware the driver was eating his meetball heero he no longer occoopys the drivers seet he must hav fled the car wen the shooting started then seen me hedding his way he is now cowering behind the drivers side reer weel. Seeing no thret from him I chek bak over my left sholder to make shure no one else is giveing chase perhaps the Mexican from the pikup truck is in persoot thankfuly he is smart enuff to stay rite ware he is. I see the polise car aggen pitcher the cop his body falling to the gruond the sikening thud it made wen he hit the rode. Poor dum cop I mutter to myself then say it aggen shakeing my hed. Rong time rong plase. If he had cum allong jus one minit erlier or later I wood now be on the bus hedded for the border he wood soon be finnishing his shift going home to eat stake and three veges with his wife and chillren. Now he will be karted off to the neerest hospitel probly the Methadist on Nth Beckly and Collorado jus a blok from the rooming house then on to a funeral home ware they will keep him on ice until buriel. No dout he will be farewelled with full polise honners considdered a heero for dyeing in the line of dooty hopfully that will be sum consolashun to his famly altho I am not sure it will be I do not think it wood be to mine. Wot wood you rather Junie a ded father who evryone considders a hero or a living breething father to gide you thru life evry step of the way? I think I kno the anser to that.

The need to ekscape overwelms me I dash down Patton towards Jeferson. At the end of the street stands Harris Motor Co they hav been feeding the grate American thurst for autos for over twenty yeers acording to a banner and colored flags flutering in the breeze. In the bak of the lot faseing Patton two peeple are stareing at me a wite fella maybe forty-five yeers old wite short sleev shirt navy tie stomuck hanging over his belt beside him a young blak man wareing overalls and cap holding a wet peece of clothe. They are standing in frunt of a new blew Chevvy stashun waggon I rekkon the blak man is shineing the car the wite man telling him ware to shine same as it ever was.

Man wot in the hell is going on? the wite fella yells at me.

I slo down not qite to a stop deside tawking to them is the best way to defoose the situashun convinse them I am not involved.

Sumones gone crazy up there I say A cop has been shot.

The wite fella shakes his hed the blak fella looks more scarred than confoosed.

Wots that? the wite man says cupping a hand to his ear.

I shrug my sholders as if to say I dont hav a clew wots going on wich isnt that far from the trooth. I wave my free hand prettend that even if I did unnerstand I dont hav time to explane it.

Im getting out of here I say.

I pass them run ruond the corner onto Jeferson a mane rode with sevral lanes in both direkshuns. I slo down to blend in lower my gun from the raysed posishun tukk it into the wasteband of my truosers.

Sirens suond in the distanse sumone perhaps one of the wimmen who appeered in the doorway of the huose must hav alreddy called the polise. Sinse the viktim is a cop a bluecote I beleev there own call them all hell is abuot to brake lose. Dallas PD will send evry avalabel man to the scene granted that may not be menny sinse the President was shot less than an huor ago. It must be all hands on dek down at Deely Plaza litle do they reelize that JFKs killer has excaped the area gotten cleen away without this lattest hiccup he wood not be seen for dust and small pebbels.

It soon becums aparent that Jeferson Boolavard is too well traveled for me to go unotised. I cut thru a Texaco stashun hed towards a reer laneway that runs paralel. Aprocheing the alley a mekanics legs poke out from under a cars engin bay he is the only person I see. A row of parked cars awateing repares lines the bak of the gas stashun it is here that I deside loozing my jaket is a good idea. All those eyewitneses to the cop shooting the Mexican in his pikup the screeming woman on the corner the cab driver with his meetball heero even the workers at the car yard they will all cleerly recall the color of my jaket as it cuvvered the top half of my body. I shrug it off let it drop to the gruond shuv it under the trunk of a Ford with my foot out of site out of mind. The pistol in my wasteband now ecksposed I untuk my shirt to cuvver it.

A breeze hits my damp skin sends a chil thru me I am swetting up a storm hardly surprizeing givven the circumstanses. I hed towards the reer laneway then chang my mind if I folow Jefferson I mite still cach the bus I had originly intended to meet at Marsallis and Jeferson.

I cross over Crawfurd start hedding down the sidewalk of Jeferson looking for the neks bus stop its exak locashun ekscapes me. As I cross Sth Beckly a sqodron of polise cars sudenly appeers on the other side of the rode sirens screeming in frustrashun at the stalled trafik rubber neckers sloing down to look at the kaos I hav cawsed. I lower my hed prettend to browse a hardware store windo look intently at cans of paynt arranged in a piramid for dissplay. They remind me of paynting the walls wen we first mooved into Elspeth St I wunder if I will ever hav use for same aggen this prisun sell cood sertenly do with a few cotes ha.

The polise cars eventully forse there way thru the traffik procede down Patton. The imediate thret gone I continoo for sevral minits until a secund set of polise vehicals approches this time from the other direkshun they are on my side of the rode. I panic unsure wether to run becos I hav been spotted or hold my gruond to attrak less atenshun. I am standing outside Hardys shoo store a few doors past S Zang a shop I hav frekwented onse or twise but never made a perchase. The stores entranse is set bak from the street one can wander in to look at windo dissplays on eether side without entring the store propper. I step inside the entranse prettend to be absorbed by the footware on offer tenniss shoos wite buks reglar work shoos all qite reesonabley prised I spose if new shoos are that importent to you personly I can make one pare last for yeers.

Inside a cleen cut yung man is wurking behind a cuonter that runs down the left hand side of the stor he wares blak trowsers blak jaket wite shirt thin dark tie. He is lissening to a raydio repport about the presidents shooting also wotching me I rekkon he is trying to deside wether he can keep lissening or if I need

131

asistence. I look down at the shoo dissplay then bak at him now he is wotching me more closely howevver I dare not tern away better to fase him than reveel myself to the passing polise. We manetane this danse for a few minits our eyes ocashonly meeting then I heer tires screech the polise cars performing a U tern on Zang to return to E 10th. There sirens gro distent more like moskitos in the nite than herelders of doom I take this as my kew to leeve the salesmans wotchfull gaze folows me out the store.

Glanseing over my sholder cheking onse more that the polise cars hav gone east I continoo west along Jeferson. About a harf blok ferther on the neon sine of the Texas theeter looms overhed brite blew vertikle letters speling out

T
E
X
A
S

muonted on the red and yelow stars of the Lone Star state the awning belo striped blew and yelow. In the brillent sunshine the creem bldg looks like sum kind of nervana. I hav allways liked the Texas Theeter spent menny a happy huor here hideing away from your mama wen we were argewing now as I heer more sirens approcheing in the distance I reelise that it may vry well be my salvashun. I can hide in the dark untill all the hullabaloo blos over the polise will never think to look here I can make myself disapeer for huors if need be.

The theeters hording announses a dubble feeture Cry of the Batle with Van Helfen and War is Hell with Audy Murfy both strike me as sumwhat apropriate givven my currant predickment.

I walk up to the entranse a semi sircular tiket booth set in the middel of a rectanguler lobby movie posters in lite boxes to eether side. The flor is mostly yelow tiles altho sum red ones make up two large stars in frunt of the twin dubbel doors that flank the tikket booth. The doors are paynted the same red as the booth six circular windos set into them two vertikal rows of my lukky nummer three ferther proof that the theeter will be a havven for me.

Inside the tiket booth sits a woman approx forty yeers old pritty as a peech dark hare a litle like I imagin your mama to look in twenty yeers wen she has attaned middel age. She is wareing the theeter unifform blew cardigen over wite blowse a yelow stripe running down each side of the butons. KLIF plays inside the booth I can here the anounser talking in frantik tones about the assassinashun his voise a strange combinnashun of seriusness and exsitement he probly can not beleev he has the good fortoon to report on a story of such magnitood your wellcum ha. The clerk bundels tikkets as she lissens her hed bent down her fingers bizly werking rolls of paper she is cleerly not aware of my presense as I slip thru the clossest dubbel doors she does not look up. My luk continoos onse inside a yung fella in simlar uniform who works the conseshun stand also colleks the theeter tikets wen rekwired is busy stokking the candy cuonter refilling shelvs with juju froots junor mints reeses peenut butter cups compleeteing paper work as he goes. His brow nitted he takes sum boxes of junor mints tikks a sheet of paper bends down to put the candy inside the glass cuonter case. Wile he is distrakted I bolt up the starecase to the balcuny levell push open the doors stumbel into the welcumming dark.

I stand inside the door for a few minits as my eyes adjust to the blak. The balcny appeers emty until I make out a bunch of skoolkids playing hooky in the frunt row. They are stinking up the plase with cigrets also giggeling throing popcorn aruond genrally makeing merry hell and liveing up to the ole saying boys will be boys.

I settel in the bak row to collek my thorts the urgensy of figgering out my neks move imposibel to ignoor. If I can jus make it to Lancaster then the border and Mexico City the Cuban embasy will obviusly grant me a veesa howevver I am also acootly aware I must bide my time wate untill the coast is cleer befor recommensing my moovements.

After who knos how long I reelise I hav been stareing blankly at the screen. The first part of the dubble feeture is playing. I recognize Audy Murfy from your mamas magazeens she considders him qite hansum I personly do not see wot all the fuss is abuot. War is Hell only came out in the theeters a munth or two ago I hav not seen it munny too tite to waste on sinama tikkets. I hav howevver redd about it in the noospaper the story of a US sargent in Korea who does not tell his troops that a seesefire has been agreed to he wants to leed his platoon on one last mishon win hisself more meddals. That may suond far feched to a civilan howevver after my time in the Marines nuthing wood surprise me evryone in the millitry is looking to play the heero the cost to others be dammed. In fack it is jus like the Koreen war itself tipical behaveyer from the U.S. prettending to be the heero akting in others interests wen in fack they are jus looking after nummer one. Mark my wurds one day that will cum bak to bite them on the you kno wot that time mite well be Veetnam.

War is Hell is rite up my allee tho lots of soldeirs shooting at each other in the heet of battel howevver I dont follo the story forse myself to stay allert aware of my suruondings in case a persewer shood pressent hisself. I am not shure how the polise wood even kno I am in the theeter howevver I must not let my gard down must be preparred just like any boy skout erning his merrit bage ha.

After a few minits my hart rate reterns to normal my swetting also not as profooss. The theeter is the perfeck plase to gather my thorts cool dark allmost emty excep for the rabbel rouseing skool boys who are a constent distrakshun. If I were a paying kustamer I wood complane to managment about there tomfoollry a person shood not hav to put up with that kind of nonsens after paying hard erned munny for a tiket unfortoonetly Junie I am obviusly in no posishun to register my displesure.

I stay still for five minits maybe ten jus sit in my seet stareing vakantly at the screen not takeing in any of the akshun makeing plans for wen I reech Mexico City. Furst I will go strate to the Cuban embasy restate my desire to asist in Fidels cawse also advise them of the grate deed that I hav purformed in the name of freedum altho no doubt they will hav herd about same by the time I arive. Then I will vissit the Russian embasy tell them simler shurely now they will ekspedite my veesa the wateing time will not be anyware neer the four munths they tole me previus. After spending sum time in Cooba perhaps werking direkly with Fidel hisself fated as a heero I will retern to Russia send at onse for you Junie your Mama and Rachel. The US by that time will no dout be glad to get rid of your mama and her conecshun to Kennedys demise we will all be reunited onse more one big happy famly in Minsk Mama joyfull to see Aunt Valya aggen I drinking vodka with my old frends perhaps retern to my old job at the raydio faktory altho the Russians may vry well hav bigger things in mind for me after wot I hav acheeved.

Howevver I hav gotten one step ahed of myself for I now notiss trubbel brooing downstares in the mane secshun of the theeter. Two men one the wurker from the conseshon stand the other it takes me a momment to recognize is nun other than the shoo salesman from the stoor on Jeferson they are both makeing their way towards the doors at the reer of the theeter. They walk down the isle looking left and rite down each ro it can only be me they are serching for. I realise that if I sit here and wate for them to check the balknee I am a ded duk. I stand up the seet flips bak with a hevvy clunk fortunatly they are too far away to heer it over the ackshun on the screne. I chek my revolver in my wasteband then leeve thru the balknee doors take the stares dubbel time to beet my pursooers befor there serch downstares cums up emty.

I reech the frunt doors leen on one to push it open wen tires screech out frunt folowed by anuther screech and anuther. I do not look out the door for feer of being spotted howevver I kno that cars pulling up with such urgensy can only meen one thing. Feeling like a mowse cornered by two cats I dash bak inside the theeter. From my spy reedings I kno that the saffest plase to hide is warever an adversry has alreddy serched. I slip into the theeter propper take a middel seet about three ros into the orkestra secshun try to look like I hav been there all the wile.

The movie still plays the handfull of pattrons oblivius to the reel drama unfolding aruond them. The consesshun stand kid and shoo salesman hav now reeched the bak doors they chek the ones on the left side of the stage reasshure themselvs that I hav not alreddy slipped out that way oh how I wish that were the kase. Finding the doors lokked they cross to the other side of the stage chek those doors too same ressult. Reeliseing that no one has left thru the reer doors they hed bak up the isle no longer looking down each row my taktik of reterning to ware they hav alreddy serched paying off hansumly. I stay put hopeing that is the end of it howevver after a few minits presoomably after chekking the balknee they retern walk bak down to the reer doors onse more. Jus as the kid reeches the bak door on the rite there cums a furius puonding from outside he pushes down on a bar releeseing the lok the doors burst inwerds fludding the theeter with lite.

Hey shut the door! sumone yells.

Sevral figgers stand silhooetted in the doorway. I can make out the shaype of a Stetson and the barrell of a shotgun whoevva is out there meens bizness.

Over the suond of the movie cums a burst of yelling a short struggel then silense. The polise hav misstaken the salesman for there qarry but hav been swiftlee set to rite.

The conseshun kid heds bak up the isle towards the lobby the salesman stays with the two cops togetther they turn to fase the theeter.

Turn up the huose lites! yells one of the cops Will sumone pleese turn up the huose lites!

Five or ten secunds pass I consider makeing a brake for it then the lites go up I dar not moove. The two cops and the salesman take a set of steps up onto the stage like they are abuot to take a bow. They wisper to each other I can not make out wot they are saying then the salesman poynts in my direkshun seemingly rite at me I tell myself its my gilty conshense talking howevver with each passing seccund I beleeve I am well and trooly cooked. I manage to carm myself but wen they start leeeving the stage I stand up hedd to the isle preppared to shoot my way out if nesesry. But common sense reaserts itself there are too menny polise out frunt judgeing by the nummer of sqod cars I herd arriveing I wood be apreehended in an instent shood I try to flee. My only remaneing hope is that the men serching the theeter do not recognise me. I take a seet two in from the isle tell myself to relacks the polise hav no idea wot I look like and the salesman may not remember so well he was qite sum distanse away wen wotching me at the store. I repeet to myself stay carm stay carm I must remane same to hav any chanse of eckscapeing this predikament.

The two cops hed down the left senter isle the salesman trayleing by sevral feet. They stop behind two men sitting maybe ten ros in frunt of me begin to qesshun them. I can not tell if they seriusly considder them suspecks or are jus putting on a sho to dellay our confruntashun until shure I am the man they seek perhaps also to wate for bakkup.

Get on your feet! barks the ferst cop a uniform patrollman like the man I jus shot. His is a soft babys fase it is sumwhat surprizeing to heer a stern voise cum out of its pudgey mouth. He is also a larg man tall wide sholdered hevvy set probly be vry diffcult to beet in a fist fite I may find out soon enuff.

The two patruns stand up fidgetting all pale and nervus unabel to look the cop in the eye. Maybe they are theeves maybe they are preests it doesnt reely matta no one enjoys being harassed by the cops howevver the cops most sertenly enjoy doing the harrassing. It is all abuot power for them sum cops no dout good peeple but for the most part they are bullys in uniforms plane and simpel. I hav fuond same in cuntrys all aruond the world it takes a serten kind of persson to want to be a cop.

Arms out legs appart! he commands then starts frisking.

Wile he serches him the secund cop stands by wotching. The saleman does same from sevral ros away. The cops baks terned I aggen ponder makeing a brake for it but ware wood I run? There are cops out frunt I kno for a fack that there are more cuvvering the bak. There is nuthing to do but wate for the inevitabel see if I can tawk my way out of it I hav always been good with werds wen needed Junie jus aks your Mama.

Sit down! the cop kommands wen he finnishes with the first fella. Then he starts in on the secund folowing the same rootine patting down his arms his boddy his legs then bak thru them aggen in revers order makeing sure he has missed nuthing. Then for jus a split secund he glanses over his sholder at me I kno then with sertenty that he has made me. I steel myself for the battel ahed there are two of them one of me I am small they are big if I am to hav any chanse of ekscape I need to get the ferst punch in then shoot my way out of trubble.

Sit down the cops says the man qikly does as he is tole.

The cops tern aruond scan the theeter continooing to put on a sho of looking for there man. Howevver they giv the game away by not looking at me if they had not identifyed me they wood be studying me hard there behavur is in fack the oposit I am

139

seemingly the last persun in the world they are interested in.

As they march up the isle towards me cold swet trikles down my nek. They reech my row stop look left look rite. Then the cop whose been doing all the frisking spins to fase me.

Get on your feet! he snaps.

I stand up. As I sed he is a big fella sevral axe handels across the sholders I hav to tilt my hed bak jus to look him in the eye. I raze my hands towards my chest as tho in surender keeping my rite hand slitely lower close to the gun conseeled in my wasteband.

Well it is all over now I say.

The werds surprize him he does nuthing but stare at me. Then he reeches for my waste he has spotted the bulge of my gun. I can not let him dissarm me I hit him rite between the eyes with a left. His cap flys off he stumbels bakward. But for a big man he mooves awfull fast he is soon upon me we grappel as I go for my gun with my rite hand.

Hes got a gun! sumone yells.

The cop givs me a qick rite to the chin stuns me but I feel litle pane as I am litrally in the fite of my life. My hand reeches the gun a split secund befor his I rayse the pistol to stomuk level sqeeze the trigger to get a shot off but his left hand clamps over mine jus befor the hammer falls. It cliks lamly sumthing perhapps one of his fingers has prevented the gun from fireing. We tumbel sideways tusseling for control of the weppon we fall between two ros of seets this is wen his size cums into play it is like wressling a grizzley bare who has not eeten for days.

Ive got him! he yells in triumf.

Now that his size has givven him the upper hand he raps his

hooge poor aruond the gun renches it from my grasp. He holds it out by the barel his partna snaches it away. Now the thret of been shot has passt cops appeer from noware jumping in to play heero. I take my hat off to the cop who subdewed me he at leest showed sum reel gumpshun leeping in wen danger was pressent insted of wateing for sumone else to do the durty work.

It is now at leest three or four cops agenst one I am not shure exakly how menny are upon me we are a tangel of arms and legs like a kartoon fite. I put up the best battel I can Junie but no man can beet those odds. One cop grabs me aruond the nek from behine anuther grabs my left arm anuther from the row in frunt grabs my body I am compleetly outnummered. Fists fly in all direkshuns I wood like to say I gave as good as I got Junie but that is not the case. They soon hav me in there kontrol but evven so blos continoo to rane down I am struk on the side of the hed my left eybrow splits it still throbs as I rite these vry wurds.

Shoot a cop wood ya! one yells strikes me in the ribs.

Cop killer! anuther snarls more blos cum thik and fast.

Dont hit me any more! I say I am not ressisting arest! I am not resisting arest! Howevver my words fall on deff ears.

Eventuly there arms tire of delivring there savagry. Three of them pik me up off of the flor drag me into the isle.

Bring his arm aruond sumone says I hav the cuffs.

One of them bends down plants his nee fermly between my sholder blades anuther snaps a cuff aruond my left rist wile sumone else pulls my other arm behind my bak then he cuffs them together more titely than nesesary no dout trying to inflick as much pane as posibel. I do not utta a wurd of complaynt I do not want to giv them the plessure howevver I do kno my rites proseed to tell them same.

I protest this polise brutalty! I shuot to anyone hoo will lissen wich I freely admit is few.

On your feet is all sumone grunts in respons.

Two cops put there hands under my arms hawl me up. Onse uprite I am determinned to sho them that they hav not hert me that I can stil oprate under my own steem I am far from a brokken man. I stand on my own two feet I am now fase to fase with the cop who apreehended me see that he is also injered a long shalow scrach runs down one side of his fase from ear to muoth. The cut is probly from wen he snached the gun from me perhaps the barel grazed his cheek no matta wot the cawse it pleeses me grately.

I kno my rites I shuot.

Shut up wise guy the cop who cufft me says.

I want a loyyer.

The only thing your getting is a trip to the chare sumone else says.

By now the theeter has more cops than pattrons. A bunch of them form a sircle aruond me leed me to the lobby. On the way up the isle the shoo salesman wotches me as one mite a mad dog I glar bak hateing him with all my sole. If not for him I wood be harfway to Mexico by now. Now hoo knos wot mite happen. As the cop jus statted the chare is not out of the quesshun Texas more than happy to carry out the deth penaltee only resently doing same to a blak man named Lavan who robbed and killt a shop keeper in Hooston. The salesman averts my gaze he knos exakly wot he has dun.

These cuffs are too tite I say to the cop on my left They are digging into my skin can you loossen them?

He stares strate ahed no response his anser.

We poosh thru dubbel doors into the lobby. The conceshon stand kid and tiket offise lady stand neer the candy cuonter the woman has jus brushed her hare probly in antisipashun of attenshun from the press the kid howevver jus looks confoosed I dont think he reely knos wot is going on. I grin at the two of them both trapped in ded end jobs they will nevver kno wot it feels like to ekscape. My kapture mite be the only momment of reel exsitement in there tawdree litle lives.

The cops leed me past the candy cuonter britely lit Holywood posters red vellvet ropes into the lobby propper. I cant see thru the frunt doors but heer one hek of a comoshun as we approch. Even so I am totly unprepared for wot greets us on the other side never in my wildest dreems wood I hav envissaged such a recepshun. Wurd has spred about the cop getting shot a croud has gathered wot looks like hunnerds of peeple mill aruond wateing to see who emerges from the theeter. They serge towards us voises swelling all kinds of yelling and obsennitys fill the air they are cleerly nun too pleesed.

Let us hav him!

Let us kill him for ya!

We want him! Hand him over!

A teenage gurl most probly a freshman in hi skool blond bangs blew eyes vry cute fase is the vry pitcher of innosense untill she opens her muoth.

Kill the sun of a bich! she screems madder than a wet hen then does the unthinkabel spits on me. Evven the cops look at each other agast at the venum that has spewed forth from this angellic litle gurl.

I protest this polise brootalty! I shout bak smurking. This insenses the croud further they are like a rabbid mob from romen times baying for blud in the coliseem revenge most deffinitly on there tiny minds.

The cops close in tite lineing up in frunt of me also one on eether side anuther two behind. Forming a wedg we start to forse our way thru the croud to a patroll car parkt at the kerb. A plane cloths cop on my rite takes off his Stettson puts it over my fase a vry stoopid idea as no one knos who I am plus I hav no problem with peeple seeing my fase for I hav dun nuthing to be ashammed of. I try to tell him this to no avale. I then reelise the danger of the situashon for if sumone were to brake thru the polise line lunge at me I wood not see them cumming who knos wot injurys I mite sustane befor they cood reskue me. I shake my hed vigrusly from side to side untill the cop remooves the hat.

Feeling safe aggen inside my coccoon of lawmen I deside to hav a litle fun.

I protest this polise brutalty I shuot aggen luoder than befor.

This stirs up the masses no end there is shuoting shoveing the polise aruond me hav to fite hard to manetane kontrol. Despite the danger inherrent in the situashon the crowds reacshun pleeses me grately peeple are so eesly manipoollated perhaps that is why politishuns luv there jobs so much. To hav hunnerds of peeple reacting to your evry wurd is as I am now discuvring vry intoxikateing indede.

We poosh thru the mellay reech the sqod car parkt out frunt of the theeter. A cop opens the reer door jumps inside slides across the seet to sit behine the driver. Anuther cop shuvs me in after him useing a hand to hold my hed down so I dont strike it on the door fram. A secund cop folows me in a detektive in a soot he slams the door shut. I hav a cop on eether side of me I spose to prevent me from leeping from the car onse it is is in moshun I must admit the thort crosses my mind I mite be handcuffed but I am not hepless I must look for any possibel avanoo of ekscape.

Three other cops pile into the frunt seet then we are off siren blareing the croud reluktently parting to let us thru there jeering reeching a cressendo. The cop on my rite smokes a siggar throing out thik ransid fooms the air in the car soon turns fowel. I feel nawshuss bile caches in my throte it is not jus the siggar smoke the shock of kapture is also upon me.

The driver thros a fast U-tern at the neks set of lites tires sqeeling. The cop on my left is throne hard up agenst me I am forsed agenst siggar man the meet in the law enforsement sandwitch. We take Jeferson bak past the theeter the croud onse aggen jeers shakes there fists we take a qik left onto Zang.

I swalo the nasty tast in my muoth shake my hed to cleer it.

I kno my rites I say to no one in partiklar a few bloks down Zang.

The five cops all look strate ahed.

Wots this all abuot? I aks.

You are a suspekt in the merder of a polise offisser one of them finely says.

A polise offisser has been killed? I heer they burn for merder. I grin as I say it try to get a rise out of them. Sure enuff siggar man tenses up his hands on his legs clench into fists.

You may find out he says thru the smoke.

Onse aggen I feel the rush of exsitement I felt wen the croud

145

outside the theeter responded to my evry wurd. I knoo that one day I wood hav the power to kontrol peeples emoshuns it is confirmmashun that I hav folloed the rite path my kapture is but a small hicup on the rode to well desserved fame.

Well they say it jus takes a secund to die I say.

There follos sevral momments of silense the cops no dout wundering wot kind of persson wood joke about there own demise. Litle do they reelise that today I hav fullfilled my lifes ambishon wot happens to me now of litle consekwense. Of corse I wood deerly luv to hold you aggen Junie and your mama and Rachel howevver if deth is wot awates me then I will die a happy man.

As we neer the viaduck siggar man aks my name. I employ there tack respond with silense.

Adress? he ferther probes.

Aggen I giv no anser.

He sighs reeches over ressles my wollet from my bak poket.

I dont kno why your treeting me like this I say The only thing I hav dun is carry a pistol into a pitcher theeter.

Lee Oswald he says reeding off of my libry card.

I keep my eyes on the rode ahed. Furst rool of interogashun consede nuthing.

He flips thru ferther takes out a selectiv serviss card.

Alek Hidell he reeds off of that.

Aggen I offer no explashun neether confurm nor deny it is a patern that I plan to folow for as long as posibel. No sense makeing it eesy for the authoritees best to keep them gessing.

He flips the wollet shut tucks it into his jaket poket.

I rekkon we are going to hav to wate till we get to the stashun befor we find out who he actully is he says. He passes the two peeces of ID to the cop in the pasenger seet tells him Wire those thru to deespatch.

The cop in the frunt seet piks up the two way raydio.

Five forty here. Car two. We hav aprehended a suspekt in relashun to the Tipit shooting. We are on root from the Texas Theeter. Destinashun homiside and robbry for ferther quesshuning.

Name? says a woman on the other end.

We hav two.

Two?

Thats rite.

Go ahed.

He looks down at the cards.

Alek Hidell. H-I-D-E-L-L.

And?

Lee Oswald. O-S-W-

Oswald? the deespatcher says There is a Lee Oswald wanted in connecshun with the shooting of the president. Offisers hav jus been deespatched to a locashun in Irving to bring him in for qesshunning.

Well I think hes sitting rite here in the car with us.

One momment pleese. There is a berst of statik then silense befor she continoos Bring the suspeck direckly to Captan Fritzs offise.

Ten four.

The two cops on eether side look at me. Siggar man lets out a clowd of smoke.

Did you shoot the president? he aks looking at me like he is seeing me for the furst time.

I shake my hed do not utta a respons. Let them work it out for thereselvs if they are capabel of doing so I am willing to litrally bet my life they are not.

We hurtel across the viaduck toward the city. A mile away the depossitry stands on the horizen. The Hertz clok reeds 1.52 less than an huor and a half has past sinse I shot the president. It shurely did not take long for me to get kaptured altho it is a mirracle that I exscaped the bldg in the first plase. I never reely expekted to make it out allive let alone reech Oke Cliff. It is a creddit to my ingenooity that I came within a wisker of freedum if not for that dam shoo salesman I wood be on a bus hedded for Mexico rite now. I consoll myself with the knoledge that now there will be a tryal my reesons for commenseing the clensing will cum out it is the chanse I hav been wateing for to edukate the peeple of the world about the grand charayde in wich they dayly partisipate. I jus need to determine the rite time to tell all I leen towards the tryal.

The downtown traffik has freed up sum howevver the driver flips his siren bak on to smooth our pasage. Cars part like the Red See we crooze down Market tern rite onto Mane in a few minits we approche old City Hall on Harwood ware the polise dept is huosed. The car terns rite off of Mane into a drivway on the left side of the bldg we disapeer down a bassment ramp into an undergruond garage entring the bowells of Dallas itself. I cant help but feel I mite disapeer down here forever swalloed up never to see the lite of day aggen. The fack that the FBI are no dout wateing inside only adds to my feeling of dred they hav been after me ever sinse I reterned from Russia now that they hav me they will never let me go.

The ramp flattens out at a stop sine we pull over besside a passage way leeding into the bldg. A clusta of press wates by the doors a reporter from KLIF cluching a microfone also newspaper men brandishing notepads and fotografers aiming camras at us. They swarm the vehikel elboing each other as they jokkey for posishun. How they herd about our arivel I do not kno no dout sum form of bribry was involved menny involved in law enforsement like to take fiscel advantag of there posishun MPs in the Marines sertenly behaved same in that respeck.

Lissen the fella seeted neks to me says thru his siggar Wen we get out we are going to hold you in such a way that you can duk your hed if you want. There are going to be scads of press out there you mite not want to hav your foto takken.

Why shood I hide my fase? I say looking him sqarely in the eye I havent dun anything to be ashammed of.

He mumbels sum wurds not to be repeeted in your cumpny Junie then gets out of the car. The cop on my left nudges me I scoot across the seet as best I can with both hands cuffed it is no eesy feet. Reeching the car door siggar man helps me stand. I tern to fase the press who do not hold bak they asale me with qesshuns.

Did you shoot the polise ofisser?

Wot are they bringing you in for?

Do you hav anything to do with the shooting of the president?

I ignoor them it is far too soon to tell my side of the story. The cops form a tryangel aruond me same as wen we left the theeter gide me thru the press pak towards the doors. I hold my hed hi look strate ahed I hav zeero to hide. Microfones are shuvved in my fase camras flash all aruond blinding me I remane as strong as steel I will not bend to there roodness.

Siggar man pushes open the dubbel doors there is one last berst of qesshuns and camra flashes then the doors shut behind us cutting off the noize. I am led past a booking area ware a cop sits eeting a sandwitch with litle enthoosiasm. A few reporters hav slippt thru the door after us the cop stops mid choo wotches thru sqinty eyes as we navigate a narow hallway to the elevater. The doors open we pile in. Sumhow a few reporters sqeeze in with us also a fella with a movie camra on his sholder.

You guys are like cokroches says siggar man his wurds are like water off of a duks bak.

Sumone punches the buton for the 3rd flor the elevater assends. The camraman trayns his lens on me I try not to look gilty but the glass eye is unrellenting I hav to turn away.

The doors open the reporters and camraman dash out furst then turn to fase me walking bakwards shuoting quesshuns at me as siggar man leeds me down the coridoor. Soon they murge with anuther pak of newsmen we are all cramed into a long narro hall its walls scuffed in plases copiuss doors leed off to diffrent offisses.

Like a pak of hyeenas the newsmen savage me with there quesshuns.

Why are you here?

Wot hav you dun?

Did you shoot the cop?

Woodnt you like to kno I think but dont utta a wurd. Why the authoritees hav givven the press such free rane I do not kno but I hav few complaynts as it will soon play rite into my hands.

No more being ignoored no moor crazy old Lee and his crazy ideas it is cleer that peeple will be eeger to heer wot I hav to say. Jugeing by this rabbid exhibishun my acshuns hav set off a pouder keg the size of wich I cood never hav hoped for the reacshun to my deed swift createing the perfeck platform from wich to esspouse my veiws wen the time is rite. This I reelise is my life from now on the rarafyed air of cellebrity and Junie I plan to use it to its fulest affeck. Howevver for the time been I must keep my pouder dry I must wate till the rite time to delliver my messige with macksimum impack also hold bak untill I kno exakly wot the cops hav on me.

Eventuly we push our way to a door its glass windo stampt 317 below that in blak letters Homiside and Robbry Burow a sine abuv also anuonseing same. The cops push me thru the door slam it on the press. We pass other offisses within the offisse untill we reech a door marked Sqod Room. A few reporters hoo hav managed to slip inside trale us rite up until the secund door is slammed in there fases.

The sqod room is fernished with metel tabels and chares a poster for the polisemans unun pinned to the wall. The room is nuthing speshul perhaps twise the size of this sell in wich I now sit. The cops lower the blinds on the door then ecksit leeveing two unifform men stashuned outside. I sit allone the tik tok of the clok my only cumpany it tells me it is 2.04pm.

Minits later the door bersts open. A detektiv in a rinkeled soot I hav not seen him befor slides two peeces of paper in frunt of me. It is the two IDs siggar man took from my wollet in the car one reel the other fake I shood kno I made the fake one.

One says Lee Harvey Oswald and one says Alek Hidell the decektive says Wich one are you?

Your so smart you figger it out.

He stares wates for more wen I giv him nuthing he leevs in dissgust.

Anuther minit passes. Then a tall man enters wareing a lite collored soot cowboy hat cowboy boots. He sits down acros the tabel from me. In those plane clothes I figger he is a detektive he conferms the qality of my observashunal skills with his ferst wurds.

Detektive Level homiside and robbry. He looks at the cut abuv my rite eye and the brooz on my left cheek. Are you OK?

I am a litle takken bak by his consern. I am fine I say. I do not want him to think that I am afrade of a litle fizcal injery.

Do you kno why you are here? His deep voise is full of wurry he is like John Wayne tawking to a pritty litle thing out on the planes.

Im not shure I say I was sitting in the pitcher theeter wotching a movie wen the polise arrested me I do admit that I poppt one of them in the fase but I was only deffending myself.

He sits bak crosses his legs. Do you kno anything abuot the shooting of a polise offisser in Oak Cliff?

I didnt shoot anybody. The wurds cum out luoder than intended I am obviusly keyed up wich is to be expekted givven the situashun.

Well he says leening foreward elbos on the tabel rubbing his chin with his fingers Heres the problem. You strike me as a reesonabley intellgent man.

Thats a probblem?

I kno his game he thinks flattry will work he does not kno

who he is deeling with. I am well versed in the art of interogashun it is sumthing the Marines drill into you in the evvent of kaptur also I am vry well red wen it cums to any toppic espeenage related. He is obviusly takeing the good cop rout but I kno that a bad cop will cum allong soon enuff.

You kno he says We can take the pistul that you had on you in the theeter and run a balistics test on it that will proove your gun was the one used to shoot the offisser.

Well youll jus hav to do that I say then clam up. There is no way I will respond to hypathetcals wen no one has so much as redd me my rites.

I rekkon we will he replys.

At that momment the door flys open. Anuther cop wareing a ten gallon hat stiks his head in the door.

Wots this fellas name? he aks.

Oswald. Lee Oswald.

The cop at the door perses his lips. He has sum burst blud vessels on his nose probly from hevvy licker a vise I never much partispated in altho if I made my liveing as a cop it may proove more tempting.

Thanks he says slams the door.

So you kno nuthing about the shooting? Level aks aggen.

Thats rite I say If that is wot this is all about you hav got the rong man.

We will see abuot that.

Yes we will.

We go aruond in sircles like that for a few more minits the convasashun not going anyware becos qite ritely I am not willing to consede anything.

Then the door flys open aggen. This time four or five men pile into the room and croud aruond Level. One of them I later cum to lern is the cheef of the homiside and robery burow Capten Fritz.

This Lee Oswald? Fritz bellos. He dabs at his cheeks with a hankercheef he is swetting up a storm his pudgey fase leeking evry wich way no dout he has been run ragged sinse the president and a cop were shot on his wotch.

Sure enuff says Levell.

OK boys get him to my offise he says speeking softer now almost like he regrets haveing to aks same. His voise is crokey like he has been tawking too much. His ears are larg his jowels saggy his eyes fix on me with a sadness. In sum ways he resembels a elefant that I sumtimes vissited at the Bronx zoo wen playing hooky I wotched that beest for huors Junie they are hily intellgent creetures capabel of feelings and emoshuns jus like us hoomans.

Two cops cum aruond to my side of the tabel hawl me to my feet manhandel me out the door. Fritzs offise is rite neks door in fack wen they dump me in a seet I can see the room I was jus in thru a glass windo set in the wall that is until a cop lowers the blinds.

Fritz sits down oposit with a pad and pen same as the ones I use to rite now. The rest of the men croud into the room a few take seets most stand in the small spase neerly all smoke fowling the air.

I am Capten Will Fritz hed of homiside and robbry he says. He gestures to a man standing agenst the wall with vry promnent eyebrows they are archt like he is perpetuly aksing a quesshun.

This is speshul agent Bookout of the FBI continoos Fritz then he chooses not to introduse the harf duzzen other men in the room. Befor I aks any qesshuns he says I want to be cleer about your rites here today. You do not need to make any statment. Any statment that you do make may be used in a cort of law agenst you. Any statment made must be free and voluntry and you hav the rite to consult with an atterny. Do you unnerstand?

Yes.

Wot is your name?

You alreddy kno that.

Well there seems to be sum confushon wether its Oswald or Hidell. But I beleev you are Lee Oswald. Is that correck?

Yes I say not seeing any poynt in denying who I am. In any evvent it will be useful for the press to kno my identaty.

State your ful name for the record pleese.

Lee Harvey Oswald.

Do you work at the Texas Skool Book Depositry?

Yes.

Wich flor?

2nd I say even tho that is not strickly correck the 2nd flor is ware the publishing cumpnys resside. I dont kno why I say 2nd flor it jus cums out I kno I am lying jus for the sake of lying but that is sumthing that I must admit I am prone to jus aks your Mama. Sumtimes I lie with good reeson for exampel I want to conseel sumthing other times I lie jus to keep myself amoosed to me it is all part of the game of life. Bessides any good oprativ must practis the skills of the trade of wich lying is most sertently one I hav red enuff spy novvels to kno same.

Jus the 2nd?

My work takes me to all diffrent flors.

Wich ones?

Four five six and seven.

Were you on those flors today?

Well yes if my job reqires me to vissit those flors then I was on those flors.

At that momment the fone on the desk rings. Fritz scowels piks it up. Fritz he says then lissens. Yes hold on one momment. He holds the reseever out to the FBI man. Its for you. Shanklin.

Bookout looks wurryed takes the reseever. Sir? he says then there is a pawse as sir speeks. Yes sir we are intervewing the suspeck rite now. I see. Yes sir. Rite away. He hands the fone bak to Fritz who plases it in the cradel.

Shanklin wants one of his lokal agents in here with us wen we interview Oswald says Bookout.

Wots this agents name? aks Fritz.

Hasty.

Fine go get him.

Fritz his faseless men and me sit in awkwerd silense as Bookout leeves the room. On the outside I am a cucummer inside I am Krakkatoa knoing that I will hav to sit in the same room as Hasty. Altho we hav never met it will be a grate chalenge to keep myself under kontrol after the harasment he has inflicted on your mama I will jus hav to grit my teeth.

A momment later Bookout reterns with Hasty in toe he is a qeer looking fella thin lips red fase. I sneer wen he givs me a butter woodnt melt in his muoth look for I kno how obnokshus he can be jus aks your Mama. He retreets to the safty of the other men lineing the bak wall he is acting like he remembers the thret to his person I left at his offise I sertenly hope so.

This is speshul agent Hasty joyning us says Fritz not reelizeing Hasty and I hav a histry. Lets pik up ware we left off. Mister Oswald you were saying you work on menny flors at the book depositry?

I am shure your notes refleck that why dont you chek them?

Wich flor were you on at the time the president was shot?

Wot time was the pressident shot?

Fritz takes a deep breth. I am employing a classik interogashun technik anser a qesshun with anuther qesshun it frustrates your interogator also slos down the pase of the intervew.

Aproximetly twelve therty pm he dralls.

I am not exakly shure ware I was at that time. But I beleeve I was takeing my lunch on the first flor.

I see.

He scribbels sumthing on his note pad. I am surprized to see he does not hav a tape reccorder at his disposel howevver this is to his advantag he is in compleet kontrol of wot is reflekted in any offishul reccord of intervew.

Anyone in the lunchroom with you? he aks.

Who sed I was in the lunch room?

You jus did.

No I didnt I sed I was takeing my lunch.

So woodnt you be in the lunch room?

Thats not ware I ate my lunch.

Then ware did you eat it?

The domino room.

The domino room?

Thats wot we call the first flor lunch room.

Why?

Isnt it obvius? On acuont of the fack that the men play dominos there.

I see. All rite. Well in any case was there anyone in this domino room with you wile you were eating lunch?

A few of the collored fellas.

Do you kno there names?

Junor was there. Not shure of the other fellas name.

This Junor fella hav a last name?

Jarman.

Fritz rites that down. Wot did you eat for lunch?

Wots that got to do with anything?

Mister Oswald...

Fine. A chees sandwitch sum froot.

Ware did you get this lunch?

Brort it from home.

Ware were you wen Patrollman Brown stopped you? he aks changeing direcshuns trying to cach me off gard. It does work sum I am surprized he alreddy knos that one of his patrollmen stopped me just after the shooting of corse I dont sho it.

Patrolman Browen? I say.

Thats rite. The offiser who stopped you inside the depossitry jus after the shooting took plase.

Oh that offisser. I was on the 2nd flor.

Ware exakly?

In the 2nd flor lunchroom drinking a coke.

But you jus sed you were on the 1st floor.

I got thirsty.

I see he says aggen scribelling in his pad. One of the agents standing at the bak of the room cleers his throt my ansers obviusly getting under his skin I shurely must be doing sumthing rite.

Can you tell me wot happened?

Wen?

Wen Offisser Brown stopped you.

Why dont you aks him?

I alreddy hav. I want to heer your side of the story.

Oh well I was jus abuot to buy a coke from the pop masheen wen this cop berst thru the door with his pistol drawen. He shuoted at me to cum over then aksed if I wurked in the bldg.

Wot did you say?

I work there so of corse thats wot I tole him. I am not sure if he beleeved me. He seemed vry adgitated. I was wurryed he mite shoot me.

Wot happened neks?

He left the room.

Nuthing hapened befor that?

Befor that?

Yes befor he left the room.

Well Mister Trooly entered the room.

Mister Trooly?

My supeviser. I rekkon he came in to see wot all the fuss was abuot. The poliseman this Offisser – wot did you say his name is?

Brown. Patrollman Brown.

Patrollman Brown aksed Mister Trooly if he noo me and Mister Trooly sed yes I wurked in the bldg. That seemed to settel the matter as they both left the lunch room and hedded upstares.

And wot did you do at this time?

I left the bldg.

You left the bldg?

Yes.

Why?

Why? Isnt that obvius? I wanted to kno wot all the fuss was abuot. I had not yet herd that the president had been shot and it is not evry day you see a cop in the bldg you work in. I figgered sumthing big was up.

All rite. Wot came after that?

I took the stares down to the first flor lobby and stood at the frunt door. A forman Mister Shelly was there. He tole me that the president had been shot.

This was the first you knoo of it?

Yes sir.

Go on.

Wot exakly do you want to kno?

Well did you see anyone you kno wen you came downstares?

Yes.

Can you remember there names?

Of corse I can I am not an iddiot.

Mister Oswald pleese.

Wesly Frazer and Billy Luvlady were there.

Did you tawk to them?

No I only tawked to Mister Shelly.

For how long?

Five maybe ten minits.

Who is this Mister Shelly?

Anuther of my bosses.

I see. For five maybe ten minits?

You got a heering problem? Thats wot I sed. Five or ten minits.

Wot did you all tawk about?

He tole me there wood probly be no more work for the day becos of all the confooshun.

And you aksepted his word?

I saw no reeson not to. He is one of the formen.

So wot did you do?

I went home.

You went home. Fritz wipes his brow looks aruond the room at the other men. Is it your usule praktise to leev work at lunch time?

Well no I say But this is not a usule day.

You can say that aggen.

I smirk tempted to repeet same as he has sugested howevver I manage to hold my tung.

So you didnt think twise about leeveing erly?

The depossitry is not vry partiklar about such things.

You dont hav set huors?

We work from eight in the morning untill fuor forty-five of an afternoon but never punch a clok or anything like that.

So you thort it was best to jus leeve?

After Mister Shelly had tole me abuot wot hapened I saw no reeson not to. It did not appeer to me that there wood be any more work dun today.

Fritz looks aruond the room at the FBI men the other homiside offissers. They are qiet thinking about wot has been dissclosed.

Fritz aggen wipes swet from his forehead altho the room is not hot. I am the one who shood be swetting howevver I am carm haveing sucesfully terned the tabels on him.

Fritz revews his notes for a moment then continoos.

Do you own a rifel, Mister Oswald?

No.

Hav you eva owned a rifle?

No.

Never?

Never.

Never had a rifel at your plase of employment?

Me personly no I say seezeing the chanse to plant sum seeds of dout.

Wot do you meen me personly? Hav you seen others with a rifle at work?

Yes sir.

Wen was this?

A few days ago.

Wot were the cirkumstanses?

Mister Caster from one of the publishing cumpnys was in Mister Troolys offise with two rifles.

Do you kno why?

I am not reely shure. I think Mister Caster sed he had jus bort them at lunch time.

Did he say why?

He claymed one was a Cristmas pressent for his sun wich seemed strange to me.

Why so?

Cristmas is more than a munth away.

I see. Wot abuot the other rifel?

He sed it was for hisself to take deer hunting.

And this was jus a few days ago?

Thats wot I sed.

Vry intresting. We will folow up on that.

Happy to be of help.

He ignoors my comment. Now wot were your moovements after you left the book deppositry?

Is it possibel to get a glass of water? I aks All this tawk is makeing me thersty.

Of corse. Fritz nods at Hasty who leeves the room to fech it. Thats probly all he is good for running erands for his masser like a litle puppy dog.

Also I say sqerming in my seet these cuffs are vry tite they are digging into my rists. Can I pleese hav my arms mooved to the frunt?

Fritz thinks for a momment then nods at one of the cops. He uncuffs me brings my hands foreward onto the tabel cuffs them aggen loosser this time. The circulashon cumming bak into my hands feels good the pins and needels disapeering. Releef also fluds thru my sholder mussels they ake after being pinned bak for so long it is almost an huor sinse they brootally aprehended me in the theeter.

That better? aks Fritz.

Yes thank you.

Mister Oswald wot were your moovements after you left the book deppositry? he aks aggen.

I went to my rooming huose.

Ware is that exakly?

I wood rather not say.

Mister Oswald I can eesly get this informashun from your employer.

Oak Cliff.

Adress?

1026 Nth Beckly.

How did you get there?

Bus.

Why did you go there?

Its ware I live. I stare at him he obviusly wants more informmashun I let him wate for a few seccunds befor continooing. I also wanted to chang my clothes I say Working at the depossitry can be a durty job. I work up qite a swet lifting boxes and carying books up and down the stares all day.

I can imagine. Ware did you put your durty clothes?

Ware I allways do.

Wich is?

Botom draw of my dresser.

Wot did you do after you changed your briches?

Put on a cleen pare.

Fritz sighs. And then?

I grabbed my pistol and went to the pitcher sho I say wanting to adress the elefant in the room if I menshun the pistul ferst it will appeer as tho I hav nuthing to hide.

Why did you carry your pistol?

You kno how boys are wen they hav a gun. They jus carry it. I smile at him he does not retern the favver.

Hasty returns with a paper cup of water slides it across the tabel. He glanses at Fritz with razed eyebrows Fritz wates a secund then nods.

Hasty stares down at me then says Mister Oswald hav you ever been to Russia?

I glar at him. It takes a tremendus amuont of willpower not to explode at this man who so cazully terrorized your mama.

I do not care to relive the past I say my lips tite.

Fritz stratens in his chare senseing for the ferst time that there cood be sumthing between Hasty and me well it is not jus bad blud it is rotten to the core.

Cum now Mister Oswald says Hasty We kno you lived there.

Then why did you aks?

How long did you liv there?

Three yeers I grunt.

Ware did you liv?

Minsk.

Hav you ritten to the Russian embassy sinse your retern?

Yes.

Wot about?

That is nun of your bizness. I see no reeson to tell him that I rote to the embassy on your mamas beharf seeking permishon for her to retern to Russia. I did this for sevral reesons one being that we were fiteing like cats and dogs I thort it mite help to hav sum time appart the other reeson I was not sure wot the future mite hold for us in the U.S. I had varius plans running thru my hed todays triumf being one of them. I thort it mite be best for Mama you and the baby to retern to her homeland wate for me there.

I tell Hasty nun of this. Anger is corseing thru my body riseing up my nek into my brane it feels jus like wen your mama and I fite and mama ansers bak. In those momments I can not kontrol myself can not think strate hot blud rushes to my hedd a red curtin lowering over my eyes. I am capabel of anything my fists take on a life of there own I am ashammed to admit to you Junie that I hav struk your mama more than onse in this condishun.

Hav you ever been to Mexico City? Hasty aks leening closer.

No I say. This qeusshun surprizes me it sugests the FBI knos my moovements in more detale than I thort. Perhaps there agents hav been wotching me closely sinse our return from Minsk a most sobring thort indeed.

Are you shure?

I hav been to Teeawana howevver onse aggen that is nun of your consern.

I think the FBI is more than capabel of desideing wot is and isnt our consern Mister Oswald.

This is wen I deside enuff is enuff. A man can only take so much. I raize my hands puond down hard on the desk the combined wate of my hands and the cuffs makes a booming thud like a watermellun dropped from a grate hight it suonds even lowder in the tite confines of Fritzs offise. Sevral of the men take a step bak altho cuffed I hav still managed to scare them grately.

I kno you I yell at Hasty You hav been out to my wifes huose twise acosting her!

The door opens a unniformed man peers in conserned about the rukkus. Fritz waves him away.

Mister Oswald says Hasty I was meerly aksing your wife sum qesshuns to try and assertane your wareabouts sinse your return from Loosianna.

It is harasment pure and simpel! I bang the desk with my fists aggen. I want you to leeve her alone!

Mister Oswald I –

Befor he finishes I thump the desk aggen then continoo to do so each time he opens his muoth to speek.

All rite Fritz finely says Thats qite enuff Mister Oswald. He reeches over plases a hand on mine to still them. His eyes are wide with unsertenty it appeers he dusnt kno that the FBI has had me in there sites sinse my retern from Russia. Agents hav twise stopped me onse outside our huose in Fort Wurth they pulled me into there car for a sposedly frendly chat anuther time in New Orleens I had a run in with them over my work with the Fare Play for Cuba comitee. I spent the nite in the pokey tawked with them the neks morning it was all qite amikabel reelly. But now this Hasty is knokking reglarly on the Pains door aksing your mama all kinds of qesshuns there reely is no end to it.

Mister Oswald Fritz says trying to be the voise of reeson Wot do you meen eksactly wen you say speshul agent Hasty has been acosting your wife?

I take sevral deep breths to get myself under kontrol befor anserring.

I meen that on at leest two srepret ocashuns he has visited my wife in her home and interogated her. He practikly tole her she will hav to go bak to Russia.

That is simpley not troo says Hasty.

Lissen says Fritz Lets all try and carm down a litle. He takes off his hat runs his fingers over his skalp puts it bak on. Mister Oswald take a sip of water.

Im not thursty I say not wanting to drink from Hastys cup.

Your choise Fritz says But we do need to continoo. Are you

reddy to go on or do you need a momment longer to compose yourself?

I am reddy I say. I wood not give Hasty the satissfacshun of thinking he has throwen me off of my game.

Vry well then maybe we shood start at the begining. Ware did you gro up?

Noware in partiklar.

That is not vry helpful Mister Oswald.

New Orleens.

Is that ware you went to skool?

Sum of it.

Sum of it?

I also went to skool in Fort Wurth and New York.

So it wood be fare to say that you hav mooved aruond qite a lot?

Wots qite a lot?

You tell me. Evry few yeers?

I rekkon so.

Why is that?

Why does anything hapen? I say not wanting to menshun the mooves were mostly a result of my mothers disfunkshonal marrages and relashuns with others. By my rekkoning we mooved over twenty times befor I sed enuff and joyned the Marines.

Must hav made for a tuff chilehood he says.

Yes and no you get used to mooveing I say. But in trooth Fritz is rite. I found it vry diffkult to fit in make new frends. I admit my upbringing was sumwhat unstable for ecksample wen my mother and step father split up I was only five yeers old I stayed home from skool with a puppy our naybor had givven me refoosed to tawk or later testafy at the divorse procedings. Of corse with hindsite I am amazed that they wood aks a child of that age to do same.

Fritz glanses down at my hands. I see your wareing a Marine Core ring.

Vry astoot of you.

Wen did you joyn up?

At seventeen.

Seventeen? Thats yung.

Well I first tryed at sixteen but they sed I had to wate a yeer.

How did that make you feel?

How wood that make you feel?

I dont kno. Dissapoynted?

There you go I say altho in realty I was more angry than disapoynted onse aggen the govt getting in the way of a mans plans.

Isnt seventeen also too yung to joyn?

Not with consent. My older bruther Robert sined sum forms and they let me in.

This wood hav been wen?

1956.

Well the cuntry thanks you for your serviss he says solemly.

I smile to myself I hav indede dun the cuntry a grate serviss of corse I can not admitt same to Fritz.

Wen did you leev the Marines?

1959.

Honrabel discharg?

Of corse.

Did you hav any cawse to use weppons wile in the Marines?

Its the millitry of corse I used weppons.

Did you excel at rifel shooting?

I was no better or wurse than the neks man I say not about to admitt to Fritz that I attaned the stattus of sharpshooter. I take a sip of the water Hasty brort in holding the papper cup clumsly in my cuffed hands. I stare daggers at him over the rim he shuffels looks at his feet.

But you are familler with rifles? Fritz says.

I hav seen a few.

Do you hold any politikal beleefs Mister Oswald?

Here he goes aggen jumping aruond trying to cach me off gard not reeliseing I am too clevver for that.

No.

Nun at all?

No. I did hav sum involvement with the Fair Play for Cuba comitee I say knoing that my arest in New Orleens will sho up on my rekord I may as well get it out in the oppen now.

I see. And wot is this comitee exakly?

It is an organizashun bassed in New York that suports a free Cuba. I was secretry of the New Orleens branch wen I lived there.

A free Cuba? Wot do you meen by that?

Free trade and such.

So you are a suporter of Fidel Castro?

I am a suporter of his revolushun yes sir all men hav the rite to be free and to fite for that freedom.

To be honnest Junie at one time Fidell was a heero of mine I even hung a pitcher of him over the mantel at W Neely St sumthing that did not amoose your Mama grately. Howevver I looked up to Fidell as the leeder of the only troo communist cuntry left Russia corrupting there sistem by catering to the party ellite. This luv of Fidel I mantaned until the day his embessy in Mexico City denyed me a visa terning there bak on a fellow freedum fiter a most shameful act indeed.

A knok cums on the door it swings open.

Can I hav a moment sir? a uniform cop aks Fritz.

Fritz stands up navigates his way thru the crouded room. He steps outside closes the door so we cant heer wot is been sed. No one else in the room speeks durring his absense. After my outburst with Hasty they are probly too afrade to aks me qesshuns wich soots me jus fine.

Fritz finnishes his conversashun cums bak in closes the door behind him.

This rooming house in Oke Cliff on Nth Beckly he says sitting down Wot name did you register under?

Wot do you think?

I dont kno. Thats why I am aksing you.

My own of corse.

Intresting. One of my offissers has jus tole me that there is no one liveing there by that name.

He must be misstaken.

He spoke to your landlady. A Mrs Roberts. She seemed to confurm this.

Then she is also misstaken. She is easly confoosed.

There was howevver he says a room rented under the name O H Lee.

Oh well it is simpel then.

How so?

She must hav missunderstood my name wen I tole it to her.

I see he says but I can see that he doesnt see at all. I look aruond the room there are menny furroed brows. In fack it is almost komical to see so menny confoosed fases in one plase. If only I had my camra I cood sell a foto of these dumfuonded cops to Life magazeen for hunnerds of dollers Our Finnest Lawmakers At Work the kapshun wood reed ha.

Onse aggen a knok cums at the door Fritz disapeers for a good twenty minits. Over the neks few days I lern that this is the usule corse of events Fritz frekwently leeveing our conversashuns presoomably to tawk to witneses the press perhaps also other offisers and such.

Wen he reterns he aks me if I hav any objekshuns to partissipating in a showup.

A showup? I say.

Yes you kno a lineup to see if any witneses can identafy you.

Witneses? To wot?

The shooting of the polise offisser.

Do I hav a choise?

Not reely Mister Oswald. You hav been legaly detaned under suspishon of comitting a fellony. A showup is a cort aprooved methud of investigateing the crime of wich you are suspekted.

I lift my cuffed hands to put an end to his legal mumbo jumbo.

I spose I hav no objecshun I say knoing a fat lode of good it wood do me if I did. Howevver I say I wood like to kno if I am alowed an attornee.

You can hav any attornee you like Fritz says Wen you get up

to the jale huose there will be a telefone made avalable to you and you can call anyone you wish.

There is an attornee in New York I shood like to speek with.

Wot is this felows name?

Abt I say John Abt.

I reserched Abt at the city libry last munth it shood be abuddently cleer by now Junie that I leeve no stone unterned. Abt represented Hall and Davis the leeders of the US communist party wen charged with conspirasy to overthro the govt. Shood it cum to a triel Abt will be the best man to advise me and giv me the best chanse of explaneing my motivs. Perhapps if I pleed gilty he can also help me bild a sucessful defense my akshuns well and trooly justifyed by histry and the ongoing ill treetment of my fello man shurely twelve good men strate and troo will see that.

You woodnt prefer a lokal loyyer? aks Fritz.

I wood not I say I want Abt.

Well then we will see wot we can do abuot that.

Fritz leens bak opens the top draw of his desk slides his notepad inside for safe keeping.

All rite men he says standing up glanseing at the time it is a few minits to four There are peeple in the bassment we dont want to keep wateing. Elmer he says nodding at one of the detecktivs You take Mister Oswald and leed him to the elevater. The rest of you keep the press bak. Understood?

Yes sir they all mermer.

The fella Elmer cums aruond the tabel helps me to my feet. His persnal higene is sumwhat lakking his body odor extreeme but it has been a vry long day no dout sum strange smells also eminate from my person.

As soon as sumone opens the door to Fritzs offise a wall of noize assales us from the other side of the homiside burow door. Fritzs men push there way thru sed door with Elmer and me close behind. The crush of reportters has intensifyed in the last huor fotografers and camramen hold there eqipment above there hedds trying to cach a shot of me. Elmer stiks close to the wall to keep sum distanse between us and them howevver it is imposibel to ignor there relentless verbel attaks.

Did you kill the president?

Tell us about the cop shooting!

Was anyone else involved?

Is it troo your a communist?

You fools I want to shuot you hav no idea why I hav dun wot I hav dun but that of corse wood be downrite foolish a cleer admishun of gilt that I am not yet reddy to make. Insted I rayse my rite arm make a clenched fist the globbal simbol of soliddarity. I want the world to kno that anything I hav dun is in serviss of the brutherhood of man.

As we inch down the hall my shert snags on a water cooler Elmer stops to free it then we turn left into the lobby ware an elevater is been held for us. Elmer hits B we dissend to the bassment insted of going out to the parking garag we walk strate ahed past the booking cuonter thru a door to the left down a hall towards anuther door markt Asembly Room. This I presoome is ware patrollmen are breefed each day befor hedding out to manetane order in our fare city. Thru a glass windo in the door I see it is a larg room with paralel hite lines drawen along one wall a razed platform in frunt of it. Oposit perhapps twenty feet away stands a screne made of wot looks to be nilon probly one way so witnesses can see us but we cant see them. Even tho they are hidden I kno who awates me behind that screne at leest one of the sevral peeple who saw me shoot the cop in brawd daylite.

Hold up a minit says Elmer.

He stops at a tabel outside the door procedes to serch me sumthing the cops who brort me in shood hav dun but overlooked in all the hullaballoo. He finds the transfer from my abortted bus ride in my top poket also five ruonds of ammo in my left trowser poket.

Wot are these for? he aks.

Jus to hav.

He harumfs then remooves the braselet I ware to cuvver a scar on my left rist the result of an act of decepshun I undertook during my erly days in Moscow. Wen I first arived I was soon tole by the Russian authoritees I wood hav to leeve I tryed evrything to convinse them otherwise even offered up millitry secrets I obtaned as a radar oprator in the Marines. Howevver wen that did not satisfy them I was destinned for expulshon like sum comon toorist overstaying his visa forseing me to act out a suiside attemp to show my desperation it werked a treet. After recooperateing in Botkin hospitel the authoritees who inishally thort me insane saw the greevus errer of there ways not only sending me to Minsk but allso provideing me with an apartment overlooking bootifull Janki Kupaly Park on the Svislak River the kind of houseing normly reserved for party elite. I was also assined a job at Gorizont electronnics a maker of raydios TVs etc. Sertenly the faktory work was beneeth me that of a common sheet mettal worker howevver at leest I was provided with a job

175

unlike here ware menny men fite for scraps on a daley basis jus to keep there hed abuv water. Then I met your Mama we marryed had you Junie nun of that wood hav happened if not for the extreem messure I took in that hotel room a few scars a small prise to pay for keeping my dreem alive.

Elmer remooves my Marines ring a cop takes a paper bag slips all of my persnal affecks inside.

Be carefull with that I say I want it all bak wen this is over.

You shood be so lukky.

He scrawels my name the time the date on the bag sornters off down the hall. Jus befor he reeches the door out to the lobby it swings open three men march in hed towards us. They wink at the cop holding my belongings then nod at Elmer as they approche.

Thanks for takeing part boys says Elmer.

Not a probblem. This the asshole shot JD? one says if looks cood kill I wood be in Parkland rite now.

One and the same says Elmer Alegedly of corse. He winks then unloks the cuff aruond my rite rist. Gonna hav to cuff you boys together.

Wate a secund I say Your putting me in a showup with these fellas?

You got a problem with that?

Of corse I do for a start hes wareing a brown sports cote him a red vest I am dresst in a torn shurt. I turn my arm sho him the rip in my sleev.

Objecshun noted he says.

Also look at my fase I say. I hav not seen it but I must look like hell after that savage attak in the theeter. Who wood you

176

think is the gilty party? I demmand.

Mister Oswald as you can no dout observ for yuorself these men are the same size age and hite as you. Those are the genral critera for any showup. Now we can stand here all day and argew about it or we can jus get this over with. Wich ones it gonna be?

I want to make it cleer I objeck to this treetment I say You are railrodeing me.

Dooly noted.

I sigh hold out my rists. There is no poynt fiteing any ferther I can not win. He unloks the rite cuff puts it aruond the left rist of one of the cops reppeets same on the other side. I now hav a cleen cut cop handcufft to eether side of me who will no dout do a poor job of prettending to be gilty I am not expekting any Oscar winning purformanses out on that stage.

Wot are you wateing for? Elmer says to the thurd cop who is jus standing there as useless as teets on a bore hog as my stepfather used to say.

He shrugs his sholders Forgot my cuffs.

Shoot I dont hav mine eether says Elmer Well dont wurry jus walk in as the forth.

Elmer takes the first cop by the elbo opens the door leeds us into the showup room singel file. The room is cold the air condishuning set for larger gathrings. Strips of brite lite hum overhed. Feet shuffel behind the screen a person coffs then a few wurds are murmered.

Elmer steers us to the wall ware horizontel lines are paynted to indikate hite. We take a step up onto the stage. I must stik out like a sore thum a broozed and bluddyed man in a torn shert handcuffed between two cops it does not take Einstine to figger out who was jus bort in for qesshuning. The forth guy is not even handcuffed to us any eyewitness wood shurely think he can not be the gilty party as no one has takken any messures to prevent his ekscape.

Look strate ahed! a voise barks from behind the screen jolting me makeing the showup reel for the first time.

We all do as we are tole. There folows more mermering then the same voise yells Tern to your rite!

With sum diffculty the three of us handcuffed together manage to do same putting our left hands in frunt of us our rite hands behind we are like the elefants on parrade at Ringling Bruthers cirkus.

Left! yells the same man. His voise sounds familler I realize it mite be Jon Wayne the cop who tawked to me in the sqod room befor Fritz got a hold of me. I recall his name was Level but by this stage I cood care less who he is in fack I am grinning at the stupiditee of the situashun. I look so diffrent to the other three men they may as well hav marched me in here with three green marshuns aksed the witness to confirm wich one most resembels a human been.

Fase the frunt!

We all turn bak towards the screne.

I heer sevral men tawking low also make out a female voise probly that stoopid woman who wood not stop screeming wen I shot the cop I shood hav put a bullet in her wen I had the chanse.

Nummer two step foreward pleese.

I look at Elmer he nods confirming I am nummer two. I take half a step foreward the men on eether side of me raize there left and rite arms alowing me the freedom to do so. I stand strate my sholders bak my chin up no trase of feer in my eyes as I look direckly at the screne. Lady if you sware on the bibel that I shot the cop then so be it. The act was comitted in the name of a much higher cawse namely you and evryone else on this plannet sumthing you will probly never be cappabul of unnerstanding.

Nummer two step bak.

Aggen tawking cums from behind the screne. Sumone presoombaly Level is repeeting the same quesshun over and over Wich one? Wich one? I am not shure how that woman cood be unserten who the kulprit is she got a good sollid look at me wile she was screeming blew bluddy murder out there on 10th St.

Thank you gentelmen Level finally shuots suonding pleesed with hisself he must hav gotten the anser he was looking for.

Outside Elmer uncuffs the two cops cuffs my hands to the frunt aggen then we go thru the same rigmaroll to get bak upstares take the elevater to the 3rd flor forse our way past the press pack wich has growen more in the last half huor sumthing I wood not hav thort possibel. It is now a heeveing mass backlit by floodlites TV camras stand on trippods bunched cabels as thik as my leg run along the flor then out the windo to the street below. I heer sum acksents how forinners got here so fast I do not kno.

How are you being treeted? sumone yells.

The floodlites fill my vishun with yelow dots I saloot with clenched fist in his direkshun.

Wot does that meen? annuther aks.

You figger it out I say.

We push thru the door to room 317 find Fritzs offise Elmer sits me down in the chare I occupyed not twenty minits erlier.

I havent eaten sinse lunchtime I say Any chanse of sum grub?

Yeah I rekkon you hav been kind of busy Elmer says Fortunatly thats not my problem.

You shure its not your problem? I woodnt want to hav to tell all those press fellas out there that your mistreeting me and depriveing me of my basik rites.

He leens over the tabel his fase reel close. His breth smells sower too much coffee.

Let me see wot I can do he says nods at two uniform cops standing at the door. One of you boys go and see wot you can skare up will ya?

One terd on rye cumming rite up says one.

Charming I say.

He slams the door behine him leeveing me alone with Elmer and the other uniform cop who givs me his best deth stare.

Fritz will be bak soon says Elmer.

I cant wate.

The uniformed cop cums bak into the room bearly therty secunds later.

Kichens closed he says and smiles like it is the best noos he has had all day.

I wasnt that hungree anyway I say knoing they are jus testing me. By keeping me hungry they think I will weeken nuthing cood be ferther from the trooth.

Minits later Fritz barges into the room like a buldog chaseing a pork chop. An ontoorage of soots and uniforms folow it is like he has his own persnal polise dept warever he goes.

All rite Mister Oswald he says parking his bakside in his seet Lets pik up we left off. Do you still unnerstand the rites that were red to you at the start of the previus seshon?

I do.

From there Fritz procedes to folow the same line of qesshuning he persued previus. He aks me aggen wot I did after leeveing work why I was carrying my pistul wen kaptured in the theeter etc. I too continoo with my aproche anser menny of his qesshuns with qesshuns wile manetaneing consistansy with erlier statments all in all Junie I put up qite a steller purformanse if I do say so myself.

After a half huor Fritz gros tired of my games.

Did you kill the president? he aks poynt blank.

Thats absard I tell him I categorikly deny the alegashun. I demand to speke to a loyyer.

This respons of corse does not satisfy him but wot does he expeck from me? A sined and seeled confeshon? Only a fool wood admit same.

By six pm nun the wiser to my involvment in eether of the shootings Fritz sends me downstares for a secund showup. The press bark at me like a pak of woolves wile I inishully selebrated there presense I am not yet reddy to speke so there constent interjecshuns are now nuthing more than an annoyanse to be tollerated.

I dont kno wot this is all abuot I shuot over there masheen gun volly of qerys.

Did you shoot the president? a reporter yells as sumone else calls me a commie bastard wich is folowed by much jeering and josseling it is like they are at a bachler party I the unwilling groom.

I didnt shoot anyone I say I dont kno wot this is abuot. I never killt anybody.

Sumhow we make it down the hall unskathed I am bundeled into the wateing elevater wisked away to the showup. This one barely differs from the furst altho myself and the three other men are at leest all handcuffed together. Howevver I am aggen fully aware how much my rufled clotheing stands out from the others the witnes wateing behind the screne perhaps meetball man or the Mexican pikup driver will hav litle trubble fingering me as the gilty party.

Look at my outfit and fase I shuot at Elmer of corse this falls on deff ears. I am parraded befor the screen singeled out to onse aggen step foreward then carted bak to Fritzs offise running the gorntlet of the press along the way.

Do you own a rifel? yells a short man with an wallrus mustash. He is dresst like all the others dark soot dark hat cluching a notebook and pen the polise ware one uniffrom the press anuther. So much for freedum of choise as I hav stated previus Junie it is all an illushon no one is free nor are there I mite add menny free thinkers arround pressent cumpny eksepted ha.

I dont kno ware you get your informashun I say I havent comitted any acts of violense.

So you clame you are not gilty?

That is correck. I want to get with a loyyer Mister Abt in New York City. I never killed anyone I shuot befor a push in the bak propells me thru the door to room 317.

I am tosst into my usule chare the clok approches six forty. I shood be worn slap out it has been qite a day but I am far from beet. In fack I feel energized I hav been wateing menny yeers for this day to arive. I wood venchure to say that it has been one of the best days of my life it is rite up there with the day you came into the world Junie at leest untill the momment the polise cornered me in the theeter took out there frustrashuns on me with fists and boots.

The uniformmed men assined to gard me stand ram rod strate two pillers of dark blew. They wotch my evry moove with blank fases howevver I kno that inside they are stooing I killed one of there own this Tipit fella not to menshun there beluved president. They wood tar and fether me do wurse things besides if they cood. To kill time I chukle litely act all amoosed this eggs them on the blud rises up there neks it is a most satisfying passtime indede.

After about ten minits of this fun and games Fritz enters with two fellas I havent seen befor also sevral detectivs and the FBI fella Bookout. The two new men are both wareing soots one a tall dapper grey hared gent with a pale blew tie the other wares ill fitting cloths perhaps from a dime store they do him no favvers the jaket too tite around the middel too lose in the sholders.

Mister Oswald this is Justiss of the Peese David Jonson says Fritz nodding at the taller fella he wares a distink air of superority And this here is Bill Alexander Asistent Districk Attorney for Dallas Cuonty.

They nod so gravly I allmost aks if there has been a deth in the famly then think better of it ha.

Captain Fritz we hav a complaynt here for your sineing says the Justiss of the Peese fella. He slides a slip of paper across the desk to Fritz who sines it without reeding slides it bak.

The Justiss of the Peese cleers his throte says Mister Oswald we are here to arrane you on the charg of merder in the deth of Offisser J D Tipit.

Arranement? I shuot This isnt a cort. You cant arrane me in a polise stashun. I can only be arraned in a cortroom. How do I even kno this fella is a judg? I say to Fritz.

Shut up and lissen the other man pipes up.

You hav stripped me of my rites I mutta.

Dapper Dan begins reeding all nise and propper from the sheet of paper This is in the name of and by the authoritee of the state of Texas personly apeered befor me the undersined authoritee this afyant who by being after by me dooly sworn disposes and says your afyant has good reeson to beleev and does beleeve that one Lee Harvey Oswald here and after stiled defenddent here to for on or abuot the 22nd day of November AD ninteen hunnerd and sixty-three in the cuonty of Dallas and the state of Texas did then and there unlawfly volluntarly and with maliss afor thort kill J D Tipit by shooting him with a gun agenst the peese and diggnity of the state atested by J W Fritz afyant sworn to and subskribed befor me this 22nd day of November nineteen hunnerd and sixty-three Henry Wade crimnal districk atornee Dallas Cuonty Texas -

I categorikly deny these charges I say.

Wich complaynt was then past to me Dapper Dan continoos dismissing my protest out of hand he ends with a bunch of mumbo jumbo Perry Masson wood be prowd of file nummers and such.

Mister Oswald does that all make sens? aks Fritz wen this Jonson fella finaly runs out of wurds.

Mister Oswald says Dapper Dan not wateing for my anser You hav the constitooshunal rite to remane silent. Any statment you make may be used in evdense agenst you for the charges stated. Do you understand?

I nod but am not reely lissening I am ponderring the charges. My extensiv legel reedings tell me that maliss afor thort will be vry hard to proove. The cops may hav me bang to rites for the shooting itself at leest one eye witness can verrify same but it will be vry hard to proove that I planned the hole thing in advanse walkt to 10th and Patton sumhow knoing that I wood encuonter this patrollman Tipit so I cood then shoot him ded. Howevver prooveing the case in a cort of law is there problem not mine.

Youll be givven the oportoonitee to contack an atornee he says Bond is denyed on this captal offense I hereby remand you to the custady of the sheriff of Dallas cuonty Texas.

The wurds captal offense ring in my ears I cood fry for this crime if that is the case then so be it it is but a small prise to pay for setting the world to rite.

Well I say I rekkon there is not much more to say until I consult with my loyyer.

Vry good chimes in Fritz trying to rap things up. He stands shakes hands with the other two men they are all pleesed as punch hav dun a stand up job in there eyes. The two men leeve the room in there plase a half duzzen felows inclooding Elmer file bak in.

Wares Hasty? I say.

Who? says Fritz.

Hasty. The FBI offisser who terorises innosent wimmen in there homes.

Speshul Agent Hasty is busy rite now he says.

Too busy to take part in the qesshuning of a person suspeckted of shooting the president? I say.

Fritz blushes I reelise that Hasty must hav been ordered not to play any ferther part in my interogashun. My erlier outberst has served a useful purpos yet annuther notch in my belt.

Good I say I will not anser any ferther qeusshuns if that man is in the room.

Dooly noted says Fritz All rite boys time to get Mister Oswald bak downstares.

Off to the bassment we go aggen for yet anuther showup this one no more or less eventfull than the previus two. Onse aggen I hav no idea who is behine the screne it cood be as I sed erlier the Mexican driver of the pikup or the cab driver with the meetball heero perhapps even one or both of the wimmin from the corner huose who saw me scatter my emty shells across there frunt lawn. I try not to wurry abuot who is putting the finger on me jus act natrel at one poynt I feel like I cood be on the set of a TV game sho the thort brings a smile to my fase. This pleeses Elmer not one bit he handels me ruffly all the way bak to the 3rd flor.

Id like sum legel repressentashun I say to the reporters as we leeve the elevater These polise ofissers hav not alowed me to hav any. I dont kno wot this is all abuot.

Did you kill the president one of them aks an unlit cigret bobbing in his muoth.

Howd you get the blak eye? shuots annuther.

Did you shoot the president?

I work in that bldg I say.

Were you in the bldg at the time?

Naturly if I work in that bldg yes sir I say getting mitey sik of heering the same qesshuns over and over aggen.

As if to proove my poynt anuther aks aggen Did you kill the president?

No theyre takeing me in becos of the fack that I lived in the Soviet Unun.

Bak up! sumone yells in the crush the smell of hunnerds of men in a small spase reeches me persperashun bad breth also the arromer of feer the situashun in the tite hallway is fast becumming unmanagabel.

Wot time did you leeve the bldg? one of them aks howevver we hav reeched the door to the homiside burow. As Elmer opens the door I deside the time is rite to reely give the press sumthing to choo on.

Im jus a patsy! I shuot as the cops bundel me thru the door.

Bak to Fritzs offise I go ware he wates with his usule hanger ons as far as I can see they hav no reel purpuss other than wanting to be in the room ware histry mite be made. The air is thik with smoke from a long day that dusnt look like ending any time soon. That soots me jus fine I feel like I cood fase Fritz across his desk forevver a part of me is enjoying our verbel dool.

Welcum bak Mister Oswald take a seet pleese Fritz says not that I hav a choise in the matta Elmer steers me to same.

A secret serviss fella beside Fritz hands him sumthing Fritz puts it on the tabel between us.

Recognise that? he aks.

Yes.

Wood you be so good as to deskribe it.

Its a wollet.

Whos wollet?

Why dont you tell me?

I hav evry reeson to beleeve it is yours.

It is your rite to beleev whatever you want.

He piks it up flips it open then to my surprize closes it aggen.

Lets start with sum basiks befor we get to that he says.

The same secret serviss man slides him sevral typed forms.

I think we hav assertaned that your name is Lee Harvey Oswald says Fritz.

Yes.

He starts compleeting the form.

Wite male he mumbels to hisself rites that down continoos to do same as I provide more informashun.

Date of berth?

Im sure you can figger that out.

You cood help save us sum time here Mister Oswald.

10 18 39.

Huh he says.

Wot?

Well you were born jus in time for world war two. Plase of berth?

New Orleens.

Hite and wate?

5-9 140.

He studys me. Hare medum brown he mumbels rites that down. Cood do with a harecut he qips reminding me of the collored boys at the depossitry teeseing me about same I wunder wot they think of crazy ole Lee now that his fase is in evry newspaper and on evry TV screen in the cuntry. Im shure that has seesed there lafter.

Eyes blew gray Fritz continoos Any scars?

Nun I say he has not notissed the ones on the inside of my left rist I am not abuot to bring them to his attenshun.

Tatoos?

No.

Mothers name?

Margrite.

Last name Oswald?

Correck.

Curent adress?

No idea.

He stops riteing glanses up. Howevver if he knoo my mother as well as me he wood reelise that it is not that much of a mistry as to why I hav lost trak of her.

Wareabouts unknowen he says rites this down.

Maybe Arlingtin I say Altho I am not shure I hav not seen her for about a yeer.

All rite. Her ocupashun?

Nerse.

Fathers name?

Robert Lee Oswald.

Curent adress?

Six feet under.

This time Fritz dusnt look up. Do you kno ware he is beried?

New Orleens.

I kno ware my father is Junie becos befor leeveing for Mexico

I trakked down his grave. It seemed importent at the time I am
not shure wot I was expekting to find but there was no more than
a fansy hedstone curtesy of vetrans affares a gravell topped grave
and a hole lot of silense. I never knoo the man by all acuonts he
was a stand up fella rellated to the grate confedrate Genral Robert
E Lee hense his name. You and I Junie we both share that same
prowd bludline perhaps that and my fathers erly passing are wot
creatted a fare meen streek of independense in me. Who knos
how my life wood be had he not left me at such an erly age.
Looseing a parent is a hooge blo to any chile Junie I sinseerly
hope you do not hav to experense same I will do evrything in my
power to prevent that from happning tho now it may be out of
my hands.

Yeer your father died?

A few munths befor I was born.

I dont spose you kno the date?

I shrug my sholders. I want to say August but I wasnt even
born yet.

Lets jus say August 1939 he says riteing that down We can
find out the exack date later. Wifes name?

Marina Oswald.

Chillren?

Two dorters.

Names?

June and Rachel.

Sibblings?

Two bruthers.

Names?

John and Robert.

Ware does John liv?

No idea. Last time I saw him he was in Fort Wurth.

Wen was that?

Five maybe six yeers ago.

How old is John?

About therty.

Ocupashun?

He works in farmasooticals.

As wot? Graduat farmasist?

No he never gradooated that I kno of.

Famly?

Wife three kids.

All rite. Now Robert? Is he also in Fort Wurth?

Uh huh.

Adress?

7313 Davenport. Marryed with kids.

How menny?

Two.

Occupashun?

He works for a brik cumpny.

Do you kno wich one?

Acme I beleeve.

It suonds like you are closser to Robert than John. Is that a fare asessment?

I considder Fritzs qesshun it is one I hav never pondered. Sertenly Robert has dun more for me than John ever did helpt me joyn the Marines at seventeen also met your mama myself and you uppon our arrivel in Fort Wurth wen we left Russia. I was glad to see his fase but as menshunned also gravly disapointed no press were in atendance well I hav there attenshun now. As far as John goes I stayed with him and his wife in New York for a spell as a chile an argooment with his wife an insident with a knife put pade to that. John is my harf bruther allways a slitely difrent relashunship as they say blud is thikker than water familys can be vry complikated afares indeed.

I rekkon so I mutter.

Vry good Fritz says. He tawks to hisself as he rites down wot cloths I am wareing blak trowsers brown shert no hat etc. I shift in the chare at this verbel descripshun of my person.

All rite Mister Oswald he says aggen useing his favrit frase Lets take a look see at this wollet shall we? He opens it up takes out the contents procedes to go thru them one by one.

Soshal securety card he says reeds out my nine dijit nummer 4 3 3 5 4 3 9 3 7 heering the words cum out of his muoth I am struk for the ferst time by the nummer of threes in it. Name Lee Harvey Oswald he says.

He puts the card to one side piks up the neks item.

Selectiv serviss card he says That apeers to sho a foto of Lee Harvey Oswald with the name Alek James Hidell and a diffrent soshal sekurity nummer aggen he reeds out its dijits.

Fritz remooves his glasses pinches the bridg of his nose replases them.

This card here he says It shows your foto but has this Hidell fellas name on it.

If you say so.

I do say so. How do you explane that?

I dont.

I sit and wate say nuthing ferther. I have no probblem

ansering qesshuns about my famly but now the fokus is bak on me it is anuther matter entirly. Fritz stares wateing for me to say more I keep my muoth shut let him try to figger it out.

All rite then lets moove on shall we? This appeers to be a unon card of sum sort with your name on it. Correck?

Yes.

Local bord 114?

Yes.

Neks he piks up a foto.

Who is this?

That is my wife Marina.

I took that foto of your mama across the street from my apartment in Minsk we were in the summa gardens of the Minsk opra huose shortly after we were marryed. She is beutifull a yung thin woman wareing simpel clotheing she cood be a pessant girl visiting the city for the ferst time. A foto of the two of us was also takken that day I aksed a passerby to use my camra howevver I much preffer the one without me the one Fritz now holds it in his fat fingers. It is a most peculer feeling seeing your mamas foto in the hands of a stranger other men leering at it over his sholder. One of the detektivs lets out a woolf wistle I do my best to ignor him but heet rises up my nek jus the same. I kno wot he is thinking he is like most men an animel if I was not handcufed I wood do sumthing about it. Howevver I am also too smart for him kno that he is jus trying to get a rise out of me I will not run off at the muoth let my emoshuns get the better of me. Best to keep a cool hed any good soldeir knos same.

Ware was this takken? aks Fritz.

Minsk.

You dont say. Wich part?

It is in the gruonds of the opra huose.

Did you like liveing in Russia Mister Oswald?

Oh yes vry much so I say hopeing to get under the skin of the men who hav jus dun same to me. I had my own beutifull apartment a good job and menny good frends.

Go on says Fritz.

Oh I cood go on forevver I say The food was marvlus cheep and plentyfull there was allways wine and vodka to drink. It is parradise over there not like here ware one has to work hard meerly to survive.

So why did you retern?

Its komplicated I say after a momment.

How so?

Well my muther needed me she is getting on in yeers.

But you jus sed you dont even kno ware she lives.

It is troo we hav growen appart I say then clam up this line of qesshuning doing me no good at all.

Fritz stares at me then piks up anuther foto this one of you deer Junie takken in our apartment in Minsk shortly after you were born. You are swadled in blankets wareing a wool cap to keep your litle hed warm.

And this? he aks shoing it to me.

My oldest dorter June.

Beutiful he says. How old is she now?

One yeer nine munths.

He piks up a plane wite card. Is this your handriteing?

Im not sure I say.

He reeds out the words Embessy USSR 1609 Decater NW

Washingtun DC Consuler. He pawses struggels with the neks word Rezhuyehko. Wot does that word meen?

You figger it out.

You must speke Russian? You livved there for three yeers.

I forgot.

He sighs. Why do you hav the adress of the Russian embasy in your wollet?

I shrug my sholders. I mite need to contak them one day.

About wot?

Persnel matters.

Wen it becums cleer that I am saying no more he mooves on. Department of Defense ID card he says neks.

How much longer is this going to take?

Why you got sumwhere you need to be? chimes in a detectiv with greesy hare. He has been standing behind Fritz sinse we entered the room chane smokeing sqinting thru the haze created by his own filthy ways.

Not too long Mister Oswald says Fritz. He puts the DOD card down it is self explanatry. Dallas Public Libry card in the name of Lee Oswald Harvey 602 Elspeth Dallas he continoos. States your skool or bizness as Jaggers Chilles Stovell. Is that a previus plase of employment?

Yes.

Wot kind of cumpny is that exackly?

It is a fotograffic cumpny. They make ads. Posters and such.

He looks at the card aggen. Visit the libry offen do you Mister Oswald?

As a matter of fack I do. I think the world wood be a much better plase if more peeple were avvid reeders.

Cant argoo with you there Mister Oswald. Wot sort of books do you enjoy?

Biografys.

Such as?

Mow Tse Tung amung others.

Anything else?

I also enjoy spy novells.

Spy novells? Fansy yourself as a bit of a James Bond do you?

I feel myself blush if I am compleetly honnest Fritz has hit a nerv I hav stiled my life sumwhat on Bond and men of a simler ilk. There is a lot that can be lerned by studying there methuds evven if fikshunal there exployts contane menny ellements of trooth.

Dont be stoopid I say.

Neks up we hav a US forses Japanese ID card. Did you serv sum time in Japan with the Marines Mister Oswald?

Wot do you think?

Im aksing you.

Well if I hav that card then yes I rekkon I served sum time there.

And this neks card? A bizness card for Enkanko hotel? Is that sumwhere you hav stayed in the past?

Yes.

Wot kind of work were you invollved in over there in Japan?

Radar mostly.

Anything of speshul signifkance?

No I say not menshuning the Gary Powers spy plane that was stashuned at my base it is usuly the subjeck of much intrest whenevver I menshun it howevver to me it is of litle importanse jus anuther plane takeing off and landing or not landing as the case may be Powers shot down over Russian territry becumming the subjeck of much internashunal uprore untill his releese. In trooth I did not much enjoy my time in Japan the ineqality between rich and poor the most aparent of any plase I ever lived the US inclooded men begging in the street for a grane of rise pressenting the strongest argewment I hav seen yet agenst captalism.

Fritz unfolds a large peece of paper from my wollet. This looks like your certifcate of servis from the Marines. Honorable discharg September 11 1959 is that correck?

Yes sir I say altho I hav amended the document to refleck same.

He puts that in the pile of items to his left that he has alreddy scrootinized.

These neks two look vry simler he says The furst says Fair Play for Cuba New York Chapter issewed to Lee H Oswald.

I tole you erlier I am a member.

And this secund one says you are a member of the New Orleens chapter?

Not jus a member. The fuonding member.

It is filed by one A Hidell. Is that middel inishul T? he says peering at the card.

I dont kno.

That is the same name on the selectiv serviss card with your foto on it.

It wood appeer so.

How do you explane that?

I dont.

The trooth is wen I started the New Orleens chapter I wanted it to appeer to hav more members than it actully did hense the need for a fake person as chappter president. I am shure they will work that out in good time but aggen Junie I hav no intenshun of makeing things easy for them.

He piks up the final card.

And lastly but sertenly not leest we hav anuther selectiv serviss card this time in your name. Most intreeging.

I say nuthing.

He pulls the munny out of the bill fold of the wollet cuonts it.

Five. Six. Sevven. Eight. Nine. Ten. Elevven. Twelve. Thirteen dollers in all he says. Not too flush are we Mister Oswald?

I get by.

He leens bak his stumik hangs over his belt an inch or two. Sumone slides a cup of coffee to him he takes a sip.

Doesnt seem like a lot of munny to get by on.

Sir I hav a wife two kids work minmum wage a buck and a qarter an huor. You do the math.

Fritz readjusts his gold tie clip. Then he leens foreward to pursoo a diffrent line of qesstuning trying to confoose me onse aggen.

Now as I unnerstand it Mister Oswald you and your wife live at sepret adresses.

Thats rite.

Wot is her curent adress?

Why dont you aks Hasty?

Aggen with Speshul Agent Hasty?

He seems to kno all about me.

Speshul Agent Hasty is otherwise ocuppyed.

Otherwise ocupped I smirk then say 2515 West 5th St Irving.

Fone nummer?

BL 3-1628.

And your rooming huose adress is…refresh my memry.

1026 Nth Beckly. It must be the tenth time I hav tole him this.

Fone nummer?

No idea I say altho I hav tole him same sevral times alreddy.

Im jus curius Mister Oswald Why do you and your wife liv at seprate addreses if munney is so tite?

Marina lives with the Pains for free.

Reely? Thats awfuly genrus of the Pains.

Rooth wants to lern Russian. Marina is helping her.

So why do you live in Oak Clif?

It is closser to my job.

At the skool book depossitry.

Wen I dont anser his words hang in the air.

Ware else hav you lived sinse reterning from Russia in…wen was that aggen?

July 1962.

Hav you lived mostly aruond the Oak Cliff area?

We lived on Elspeth for a wile.

Nummer?

602.

Fone?

Nun.

Befor that you were in New Orleens?

No after that I say he knos full well it was after he is jus trying to trip me up.

Adress in New Orleens?

Magazeen St. 4706. No fone I say antisipating his neks qesshun.

And then you mooved bak here a few munths ago.

Thats rite.

Lets tawk about your employment histry.

I thort you sed this woodnt take long. I poynt at the clok it is neerly nine.

Mister Oswald I am the one in charg here.

Of corse I say even tho I kno and he knos that without me nun of us wood be here.

He looks at the clok. Lissen there is sumthing else we need to take care of. Lets take a brake and get it out of the way. That way we can all get a spell.

He disappeers out the door for a minit reterns with two men wareing wite cotes they cood be dentists from a Collgate commershal.

Mister Oswald Fritz says This here is Detektivs Hicks and Stoodybaker of the Dallas PD. They wood like to purform sum tests on you.

To my surprize Elmer reeches over remooves my handcufs I am not about to argew. Wile suspishus of his motivs it is with grate releef that I am abel to moove my hands aggen.

Wot kind of tests? I say.

We need to fingerprint you Hicks says And also purform a parafin test.

Parafin test?

I am of corse playing dum I hav cum across this proseedur menny times in my reedings. It is a methud wareby heeted paraffin is applyed to thin banduges lade across the skin wen the parafin cools it hardens into a cast wich can then be removoed tested for trases of nitrats left behind after gunfire. Of corse sinse I hav resently fired both a rifle and pistul it shood be no grate surprise if the test cums bak positiv.

Fritz dootyfly explanes wot I alreddy kno.

I see I say And wot if I refoose the test?

That is your rite Mister Oswald but we will then get a cort order and then you will be forsed to comply. Refoosal will simpley delay the inevitabel.

All rite I say haveing herd this toon befor there is no poynt playing hardball.

The two men in wite cotes nod go about there bizness. Stoodybaker opens a brown lether docters bag lays out medicel parafernayla banduges tongs gluves etc. The other fella leeves for a few momments reterns with a bole its contents steeming. The cops all hold there noses the warmed parafin giveing off a most unplessant odor akin to a zoofull of animel droppings onse it asales the nostrills it does not let go.

Stoodybaker lays a cleen towel on the tabel aks me to plase my rite hand on it. He piks up a brush that one mite use to bast a turky it reminds me Thanksgiveing is less than a week away wot I woodnt giv to spend it with you and Mama and Rachel that seems improbabel now. Stoodybaker dips the brush in the bowl of parafin procedes to smeer this all over my hand and fingers. Onse I get past the slite berning sensashun it is a not an unplessant feeling in fack I almost giggel onse or twise I can be tickelish on occashon as your Mama will atest.

Plase the other hand beside it pleese Studebaker instrucks

after he has smuthered the rite with parafin. He repeets the prosess with the left then swoddels each hand with a layer of thin banduge repeets the aplicashun of parafin adds more banduge does this menny times over untill I hav a thik cast on each hand. Wile wateing for them to harden he does same to my rite cheek chekking for trases of nitrate from the rifel butt. The fowl smell ariseing from my cheek bothers me sum but I dont utter a wurd of complaynt I wont giv them that satissfacshun.

Stoodybaker finnishes with my cheek cheks the furmness of the banduges on both hands. Satissfyed he takes scissers cuts the banduge off of my rite hand takeing care not to disterb its shape. The cops tense up at the site of a sharp weppon in my visinity howevver the thort that I wood attemp an eckscape is laffable. How cood I posibly fite my way out of this bldg crammed as it is with unifform cops detektivs sekret serviss not to menshun the worlds press all jammed into hallways so narro one of the seven dwarfs cood not sqeeze by? I hav full fath in my abiltys Junie howevver not even I am cappabel of pulling that one off Hoodini cood not acheeve same.

Stoodybaker carefuly remooves the cast from my rite hand repeets the prosess with the left. Three dimenshunal likeneses of my hands now lye on the tabel I can not help but think of the deth mask of John Dilenger resently feching menny thuosands of dollars no dout these casts will one day be jus as sort after. The Hands That Changed the World cood be there kapshun.

Stoodybaker puts his hand on the bak of my hed twists it jus so says Hold still pleese. He takes a pare of tweezers gingerly tugs at the edges of the banduge on my cheek untill it cums free from the skin. Peeling it off he lays it down beside the hand casts. The other fella takes three plastik bags alreddy labeled with my name date of berth todays date. He slips a cast inside of each seels them tite as he is doing this Stoodybaker takes out an ink pad sevral forms from his bag.

Wots this? I say playing dum.

Time to get sum fingerprints Mister Oswald says Fritz.

Stoodybaker takes a peece of banduge applys sum cleening flewid wipes the tips of my fingers to remoove any leftover parafin. Then he takes my indecks finger pushes it down on the ink pad rolls it over the form to make a blak imprint. The fingerprint form has two ros of five boxes one ro for each hand. Stoodybaker methodikly fills each box with a print from each finger then wen all my fingers hav ink on them makes a print of the fingers all toggether underneeth the ro of boxes. Then out cums the cleener aggen to wipe away any serpluss ink.

Fritz pushes a pen across the tabel. Stoodybaker piks it up holds it out to me.

Wots that for? I aks.

Sine rite here Stoodybaker says poynting to a box that says Signatur of Person Fingerprinted.

I will do no such thing.

Mister Oswald says Fritz Be reesonabel.

I shake my hed. No I say I am not sineing this. I hav no idea wot you intend to do with these fingerprints. For all I kno you mite try and copy them onto a weppon and fake my gilt.

Mister Oswald I can asshure you that –

Tawk as much as you want. I am not sineing that form.

Fritz holds his hands up to Stoodybaker as if to say Wot can I do? Stoodybaker and the other fella pak up there old kit bag leeve the room. After a few secunds it is like they were never there excep for the lingering smell of parafin.

Mister Oswald says Fritz I think you are being most unreesonabel.

Easy for you to say you are not the one in the hot seet.

That is troo enuff. He looks aruond the room at the other men as he collecks his thorts. Now ware were we?

I beleev we were discussing the accooseds previus adresses says smokeing man fireing up anuther Chesterfeeld.

If you say so I say.

Ah yes says Fritz ignoreing me. Ware else hav you lived sinse returning from Russia? I hav Elspeth Street...Magazeen Street...he says fliping bak thru his notes.

Noware else I say knoing W Neely is missing from his list one more thing he can figger out.

That is the compleet list?

Well we livved for a wile with my bruther Robert wen we furst came bak.

That wood be at his currant Fort Wurth adress?

Yes.

Anyware else?

We rented a huose also in Fort Wurth. I cannot recall the adress.

We will look into that. Thats it?

Thats it.

OK. Lets tawk employment. We kno you are curently employed at the Texas Skool Book Depossitry.

I nod.

Wot abuot befor that?

I worked for a coffee cumpny in New Orleens.

Doing wot exakly?

Greeseing masheenry and so forth.

How long did you do this for?

Maybe a few munths.

I want to add that it was a few munths longer than any man shood hav to bare the work durty and distinkly unrewarding. My cowurkers were also a cawse for consern not a thinker amungst them happy to liv there lives in total obedeense to the establisht order. I wood play mind games with them aks how cood they stand liveing in this cuntry also prettend to shoot them with my finger as I walked by evry one of them idiots to a man.

Wot was the name of the cumpny?

I forget.

Wich street were they on? says Fritz after takeing a momment.

Magazeen.

All rite. There cant be that menny coffee cumpnys on Magazeen Street. We shood be abel to trak it down. Any other jobs sinse the Marines?

I worked for a short time for Jagger Chiles Stovelll in Dallas.

Ah yes the cumpny on the libry card. And wot kind of cumpny is that aggen?

They mostly do fotografic work.

Adress?

522 Brower.

OK. And your shure there is no other employment that we shood kno abuot?

Nun to speke of I say Those are the majer posishuns I hav held.

Vry good Mister Oswald. Now lets go bak to your moovements after the shooting.

I shift in the chare sit more uprite. I hav tawked long enuff I say I hav nuthing ferther to add. I wood never admitt it to Fritz but I am beet my mind loseing its usuley razer sharp edge. To anser more qesshuns in this condishun wood be a mistake of that I am serten.

Im shure thats not troo Mister Oswald I am shure you hav plenty wurth heering.

I dont hav anything else to say I repeet Wot started out as a short interogashun has turned out to be vry lengthee.

Jus a few more qesshuns if you dont mind Mister Oswald.

I dont care to tawk any more I say close my muoth.

Mister Oswald pleese cooprate with me here.

I am still wateing for sumone to cum foreward and give me legall repressentashun I say then shut my gob for good.

Fritz huffs and puffs like the big bad woolf goes all red in the fase but wot can he do? They cant forse words out of me. He looks at the clok it reeds 11.15pm.

I tell you wot he says There is to be a press conference at 11.30 and the cheef shood like you to atend. Wots say we take a brake you sit a spell and then we atend the press conferense together?

This is musik to my eers givs me a hole new berst of energee altho of corse I remane impassiv. Never in my wildest dreems did I expeck the orthoritys to grant me a press conference. Espeshully not so soon. Wile it is too erly to reveel my reesons for commenseing the clensing it will giv me a chanse to introdoose myself to the world perhapps sow sum ferther seeds of dout about wot transspired.

All rite I say like I am doing him a faver I will atend your litle press conferense.

Vry good he says But we need to be carefull down there. It mite get a litle hektic.

Oh capten aint no one gonna hert me.

He rases his eyebrows we both kno that now an aleged killer has been cort evryone jus wants to see him tryed and fryed it is like Roman times an eye for an eye they wood screne it live on CBS if they cood.

Fritz stands up says to Elmer Im hedding down now. I think Cheef Curry is going to say a few wurds and I want to make sure evrything is set for our frend here. Bring him down in ten minits.

The momment he leeves the room the other men skamper off to take bathroom brakes do papperwork whatevver else it is that cops do. Appart from a cop outside the door I am left with my own thorts for ten minits I will not lie Junie I spend nine of them thinking abuot you your Mama and Rachel. The impending press conferense has made me reelize that wot I hav dun has changed not jus my life forevver but the three of yours as well I hope that you can forgiv me for that. The cawse of takeing the first step towards makeing the world fairer for all was jus too importent. Sumtimes things are bigger than the individules involved I trust one day you will see my poynt of vew.

The press conferense is held in the showup room wich I am by now vry well aqainted with. Howevver on my previus visits it was ocoopyed by a dozen peeple at most myself the other partisippants in the showup the eye witnesses cops etc hidden behind the one way screne. Now as I am led handcuffed into the press conferense a see of peeple greets me it is like the mellay on the 3rd flor multaplyed by ten. Reporters sum sitting sum standing all cluch note pads. TV camras and press fotografers fase the frunt of the room a wall of polise faseing them. The two oposeing sides part as Elmer and anuther cop holding my arms leed me to the senter of the room.

The hubub of noize rises camras flash then evrything drops to a wissper as I stand faseing the croud. Sum of these men I reelise hav not seen me befor it is the ferst time they hav lade eyes on the man who alegedly shot there president. I can tell they alreddy hav me pegged as gilty they look at me like sum kind of freek a sideshow attrakshun no diffrent to a beerded lady or two hedded baby. I reckon in sum ways I am a freek takeing it uppon myself to sacrafise evrything I luv to improove the world for all mankind ninty nine persent of men content to get marryed sire three chillren sit aruond in frunt of the TV set evry nite nurseing a Bud wotching Fred Flintstone eat his brontasorus burgers. It is you who are the freeks I think as I look out over them I am the only sane one amung us.

Wot can you tell us about the situashun? a reporter who is neeling up frunt aks.

To a man evry one of them holds there breth wateing for me to speek. I am not an expereensed orrater Junie I shood be nervus as heck howevver a carm passes over me that cums from I kno not ware perhapps the knoledge that I hav acted in the intrests of all.

I positivly kno nuthing about this situashun here I say cleerly with grate control I wood like to hav legel repressentashun.

Like an ecko cawseing an avalanch my words shatter the

silense an exploshon of voises hits me I heer nun of there qesshons. I wate till the yelling dies down then anser the last qeusshun I heer Hav any charges been lade agenst you yet?

Well I was qesshuned by a judge howevver I protested at that time that I was not alowed legel repressentashun during that vry short and sweet heering.

I paws for anuther qesshun wen it is not forthcuming I continoo.

I reely dont kno wot the situashun is about. Nobody has tole me anything excep that I am acoosed of merdering a poliseman. I kno nuthing more than that. I do reqest sumone to cum foreward to giv me legel asistence.

Did you kill the president? says a voise to my left.

No I hav not been charged with that in fack nobody has sed that to me yet. The first thing I herd about it was wen the newspaper reporters in the hall aksed me that qesshun.

You hav been charged a voise calls out.

I stand sillent I hav no response to that. It is the ferst time I hav herd that they mite hav enuff evidense to charge me with killing the president. Sertenly Fritz has not sed same I reelise that perhapps he is a craftyer fox than he first appeers wateing till I am in frunt of the werlds camras to drop this bomshell.

Sir? I say.

Wot? yells a reporter.

You hav been charged the same person repetes the wurds no less shokking the secund time ruond. This time I see the muoth from whense they cum nun other than Cheef Curry the hed of the Dallas polise dept hisself.

We cant heer ya sumone yells from the bak of the hall.

Mister Oswald how did you get the blak eye?

A poliseman hit me.

Wot did you do in Russia? a man sitting on the flor aks howevver Elmer and his cohort are alreddy leeding me away. Those in authoritee hav desided I hav sed enuff. I must admit the atmosfere in the room has growen dark confooshon thikening the air like volkanic ash continooing wood not serv any useful purpuss.

The elevater passes the 3rd flor as Elmer and two unifformed men take me strate bak to my sell on 5. This is wen I dig out the stollen pad and pen from under my matress and commense this missiv to you deer Junie. Cheef Currys statment has highlited the urgensy of my situashun there is absolootly no time to waste. The faled press conferense its abrup ending hav also showen that oportoonitys to tell my side of the story may be more limited than I antissipated. If I am formly charged with the presidents murder and mooved to the cuonty jale press conferenses may ceese alltogether. I need to ajust my stratagy stay allert for a chanse to reveel my motivs. Wateing untill my day in cort cood be risky as I may not servive that long. As I hav sed Junie I am well aware of the nefarius ways of the FBI CIA Secret Serviss if they want me gone it will be so in a hartbeet the fack that the eyes of the world are upon me will not matter one jot. Also judgeing by the atmosfere in the press conferense there is alreddy vry strong sentament agenst me howevver I do beleeve that will chang onse I explane my reesons for the clensing.

Fifteen minits later Fritz reterns nods at the gard who unloks the sell door.

Cum with me he says offring no further eksplanashun.

My hed still spinning from the press conferense I alow them to steer me to the elevaters. Fritzs grim fase reinforses my wurst feers the authoritees hav alreddy cum up with a senario to sucessfuly explane away my demise suiside being the most plawsible explanashun altho why they wood remoove me from my sell to acheeve same does not make sense.

We dessend one level to the 4th flor no press are gathered ferther arouseing my suspishons. Howevver the lak of confooshon does smooth our pasage to a room marked Identificashun Berow ware two men in wite cotes and a fingerprint kit awate Fritz explaneing I am to onse aggen be fingerprinted. It is only minits sinse I was subjected to same howevver releef limits my objecshuns I will take a litle more ink on my fingers over being permnently silensed any day. After they hav takken the prints I am seeted agenst a plane wite wall an identifcashun bord plased over my rite sholder it shos the booking nummer and date 11-23-63. Mug shots are fired off from the frunt and side on. I try not to look too pleesed with myself these fotos mite well be leeked to the press I do not want to look like I am gloteing over my akshuns I manetane a serius fase with an apropriat level of gravitas thru out. Only a crazy man wood look pleesed in his mug shot I most sertenly do not want to cum across as that I am vry far from insane that will never be my defense shood the case go to tryal. Also for any prissoner the day of captur is far from a tressured momment no cawse for selebrashun so wile this mite well be my finnest hour I make shure my mug shot does not refleck same.

An huor later aruond one am I am reterned to my sell the

secund set of fingerprints and mug shots compleet. I hunch in the bak corner fase the reer wall continoo to rite these notes at a furius pase Junie panefuly aware that I do not kno how much time I hav left to finnish the job. I will also need to conseel them befor I am mooved otherwise they will be discuvvered wen I am serched at the cuonty jail. Ironikly that jale is lokated on Hooston and Elm jus yards from ware I had my rondayvoo with Mister Kennedy if I look out the windo neks week I may well see sum of my co workers Junor Wesly etc cumming and going from the skool book depossitry perhapps they will pay me a vissit in there lunch hour ha.

A half huor later my scribbleing is onse aggen interupted. I am reterned to the 4th flor Identificashun Burow ware Justise of the Peese Jonson wates along with Fritz and sevral others. Dispite the late huor Jonson looks his usul dapper self his arragense cleerly on dissplay he looks down his poynty nose at me.

You remember Mister Jonson and Mister Wade says Fritz.

Wots the meening of this? I aks.

They are here to reed you the charges layed agenst you in relashun to the shooting of the president.

I dont kno wot you are tawking abuot.

They all ignor me Jonson starts speeking all prim and propper like he is reeding a proklamashun from the Qeen of England. The wurding of the charg is the same as the one regardding Tipit the name of the viktim the case nummer the only vareenses. I am charged with murder with maliss afore thort in the deth of John Fitzgereld Kennedy. Jus like the Tipit arranement I interupt sevral times aks why are they doing this it is a frootless endevver

Jonson continoos to drone on determined to reed evry last sillable.

Well I rekkon this is the tryal then I say.

No Mister Oswald says Fritz takeing off his glasses and cleening them with a hankercheef As we explaned to you erlier this is the arranement ware we advise you of the charges agenst you.

I want to contack my loyyer Mister Abt in New York City.

That is of corse your rite and we will do evrything in our power to make that happen.

I wood like this gentelman I say He is with the American Civil Libertys Unoin.

Ferst thing tomorow we will put you in tuch with him Fritz says A telefone will be made avalable to you in the sell blok.

I shood hope so.

Dapper Dan fires up a sigret stinking up the room.

Can I go bak to my sell now? I say That smoke is giveing me a hedake.

Fritz nods opens the door tells Elmer and the two uniform guys outside to take me bak to my sell. I walk arm in arm with my captors barely takeing in my surruondings. The speed at wich the polise hav charged me with Kennedys merder has takken me by surprize. I thort I wood hav sevral days at leest befor they started putting the peeses together. Being charged with the Tipit killing is one thing there were eyewitneses galore howevver the shooting of the president had no such witneses that I kno of altho thuosands of peeple were in the plaza it wood only take one of them to look up at the rong time. Howevver that seems unlikly all eyes were on the motorcade also I made my getaway cleen as a wissle I therefor can not imagin wot evidense they hav agenst me. The only thing tying me to the crime seen is my rifel how cood they hav trased that so qikly? Perhaps that was the purpuss of the fingerprints altho I hav red it is vry diffcult to lift prints from a wood rifel stok I consoll myself with the thort that it must also be tuff to plant same.

As the sell door clangs shut I figger there are forses at work here much grater than me. Events are moveing vry qikly I hav been charged jus thirteen hours after pulling the trigger. As soon as the gards tern there bak I set to riteing aggen resolv to spend evry avalable minit finishing these notes it is imperativ that I do so befor things spyrral out of control.

I hav also reeched the conklushon Junie that I can not deppend on these notes ever reeching you if sumthing shood hapen to me then the world will never kno the reesons why I shot Kennedy commensed the clensing. Howevver the mind works in misteerius ways alreddy a plan for a grand anuonsement of my motivs is takeing shape. If I am rite and I usuley am I will soon hav the perfeck stage from wich to command the worlds atenshun evryone will soon kno the troo brillense of your papa.

Saterday

I scribbel frantikly thru the silent huors of erly morning pawse only around dawn forse myself to slepe I need rest befor the interogashuns begin. Despite being formly charged my stratagy remanes the same admit nuthing howevver I will need my wits about me Fritz is a vry deseptive qeshtuner indede. He is skilled at prettending he is folowing one trane of thort then veering 180 degrees caching me off gard even tho I kno it is cumming.

The sell block was eerly silent thru out the nite only the deep breething of the gard brakeing the qiet. Eether the cops evakewated the floor so I dont cum to any harm or it is the qietest nite in the histry of this fare city not a drunkerd or mallcontent to be fuond. Befor falling sleep I wotch the stars in a pach of blak sky out the windo I hav lived in Texas long enuff to kno that at dawn the line between land and air will glo soft yelow the sun riseing upward into the pale blew. Junie I am not much of a romantik but if I am to spend the rest of my life behind bars that is one site I will sorly miss. It reminds me of hunting on the frinjes of Fort Wurth of an evening my bruthers silloetted agenst the horizen by the setting sun.

I slepe for I do not kno how long perhapps only an huor befor I am woken by the gard banging on the bars with his batton. He slides brekfast thru a horrizontel gap in the bars. Scrambelled eggs most probly powdered cold toste no butter a plastik cup half filled with orang juse. Howevver I do not complane your Mama has sertenly served wurse ha.

Wile eatting I asess the events of the previus day no dout I hav pulled off one of the grate feets in human histry. It is one thing to aspire to sumthing of such magnitood qite anuther to make it hapen I now kno how Hitler probly felt wen he overthru the kyser. Yes his later deeds were disgraseful and I kno sum will see mine in a simler lite howevver they can not deny the skale of my acheevement nor the suond reesoning behind it. It is now my dooty to use this plase I hav created for myself in histry to edukate the peeple of the world about the menny ineqitys they fase I am more than reddy for that chalenge hopfully they are reddy to lissen.

I swalow the last muothfull of egg carry the tray bak to the sell door. The gard a short fat fella his coller almost hidden by chins stands up takes the tray plases it on the gruond retakes his seet hevven forbid he shood stand up for any longer than five secunds.

Any chanse of a fella getting sum cofee? I aks.

Wot do you think this is an a la cart resterant?

Jus aksin.

Well not up here there aint. Maybe wen we take you downstares.

Wen will that happen?

Not sure. Still wateing on word from the Cheef.

216

I turn away try to ignoor his presense as I go thru my morning abhlooshuns useing the filty wash basein and toylet. I do my bizness wash my fase run fingers thru my hare brush my teeth as best I can with a finger and sum cole water. I retern to my bunk get bak to riteing soon becum lost in the wurds. I hav always enjoyed riteing despite the fack that it is cleerly diffkult for me. I onse dreemed of riteing for a liveing wen I mooved to Russia I applyed to the Albert Switzer Colleg in Viena my plan to rite short storys about American life. The aplicashun was admitedly a roose to get to Russia they make oversees travel in the ferst three yeers after leeveing the Marines vry diffkult without good reeson. Howevver I was genewinly intrested in riteing. Then of corse wile in Russia I kept my Historic diary a record of liveing condishuns there. Perhapps now my Historic Diary will reech the audiense it deservs I had started the prosess of haveing it typed up wen I reterned from Minsk I trakked down a typist in the yelow pages but ran out of munny. Now I may well hav time to compleet the task myself if I cood sumhow get my hands on the notes and a typeriter perhapps one of those Remmington Super Riters from Montgomry Ward maybe there is a male order catalog lyeing aruond in this sell sumwhere ha.

I am not shure how much later it is wen the gard speeks aggen.

OK Oswald time to hed downstares.

I nod fake a coffing fit to cuvver stashing the notebook under my matress. Not the most orignel hideing place I freely admit howevver sinse they hav alreddy serched my person stood gard over me all nite I am hopeing they will not bother tossing the sell. My only other opshun keep the notes on my person seems highly impraktical to say the leest.

After we compleet the usul drill me putting my hands thru the spase in the bars the gard putting the cuffs on anuther gard joyns us he slides open the sell door we hed down the hall. Jus befor the elevater the secund gard stumbels sprawels across the flor stops jus short of the elevater doors.

He climes to his feet dusts off his pants and sleevs. One of these yeers theyll fix that dam thing he says stamps his foot down on a vinil tile its corner stikking up a half inch abuv flor level.

We dessend two flors forse our way thru the press to Fritzs offise the same fases fill the room. Bookout the FBI fella Sorels a man in charg of the secret serviss sum US marshel and a cupple more detektivs.

Good morning Mister Oswald says Fritz as cheery as can be I trust you slept well in our acomodashuns.

Yes sir I say matching his sunny dispossishun ray for ray.

Youve been taken care of? he aks Brekfast and such?

Yes sir I say aggen.

All rite then lets get down to it. We will pik up ware we left off yesserday. You say you left work and cort the bus home folowing the shooting of the president?

Thats rite.

Rode it all the way home?

Yes sir to the stop rite across the street.

Thats a curius thing he says scraching his cheek.

I say nuthing let him get to wot he is getting at.

Wen we serched your person yestaday we fuond a bus transfer in your poseshun.

Aggen I say nuthing.

Why wood you hav a bus transfer in your poseshun he aks If you rode the bus all the way home? Arent transfers givven to passengers changeing busses so they dont hav to pay anuther fare?

Thats rite I say as if I jus remembered The bus driver gave it to me wen I got off of the bus.

The bus driver driveing the bus you cort wen you left the depossitry gave it to you?

Yes.

But you jus tole me you rode the bus all the way home?

I shrug my sholders. The traffik was bad.

So how did you get home?

You seem to hav all the ansers why dont you tell me?

Maybe you cort a cab? he says his eyes smileing he alreddy knos the anser they hav trakked down the driver or a witness conferming same.

Thats rite I say desideing theres no harm in admiting the trooth bus taxi shanks mare my mode of transsportashun makes litle diffrense other than that they hav cort me in a lie it wont be the first time probly wont be the last.

You cort a cab yesterday?

Yes I got off of the bus becos of the traffik and cort a cab.

Wots that? he says cupping his ear prettending not to heer so I hav to repeet same.

You herd me.

Why did you cach a cab?

Well like I sed the trafic was all messt up and not going anyware. We were mooveing reel slo so I got off and cort a cab.

Do you remember ware?

Not exackly.

Remember anything about the driver?

Not reely.

Tawk to him at all?

No.

Tawk to anyone else?

No. Well I do recall that after I got in the cab an old lady aksed if the driver cood call a cab for her.

Then wot hapened?

I tole her she cood hav mine but the driver tole her to take annuther.

And thats wot she did?

Far as I kno yes sir thats wot she did.

How much was the fare home?

Eighty five sents I think. I gave the driver a doller tole him to keep the chang.

Look at the big spender. And wen you got home you changed your cloths. Is that still correck? Or did you make that up too?

That is still correck I say ignoreing his cheep shot.

Wot did you do with them?

With wot?

The durty clothes.

Why I put them in the durty cloths basket of corse.

In your room?

Ware else wood I put my durty cloths?

Yesserday you sed you put them in the botom draw of the dresser.

Thats rite. That is my durty cloths basket so to speek.

And those durty clothes were?

Red shert gray trowsers.

Long sleev shirt?

Yes.

Yesterday you sed you jus changed your trowsers.

I mispoke.

He fixes me with a glare. All rite lets tawk about wot you were doing befor the shooting.

Your wish is my comand.

You rode to work Friday morning with one Bule Wesly Frazer is that correck?

If you say so.

That is my unnerstanding. We spoke to Mister Frazer yesterday and he sed he gav you a ride to work whennever you vissited with your wife in Irving.

I say nuthing if he has alreddy spokken to Wesly best to let him leed the conversashun lern wot he has discuvvered.

Mister Frazer sed that this was usully on Friday afternoon hedding home for the weekend or on Monday morning hedding bak to work. Is this also correck?

If you say so I repete.

Mister Oswald we hav spokken to Mister Frazer there is no poynt denying it.

OK OK yes I ocashonly ride to work with Wesly Frazer. So wot?

Well Im curius why you rode with him Thersday not Friday like you usully do.

Why dont you aks Wesly? He seems to hav all the ansers.

We did aks Wesly Mister Oswald. He sed you tole him you needed to pik up sum curtin rods for sum drapes that your wife made for your apartment. Is that correck?

No.

No?

Wot are you deff?

Then why wood Mister Frazer tell us that?

Youll hav to aks him.

So you didnt bring a long pakage to work with you on Friday morning?

No.

Fritz looks aruond at the other men in the room frustrashun is rit larg on there fases.

Mister Frazer and his sister both say they saw you carrying a pakkage with you yesterday morning.

His sister?

She says she saw you thru the kichen windo.

Reely? I dont even kno his sister I say strugleing to contane my anger with the stoopid cow I hate her more than ever.

Mister Frazer says you put a long pakkage on the bak seet of his car yesserday morning befor he left the house. Wen he got in the car he aksed you wot it was you sed it was the curten rods you tole him about on Thursday wen you aksed for a ride home. Does any of this suond familer to you Mister Oswald?

No it does not.

Mister Frazer also sed that after arriveing in the car park at work yesterday morning he wotched you walk across the rale yard to the depossitry carrying the pakkage.

That is categorikly incorreck I say my world tilting on its axis for I now start to see the evidense they hav bilt up agenst me why I was charged with the presidents merder in less than twenty-fuor huors.

I deny these alegashuns I say.

So you deny carrying a pakkage to work yesterday? says Fritz.

Sumone at the bak of the room cleers there throte.

Wot was in the brown bag? aks smokeing man the ferst werds he has spokken in qite sum time.

My lunch I say desideing it is better to lie about the bag than deny its existanse they hav too much eye witness testamony.

Your lunch?

Thats rite.

Why did you carry your lunch in a big old bag like that?

Well you dont allways get a bag that jus fits your lunch. You take wot you can get.

Ware did you carry it? he says thru a clowd of smoke that seems to emmanate from his evry orifiss.

I carryed it in my lap like I always do. Then Wesly sed thro it over in the bak seet so I did.

It must hav been qite a lunch Fritz says Wot did you hav for lunch yesterday Mister Oswald?

A cheese sandwitch and an appel jus like I tole you yesterday.

Thats it?

Yes sir.

Thats all you took to work with you yesterday?

Yes sir.

All rite. This is the lunch you were eating at the time the president was shot?

Yes sir.

Ware was that aggen?

The domino room.

Thats rite the domino room he says nodding his hed like he

had forgoten but I am awake up to him. Was there anyone else with you?

I alreddy tole you yessterday.

Id like you to tell me aggen.

I kno wot Fritz is up to hes trying to cach me in anuther lie but I am too smart for that.

I ate lunch with sum of the collored boys I work with.

Names?

Junor was there.

Last name?

Not shure I say even tho I kno it is Jarman. I am pritty sure I tole him the name yesserday but if not let his men do sum legwerk burn off all that bbq and Bud.

Anyone else?

Anuther fella I say I dont kno his name.

Negro?

Thats rite.

Wot did he look like?

Short.

Mister Oswald I am curius why you liv in a room on Nth Beckly he says changeing tak aggen he is like a saleboat swiching bak and forth on the bay trying to cach sum breeze.

Why?

Well your wife Marina lives in Irving with your two dorters. Isnt it strange that you liv by yourself menny miles away?

Mrs Pain –

Mrs Pain? he interups.

The woman my wife lives with out in Irving.

Can you spell that name pleese?

P-A-I-N.

He rites that down a tiny smile on his lips. Pleese continu.

Mrs Pain is lerning Russian and my wife needs help with the chillren so it makes a nise arangment. My wife spekes to her in Russian all day long.

How much bord does your wife pay Mrs Pain?

Nuthing.

Nuthing? She livs with this Mrs Pain for free?

Yes sir. Jus helps her with her Russian.

Tell me more about this Mrs Pain.

Not much to tell reely. I dont kno her so well.

Is she marryed? Singel? Divorsed?

Her and Mr Pain are seprated. He doesnt liv in Irving.

I see. Wots his ferst name?

Michel.

Do you kno ware he lives?

Im not shure. Someware out neer Luv Feeld I think he works at the airport.

Doing wot?

Sum kind of engineer.

I see. Do you drive Mister Oswald?

Wot has that got to do with anything?

Im jus wundering why you dont hav a car. Why you ride with Mister Frazer to work.

Cars are expensiv I can get aruond jus fine without one.

Do the Pains hav one?

Yes. They hav one each. I think it is an unesessary extravaganse but to each there own.

I rekkon thats why they hav a huose with a garage.

You will hav to aks them I say pondering the relevanse of his observashun.

All rite. We mite jus do that. So your wife has lived with Mrs Pain for how long?

Sinse she came bak from New Orleens to hav the baby.

How long ago was that?

Hard to say exackly.

Well wood you say its been a few munths?

Sumthing like that.

Do you keep any poseshuns at the Pains Mister Oswald?

A few things.

Ware are they stored?

The garage I say an alarm bell ringing in my hed.

Such as?

See bags and such.

See bags?

You kno. Duffel bags.

I see. Wen did you put them there? Wen you came bak to Dallas from New Orleens?

Thats rite.

Wen did you retern?

September.

There didnt happen to be a rifel amungst those poseshons did there?

No sir.

You never had a rifel in New Orleens that you brort bak to Irving with you?

No sir I say wich is not a lie your mama brort it bak with her in Rooths car.

Hav you ever owned a rifle Mister Oswald?

No sir.

You never ordered one thru the male?

Agen he caches me off gard it suonds like he has alreddy werked out how I bort it.

No sir I say knoing that if I admitt to owning a rifel it will open up a hole new world of trubbel one that is wurth stalling for as long as posible.

Your absolootly serten of that Mister Oswald?

Thats rite I say emfatickly.

Wot about the pistul?

Wot about it?

How did you get that?

Not by male order if thats wot your insinnewating.

Then how did you get it?

I bort it.

Ware?

Fort Wurth I beleev.

Witch store?

Dont remember.

Wen?

Dont remember.

Theres a lot of not remembring going on here Mister Oswald.

I cant help it if I hav a bad memry I say resisting the erge to smirk my mind has allways been a steel trap.

Your bruther Robert livs in Fort Wurth is that correck?

Yes I tole you so yesterrday.

Maybe the gun store is neer his house.

Maybe I reely cant recall.

Does your bruther kno Mrs Pain?

Oh yes they are ferm frends I say even tho they hav never met lets see the grate homiside detektive work that one out.

Fritz looks down at his notes for a spell formulateing his neks qesshun. Onse aggen he surprises me.

Mister Oswald hav you ever been a member of the communist party?

No sir.

Never?

Never. I hav never been a card carrying member. I hav of corse been a member of the Fare Play for Cuba commitee.

Yes I remember that from our discusshuns yesterday. Are you a member of any other politikal organizashuns?

The ACLU I say altho I am not shure I wood call them a politikal organisashun.

Junie I joyned the ACLU a few weeks ago antissipateing I may need there legel asistence. Reely I hav no time for them but wen I cood see a use for there legal ackumen I was willing to coff up the dews.

Your a pade up member? aks Fritz.

Thats rite I sent them two dollers.

Why did you take the pistul to the pitcher sho?

He is still trying to confoose me jumping all aruond the plase like a Mexican jumping been he shood hav lerned by now that that technik is a rode to serten falure.

I tole you yesterday.

I beleev you sed becos thats wot boys do he says not looking bak thru his notes Any other reeson?

No sir.

He looks at me I look at him we are two hevywates sizeing each other up.

You anser your qesshuns vry qikly Mister Oswald.

Thats jus the way my mind works.

Hav you been qesshuned befor?

Perhaps.

By who?

I nod at the FBI felows.

The FBI? says Fritz Wen was this?

After I reterned from Russia I say I was intervewed on sevral ocashons. Onse I was stopped on the street in brord daylite rite outside my home in Fort Wurth.

I see. Wot did they aks you?

All sorts of qesshuns. I gather they were trying to figger out if I was an enemy of the state.

Are you Mister Oswald?

No sir.

But you were interrogatted by the FBI nun the less.

Yes sir.

How wood you deskribe those efforts?

You kno. Hard soft. Good cop bad cop. The buddy methud. I saw rite thru them.

So you are familer with interogashun methuds?

You cood say that. Much more than my wife at any rate. She and Mrs Pain were intimidatted by that horribel Hasty fella.

Well he is not here rite now so lets not wurry abuot him.

Oh he doesnt wurry me in the leest. I deside to swich tacks on Fritz giv him a tast of his own medisine. I shood also like to remind you that I hav not yet tawked with a loyyer.

As I havs tole you Mister Oswald you can hav a loyyer any time you wish.

I dont hav munny for a fone call to Mister Abt.

You can call colleck if you wish Fritz says Jus use the jale fone. You can also call any other loyyer.

I dont want any other loyyer. I want Mister Abt.

Who is this Abt fella? Wots so speshul about him? Why not jus choose one that is avalable in the Dallas area?

Well I never met Mister Abt personly but I kno he has deffended a few peeple who were in violashun of the Smith Act.

The Smith Act? I hav never herd of that.

You kno trying to overthro the guvnment.

Oh yes he says sitting up strater. Is that wot you were trying to do?

I wasnt trying to do anything I say reeliseing I may hav let sumthing slip But the president the hed of our govt has been killt by sumone and I think Abt may be helpful to me in this situashun. If I cant get him the ACLU cood also help me find a loyyer. They will also help with fees and such.

I see.

Fritz ponders this for a momment. I am surprized wen he does not rite wot I sed down insted chases the breeze in anuther direkshun.

Wot was your adress in New Orleens?

I am sure I tole you yesterday.

Well tell me aggen pleese.

4907 Magazeen.

Thank you. And you worked ware?

William Rily cumpny I say.

Oh so now you remmember there name?

It jus came to me I say forgetting that I had alreddy fayned ignoranse on the toppic.

Doing wot?

I drop my hed look at my hands. We cuvvered all this yesterday I mutter.

Lets cuvver it aggen.

I greesed the masheens.

Vry good. That wasnt so hard now was it? Hav you had any previus arrests?

He is bilding towards the Fair Play for Cuba insident showen his hand by aksing leed in qesshuns about my life in New Orleens. Sinse I kno that he knos about that evvent I deside to play along.

Yes sir.

How menny?

Jus the one.

Want to tell me abuot it? he says like a sychiatrist tawking to a payshent on his sofa rather than a homiside cop trying to send sumone to the chare.

I had a little trubble in New Orleens I say.

Wot kind of trubble?

I was working with the Fare Play for Cuba peeple handing out leeflets on Canal St. Sum anti-Castro peeple came along and started cawseing trubble. I was haveing nun of that so I defended myself.

You were detaned?

Yes sir. Sumone called the polise and myself and anuther gentelman involved were takken into custady.

Wot happened neks?

I was held overnite and releesed in the morning.

Was that your only run in with these anti-Castro peeple?

If you meen of a fisical nature, yes.

But you saw them at a later time?

Yes I debated sum of them on the raydio.

Reely? You were on the raydio?

Why is that so surprizeing to you?

Well its not surprizeing Mister Oswald its jus that…

Fritz looks aruond the room grining he has run out of wurds.

I gav as good as I got I say I acqited myself qite well under diffcult cirkumstanses thank you vry much.

I dont detale the cirkumstances to Fritz but they were more than diffcult the first interview extreemely smooth the secund extreemely hostile I was ambushed accoosed of being a communist my time in Russia used to smeer my name. Howevver I held my gruond Junie they did not get the better of me altho it is fare to say I was breefly rattled.

Im shure you did vry well Mister Oswald Fritz says I can see that you are vry qik on your feet.

I flash a smile let him think his flattry is working. I kno he is trying to ingrashiate himself to me litle does he reelise it is haveing the oposite effeck I think him stoopid for atempting such an obvius roose.

I think I understand your feelings on the subjek of Cuba he says But wot about the president?

Wot abuot him?

Wot are your feelings about him and his famly?

I dont hav any vews on the president I say.

Oh cum now Mister Oswald. A politikly minded man like yuorself and you hav no vews on the president? Of all the things you hav tole me sinse you got here I find that the hardest to beleeve.

Well I like the Kennedy famly vry well I say And hav my own vews on nashunal polisy. I hav nuthing ferther to say on the matter.

Wood you be willing to submit to a polygraf test? he aks.

I most sertenly wood not.

Junie I am not abuot to agree to a polygraph wen I hav not even fuond a loyyer. I can be one hek of a lyer wen I set my mind to it can run rings aruond most polise FBI and such howevver trikking a cold harted masheen of steel and cogs is anuther matter entirly I am not shure if even I cood fool same.

I hav had enuff for this morning I say I kno they want to grill me insesently grind me down over the corse of the day it is better if I can diktate the pase of proseedings.

Much to my surprize Fritz agrees with my sugesshun.

Vry well he says Lets reconveen after lunch. Boyd and Sims take Mister Oswald bak to his sell.

Onse there they treet me to a balony sandwitch glass of swete milk two oreos I am liveing high on the hog no dout. To make the cookies last I pull them appart eat each harf sepret. Plane food fansy food it makes litle diffrense to me as long as it is cleen well preparred. Your mama wile a teribel cook never reseeved complaynts from me altho she may well tell a diffrent story. I freely admitt that on occashon I cood be a demanding husband disapoynted if dinner arived on the tabel late or she forgot to put the butter out howevver my own muther went thru sevral husbands so who did I hav to lern off wen it came to the finer poynts of matramony? I hav always dun my best to provide for my famly Junie I hope that is obvius to you in the difrent jobs that I hav undertakken sum nun too glamrus cutting sheet metel to make loovers greeseing filthy cogs at a coffee cumpny also endless swetty trips up and down the deppossitry stares. These jobs I took to provide for you hopfully I can continoo to do same of corse that is an unknowen rite now. If I do sumhow eckscape this predikament who knos ware it mite lede we may well be invited to Cuba or Russia feted for my acheevement live with the upper eshelons of sossiety. Perhaps a palase is not out of the qesshun altho cleerly the trappings of welth meen vry litle to me.

I finnish the oreos lie bak on the paper thin matress to rest befor the neks ruond of qesshuning. Sumhow despite the madness swurling aruond me probly a result of riteing thru the nite I fall asleep. I dreem of walking thru a sweeping ranch huose with all moddern convenenses refridgerator elektric stove larg collor TV swimming pool with diveing bord visibal thru the windo. Your mama calls darling darling from one end of the huose I hed in that direkshun travel thru room after room with no end in site I can not find my way out of this suberban maze. Darling she continoos to repeet I frantikly serch for her eventuly stumbel upon a long hallway her voise cums from behind a door at the far end. I sprint down the coridoor push it open find your mama with anuther man tall and handsum. It is Anatolly a frend of Mamas from the old cuntry who we allways sed looks like Kennedy. She is gazeing into his eyes melting into his arms I speke but mite as well be conseeled behind a brik wall I am invisibel to her. Out the windo the Texas planes strech on forever as they allways hav and allways will I look bak it is now Kennedy holding your mama half his hed missing his combed hare matted with blud and—

Oswald!

I wake with a start shake my hed to loossen the fog of sleep.

Oswald! the gard shuots aggen Five minits befor we hed bak downstares.

I sit up swing my legs off of the bunk plase my feet on the flor.

Lets go I say not wishing them to think I am afrade of a litle more interogashun.

Hold your horses he says terning to a cop who has also cum to eskort me Get a lode of this fella he cant wate to get bak in there with Fritz.

Maybe its troo wot they say the other gard says He reely does hav a scroo loosse. He moshuns for me to put my hands thru the bars so he can put the cuffs bak on.

Hav to be says the first cop To do wot he has dun.

I ashure you gentelmen I say as I folow his reqest to plase my hands thru the bars I am anything but of unstabbel mind.

The afternoon interogashun sesshon piks up ware this mornings left off. Fritz aks qesshuns I defleck same the other men in the room mumbel a few words of disscontent evry now and then. Anuther fella is also present a Mister Kelly sum kind of inspecter with the postel serviss a litle old man he looks like sumones granfather who has wondered in off the street unshure if he is in the rite bldg. I asoom he is there to qiz me about male ordering the guns also probe the detales of my post offise box.

Fritz thrusts I pary things dont get intresting untill he aks me ware I hav lived in Dallas.

I hav alreddy tole you this a hunnerd times I say.

I want to go thru them all aggen he says To make shure we havent mist anything.

I sigh. Well you kno about Nth Beckly. Befor that I lived in a rooming house on Marsallis for a short periud.

How long?

Less than a week. The landlady and I did not see eye to eye. I do not menshun how I saw the old crow on the bus imedately folowing the shooting if I tell them that she will be brort in and sware on a stak of bibels that I shot the pressident and the cop probly fifteen other peeple besides.

Befor that?

Well I was in New Orleens.

Thats rite he says Magazeen Street if I am not misstaken.

You are not.

Wot abuot befor you moved to New Orleens? Were you also in the Oak Cliff area?

Yes.

Adress?

Elspeth.

Anyware else?

Not that I can recall.

Wot about W Neely St? Did you ever liv there?

I dont think so I say sik of giveing him evrything on a silver platta.

Reely?

Reely altho we hav mooved aruond so much it is hard to remember evry plase we lived.

Why hav you moved aruond so much Mister Oswald?

A few reesons.

Such as?

Id rather not say.

Jus giv me one.

Well to stay one step ahed of these fellas for a start I say nodding at the FBI agents leening agenst the wall they shift uncumfortably from one foot to the other.

So you never livved on W Neely St?

Not that I can recall I say now wurryed abuot how Fritz is shoing so much intrest in W Neely he may hav an ultereer motiv for this line of qesshoning. Sumone mite hav tole him we lived on W Neely otherwise he wood not be so persistent howevver that still does not explane why he is so intrested in that partiklar adress.

As far as your poseshons go he says They are all at Mrs Pains huose in Irving and in the Nth Beckly rooming huose. Is that correkt?

Yes.

Anything anyware else?

No.

All rite. I beleeve speshul agent Bookout has sum qesshuns for you.

Mister Oswald says the fella with eyebrows like well used pipecleeners I wood ferstly like to aks you about sumthing we fuond in yuor wollet.

Wots that?

He pulls out the selectiv serviss card from a carbbord folder. Is this here a foto of you?

Yes.

But the name on the card is one Alek J Hidell.

I thort we alreddy discust this.

It is also sined by one Alek J Hidell.

Wen I remane silent he says Wot can you tell me abuot this card Mister Oswald?

Nuthing.

Well why is it in yuor wollet?

I dont kno.

But it is in yuor wollet?

It is now.

Wot do you meen by that?

Well who knos how it got there.

Is that yuor handriteing rite there? Did you sine this?

No sir.

Did you create this fake peece of identifficashun?

No sir.

No?

No sir.

Then why is it in yuor wollet?

Your so smart I say You figger it out.

His eyebrows creep higher on his forehed they hav a life of there own a pare of catterpillas craweling up a rok.

He takes out my adress book.

We fuond this amungst your poseshuns in your apartment on Nth Beckly he says.

If you say so.

Is it yours?

I am not shure.

Your not shure?

No.

But it was fuond in your room.

Jus becos it was fuond in my room dusnt meen it is mine. Menny peeple cood acksess that room wen I am not there.

I notise there are a lot of Russian names in here. He fliks thru the pages. Kno a lot of Russians do you Oswald?

I kno my fare share. After all I am marreed to one. There are a nummer in the Dallas area that my wife and I hav becum frends with I say not menshuning that I dettest most of them they are traytors to there cuntry. Flored as the Russian sistem mite be it is no wurse than that witch exists here these Russian expats hold up the U.S. to be the be all and end all jus becos they manage to make sum munny here. They are Unkle Toms evry singel one of them excep my good frend Goerge a geollogist who is extreemly well traveled with simler political veiws to my own. Sum mite describe George as a blohard a vry harsh verdick he is highly inteligent and vry suportiv of my stanses whereas menny of his kompatriuts dont care abuot there fello man as long as they are alrite. I admire George grately gav him a copy of the foto I gave you Junie the one of me with my weppons in the bak yard at W Neely. On his I rote in russian hunter of fascists ha. George reelly got a kik out of that I think he will be vry pleesed with me for commenseing the clensing I can not wate for the chanse to tawk to him about it. I kno he alreddy suspecks I was the one who took a potshot at Walker he aksed me poynt blank if I did it of corse I denyed same but in his eyes I cood see he knoo the trooth.

Mind if we contakt sum of these Russians? Bookout says.

Why?

To confurm wether you hav a relashunship with them or not.

Be my gest I say smileing. His eyebrows arch ferther upward a feet I wood hav thort fizzicly impossibel.

Thank you speshul agent Bookout Fritz says scoweling at my smile he is a hedmaster deeling with a trewant. You kno Mister Oswald I wish you wood take all this a litle more seriusly.

It is diffcult wen yall keep aksing such stoopid quesshuns.

Be that as it may you hav killed the president and that is a vry serius offens.

I didnt kill the president.

Well you hav been charged with his murder. Dusnt that meen anything to you?

Thats OK I say Peeple will forget all about JFK in a few days. There will be anuther president and peeple will forget all about him.

At this statment there is much shakeing of heds and tsk tsking but I kno and Fritz knos and evryone else in the room knos that that is the gods honest trooth. Unless of corse world war three brakes out as cuntrys acoose each other of involvment it wood be Archdook Ferdinand all over aggen one can only hope as it cood leed to a hole new world order.

You are also charged with the merder of a polise offiser Fritz says.

I did not shoot any polise offiser I say I was in a pitcher theeter with a pistol wotching a war movie that is all.

Then there is also the small matta of woonding Guvnor Conelly with intent to kill. You will probly be charged with that at a latter date perhaps after we moove you to the cuonty jail.

Conelly was shot?

I did not kno that one of my bullits had struck the guvnor but he wood be no grate loss. I rote to Conelly after leeveing the Marines he was secretry of the navy at the time I sort reversel of my disshonorabel discharg of corse I never got any joy from him he fobbed the problem off onto the neks secretry. If he was struk by a bullit he got wot was cumming to him wot gos aruond cums around.

Yes says Fritz The guvnor was seriusly woonded but by all accuonts has servived.

I see I say trying to figger out wich bulet cood hav struk him. It must hav been one of the bulets that hit Kennedy. I only fired three shots the first I kno mist evrything the other two struk the pressident one of those must hav kept going and hit the guvnor. It is unlikly but not impossibel. Wen you hav been aruond guns for as long as I hav you kno that bullets can behav in vry misterius ways.

As I sed continoos Fritz You will probly be charged with Guvnor Conellys shooting after we moove you to the cuonty jail.

Why moove me to the cuonty jail? I am perfeckly comfortabel here I say wishing to remane longer so I can finnish my riteings.

It is standerd proseedure to moove anyone to the county jale after charges hav been lade agenst them. Also we think you mite be saffer there. It will be less kayotic so it will be ezier to proteck you.

Proteck me?

There hav been numerus threts agenst your person he says.

No ones going to hurt me I scoff prettending he is jus trying to scare me but we both kno he speeks the trooth. Why a few of the men rite here in this room probly want to finish me off for wot I did to there fellow blue cote not to menshun good old Jack. I am probly the most hated man in America rite now howevver wen evryone knos the reesons why I shot Kennedy they will qikly change there toon.

Why shood you care anyway? I aks Fritz.

It is my responsabilty to make shure you are kept safe so you can reseev a fare tryal.

A fare tryal? We will see abuot that. Wen do you plan to moove me?

We are not shure yet. Cood be today cood be tomorow.

I shrug my sholders. Now the desishun has been made it makes no diffrense wen I am mooved it is meerly swopping one set of bars for anuther. Howevver it does meen that I need to finish this diery qikly then figger out a way to stash it befor I leeve. I hope they moove me tomorow morning that will giv me twelve huors to finnish as it terns out Junie that is exakly wot happens I am riteing this in the erly huors of Sunday morning rushing agenst the iminent arrival of dawn and my kaptors.

A few minits later approx one ten pm Fritz raps up the interview seshon. Two cops escort me bak to my sell I ignor the barking repporters like the unwanted introoshon they hav becum saveing my comments for my grand reveel the plan for wich is sloly takeing shape.

I am in my sell bearly five minits dont even hav time to resoom these riteings wen a gard raps on the bars signelling he wishes to reapply the cuffs.

Wot is it now? Anuther showup?

Sumone here to see you.

Who?

Sarge didnt say.

The sell door clangs open two gards leed me to the elevater like a stray mutt. I wunder who the mistry visitor is hop and pray it is your Mama with you and Rachel in toe seeing you wood lift my spirits no end. We dessend to the 2nd floor enter an emty room ware inmates can convers with luvved ones. It is split in two by a thik screne of glass a row of metal chares fase each other on eether side of the glass a blak fone muonted to a partishun beside each seet to fasilitate two way comunicashun. Two gards one holding each ellbow steer me to a chare to awate the arrival of I kno not who.

Pressently a door opens on the other side of the glass a gard appeers then ushers in your Mama my hart rejoises untill I see my mother traleing close behind. Her pressense immediatly gets my goat my mother has allways had a tendensy to sho up at the most inoportoon momments inviteing herself into my life wen not wanted. To be frank she is the last person in the world I want to see at that momment so I focuss on your mama who is indeed a site for sore eyes. Despit the manner of our parting jus a day ago and my intense bitternes over her refoosal to aggen liv toggether I feel my hart sloly tareing in two at the thort of possibley never holding her or you or Rachel in my arms aggen. I push the thort away consentrate on the reesons why I hav dun wot I hav dun it eases the pane to sum degree but not entirly.

Your mama looks all aruond her like a baby bird who has tumbeled from the nest. She is unsure wot to do I nod at the blak reseever on the other side of the glass. She piks it up rayses it unsertenly to her ear. They say absense makes the hart gro fonder I do not dout it for the only thing I want in the world at that momment is to hold your mama. She has never looked so luvly her pale skin perfeck her eyes full of a beutiful sadness she is like Sno Wite and I one of the seven dwarfs perhaps Grumpy ha. She wares a lite coton frok meenwhile my mother wares a tired dress with no shape probly prokured from the Salvashun Army she resembals a dumpling swathed in bandiges.

Zdravstvuy Marina I say.

Zdravstvuy Alik she says we continoo to convers in Russian howevver I will rite it in English for you Junie.

Why did you bring that fool with you? I say nodding at my mother.

Shes your mother of corse she came she says her eyes wandring over my fase. Hav they been beeting you?

No they treet me fine. Your not to wurry abuot that I say my words cumming out faster than expekted my voise also slitely higher piched I will admitt seeing your Mama aggen has ratled me sum.

Did you bring Junie and Rachel? I aks reeliseing I forgot to bring the beginings of this diary to giv her no matter I cood not get it thru the thik glass that seprates us anyway. I will hav to devise annuther plan befor I am mooved to the cuonty jail that shood not be diffikult for a man of my mental fakultys.

Yes they are downstares.

I wood like to see them.

They wont let me bring them up. Her eyes dart about. Alka can we tawk about anything we like? Is anybody lissening in?

Oh of corse we can speek about absolootly anything at all I say sarcastikly. Your mama nods gets my meening strate off that the fones are tapped she can be vry shrood wen she wants to be.

Alka they aksed me abuot the gun.

Oh thats nuthing I say And you are not to wurry if theres a tryal. Its all a misstake and I am not gilty.

I dont beleeve you did it she says but I sense sum dout. Evrything will tern out well she finishes half hartedly.

There are peeple who will help me I say putting on a brave fase despit knoing Fritz and his cohorts hav alreddy trased the gun bak to me who knos wot else they may hav discuvvered to bollster there case.

Wot peeple?

A loyyer in New York City. A grate loyyer who has deffended other peeple in simler situashuns. Peeple who hav been unfarely acoosed of rong doing. I am cuonting on him to help out.

Oh Alka she says then befor she can utter anuther word her eyes fill with teers.

Dont cry I say Ah dont cry theres nuthing to cry abuot. Try not to think about it. Evrything is going to be all rite.

Your mama nods but she is unabel to speek the sobs now cumming thik and fast.

And if they aks you anything you hav the rite not to anser. You hav the rite to refoose. Do you unnerstand?

Yes she says thru more teers. It tares me appart to see her in this state to see how wot I hav dun afecks her so. Teers sting my eyes my mother swims in my vishon as she buldozes her way in grabs the reseever from your Mama.

Lee she says I am so worryed abuot you.

Mother I am fine I say my hackells riseing.

Hunny you are so broozed up. Your fase. Wot are they doing to you?

Mother dont wurry I got that in a scuffel.

A scuffel?

Wen they arested me in the picher theeter.

Well I dont trust these peeple Lee. They will do you harm I kno it.

Mother don't be such an allarmist I say even tho I obviusly entertane simler thorts.

Oh Lee this is like a nitemare. Is there anything I can do to help you?

I shake my hedd needing her help like a hole in same. Whenevver my mother interfeers evrything goes to hek in a handbasket I hav lerned from bitter expereense to keep her out of my afares at all costs aks for help only wen absolootly nesesary. On occashon she can be useful she did help me get that erly discharg from the Marines pretending she needed my care after takeing a spill at work. Even so onse free of the serviss I took off for Russia without a werd of warning made a cleen getaway befor she cood mess with my plans. That mite seem harsh but this is the wooman who put me in a orfanage the day after Cristmass day when I was but three yeers of age. I owe her vry litle but she is eckspert at playing the viktim the world allways agenst her. That may be the case I offen feel the same way but I can not allways be the one to fix her probblems.

Mother evrything is fine I say.

Do you hav legal asistance?

Yes mother I kno my rites. I hav a vry fine attornee from New York.

New York? she says haveing understood nun of my conversahun with your mama one of the big advantuges of speeking Russian in her cumpny.

Yes mother he is the loyyer who will serv me best.

Well all rite then she says.

Dont wurry about a thing evrything is going to be fine. Over her sholder I see your mama has composed herself seesed her crying.

I shood like to speek to Marina aggen pleese.

Your mama steps up takes the reseever off of Mother who dusnt want to let it go rellenting only at the last momment. I stare at her until she steps bak to aford us sum privasy.

Marina I say.

Yes Alka.

Youre not to wurry.

All rite.

You hav frends. The Pains. The other Russians in Dallas. They will help you.

In fack the lokal Russians hav helpt your mama menny times bying food clotheing even a playpen for you Junie. To be honnest there interfeering offen angered me a man likes to provide for his famly I hav no need of charitty even if I am pennyless I wood rather stand on my own two feet. The lokal Russians also onse atempted to steel your mama away from me claimeing I was a thret to her person. It is troo I onse slapped her in frunt of them but it was justifyed they were helping us moove into Elspeth St your mama had left the zipper of her dress harfway down I saw red at her brazzen dissplay of flesh. After that insident your mama left for a few days thankflee she saw sense wen I imploored her to retern thus ending a chapter in our lives I am shure neether of us is prowd of.

The Red Cross will also help you and the gurls I say.

Enuff of me she says Wot abuot you?

You mustnt wurry abuot me.

Oh Alka…

I heer the shuffeling of feet behind me the gards are mooveing in it looks like our time is up.

Kiss Junie and Rachel for me I say.

I will she says Alka remember that I love you.

I love you too.

Her eyes onse aggen brim with teers they overflo leeving two silver trales down her cheeks.

Make shure you buy those shoos I say.

Shoos?

For Junie. She cant keep wareing hand me downs from the Pains forevver.

Of corse Alka she says I will get the shoos.

This pleeses me it is the mane reeson I left the munny on her dresser yesserday.

Evrything will work out jus you wate and see I say holding her gaze saying goodbye with my eyes. She nods her chin trembeling teers gather on it then drop to the flor.

Proshchay Alka she whisspers.

I fall into her blew eyes as she hangs up the reseever then she turns leeves the room my mother close behind. The gards leed me off I insist on walking bakwards to wotch your mama untill the last posible secund. As she disapeers thru the door I think of the yung girl I met at that workers ball in Minsk swept off of her

248

feet by a yung American the girl who saled to New York City holding a babe in her arms who setled in a town far from her cuntry of berth it must hav been akin to mooveing to Mars for her. It is troo Junie your mama and I hav had our issews wot marrage dusnt but in my vew we will always be marryed no matter wot cums between us prisson bars whatever. As I hav tole her menny times durring our argooments divorse is out of the qesshun end of converssashun it is not for nuthing that the marrage vows cleerly state till deth us do part.

There all teenagers I protest.

Thirty minits after saying goodbye to your mama the low feeling still in my gut I stand in the elevater handcuffed to three yung men on the way to anuther showup. To add to my wos I hav not had a chanse to call Abt in New York howevver it is the weekend despite my new fuond cellebrity it is unlikely that any loyyer is sitting aruond wateing for Lee Oswald to call.

They are much yunger than me I say You are trying to raleroad me.

Shutup Oswald says a short detektiv wareing a tall hat These men are abuot the same size as you. They are the best we cood do at short notiss.

Oh yeah Im shure you tryed reel hard.

The elevater cums to a hard stop the doors pop open. A cop leeds the way past the booking area folowed by three planesclothes detektivs then we players in the showup all handcufft together. I am in secund posishun as usule. We pass the booking cuonter sum press men with a TV camra appeer from the doors to the garage I make a sper of the momment desishun to put on a sho.

For the last day I hav been fotograffed in a tshirt I shuot.

A cop stands at the cuonter looks at me grim fased.

Ive been fotograffed in a tshurt I repete poynting to my durty shirt And now there takeing me in frunt of a lineup amung these men and that way I will be pikked out. Rite?

Thats rite a detektiv replys admiting in frunt of the press that the authoritees will do anything in there power to stak the dek agenst me.

Outraged I continoo to complane inside the showup yell at the nilon screen seprateing me from my accoosers.

Look at these men I shuot They are not even men they are teenagers they dont look a bit like me.

Complaneing I kno is the rong thing to do I will be pikked out of the lineup for sure by wotever witness stands behind the screne. But I am so angered by the injustiss of it all that I can not stop myself from voiseing my objecshuns. The shuoting does hav one postive result howevver the showup is cut short I am qikly releesed from the conga line of suspecks bundeled bak to my sell.

A few minits latter two men from the Indentifkashun Burow turn up aks if I will consent to haveing fingernale scrapeings takken also sum sampels of hare. It meens finnishing my diary will hav to wate until tonite but the last thing I need is anuther frootless confruntashun I meerly nod my assent the sell door slides open alowing them entry. The two of them go abuot there bizness one useing tweezers to take hare from my hed armpits and down belo the other swobbing beneeth each fingernale with a wet Q tip then scrapeing them with a wooden stick. I feel like a woman at a beuty sallon I half expeck them to put my hare up in rollers neks.

Wen they finish storeing there findings in ruond pill boxes one aks me to sine a form acknolegeing releese of same. Wile willing to submit to there reqest for body sampels just like the fingerprints I am absolootely unwilling I tell them in no unserten turms to sine one singel peece of paper until I hav spokken with my loyyer.

After they abskond with sed body sampels muttring about my refoosal to sertify same I furiusly scribbel these notes for a harf huor. I am raseing agenst the clok comitted to finishing and conseeling these pages befor I am mooved to the cuonty jail. I overherd Fritz tawking to his men it seems the moove will happen Sunday morning. I hav not yet desided wether I shood hold off till after the moove spill the beens at the tryal thereby risking sumthing untoward hapning to me in the meentime or let evryone kno the trooth rite now I leen towards the forma.

Pressently the gard bangs the butt of his weppon on the bars to atrack my atenshun.

Wot is it now?

Your a popullar man he says theres sumone else here to see you.

Oh yes thats me I say tawking lowdly to dissgise shuving the notepad bak under my matress Mister Popullarrity is the name I hav always gone by. Nuthing cood be ferther from the trooth I hav always had trubble makeing frends from elementry skool rite thru middel skool high skool then on into the Marines the same problem folowed me evryware. I had but one frend in the Marines Delgado we offen tawked of leeveing the serviss and joyning Castros cawse. With our millitry traneing we wood be invalubel asets to the Coobans probly becum offissers like Morgan a fellow Marine who did same and fort with the rebbels with grate sucess. I studyed Spanish for a periud in preparashun howevver Delgado like all peeple ultimatly disapointed me he did not want to go thru with the plan I was not abuot to attemp same on my own. Russia was the only plase I made frends eesly the odd man out the funny litle American who had ingeeniusly forged his path to Minsk yuong men and wimmen alike fuond me curius I hav never had a richer soshul life. I made fast frends with menny coworkers at the raydio factory we wood go danseing drinking hunting. I even had sevral gurlfrends befor I met your muther but nun as speshul as her all even Ella who sperned my matrimoanial advanses I reelize now were but a passing fansy.

Hurry it up Oswald snaps the gard I hav becum lost in thort putting on my shoos. I get a riggle on we take the elevater to the 2nd flor visitors room. I wate for sevral minits on my side of the glass untill the door swings open my older bruther Robert walks in. I hav not seen him for qite sum time not sinse befor we left for New Orleens he looks the same as always a shineing ecksample of the American dreem a man with a nise wife nise kids nise home he has always dun the rite thing has Robert.

He walks over to the glass wall his sholders hunched. He takes the blak fone off of the hook I do same. His fase inches from mine he studys me looking for I dont kno wot.

How are you? I aks.

I am fine how are you? He poynts to his eyebrow the spot ware I hav the cut.

Im jus fine. They are treeting me OK. But you kno I can not and wood not say anything even if they werent becos this line is probly tapped.

He nods but I can see he does not reely unnerstand.

I see you hav a new baby he says.

Isnt she a beuty?

She is indeed. I was not aware of her. She came as qite a surprize wen I saw her downstares.

He is probly not alone on that scor. I also nevver tole my mother about Rachels berth as she wood hav given me a lecher about how I cood not aford anuther muoth to feed I am serprized she did not deliver same just now. She also wood hav insisted on cumming over to help that is the kind of help I can do without thank you vry much.

I can see Robert is looking for an explanashun I simpley smile reply Well I was hopeing for a boy then I shrug my sholders You kno how that goes.

He looks at me sturnly it feels like I am under interrogashun all over aggen.

Wot about Marina and the chillren? he aks Wot will happen to them?

Dont wurry about them. Our frends the Pains will take care of them.

Well who you considder to be your frends are no frends of mine.

I leen bak from the glass astuonded at the gall of this man. Who is he to say who I shood or shood not be frends with? Wile I mite hav my own ishoos with the Pains they partikly Rooth hav been extreemly kind to your mama and you girls provideing food clotheing and shelter. I dont qite unnerstand ware this atitood is cumming from altho Robert has always been a vry strate shooter ever sinse we went to Luthran Sunday skool perhaps it is the Pains qaker bakgruond that unnervs him so. There is also a litle of the big bruther litle bruther dinamic happning here he probly can not stand the fack that I hav usserped him made a grater mark on the world than he ever will.

Lee wot in the Sam Hill is going on? he says after an awkwerd silense.

I dont kno I say sudenly feeling five yeers old aggen the litle bruther berrated by his big bruther for leeveing his favrit toys out on the frunt lawn overnite.

You dont kno? Look theyve got your pistul theyve got your rifle theyve got you charged with shooting the president of the united states and a polise ofisser. And you tell me you dont kno? Well I want to kno jus wots going on.

Well that is qite the tirrade I think to myself. His body has becum as stiff as a bord he is mortly ofended to find hisself in such a situashun he shood try standing on the other side of the glass.

I push my sholders bak look him strate in the eye say I jus dont kno wot theyre tawking about. Dont beleeve all this so called evidense.

His response is to fix his eyes with mine try to stare me down will a confeshon out of me but that will only hapen wen I am good and reddy and I wont be telling it to him Ill be telling it to the world.

His eyes stay lokked on mine until I say in a hushed voise Bruther you wont find anything there.

He blinks looks away. I hav spooked him won that game of chiken if we were kids aggen I wood giv him two for flinching.

Hav you fuond yourself a good loyyer yet? he says It suonds like you may need it.

Not yet but I am in the prosess.

Capten Fritz tells me that there is a man in New York you wish to use.

Fritz? Wen did you speke to him?

Last nite.

Last nite?

I hav been bak and forth here sevral times trying to sort things out.

I see. Well yes there is a good man in New York I shood like to use.

Wot is his name?

You jus stay out of it I say. The last thing I need is to hav to explane to him why I want Abt. The fack that Abt has repressented comunists conspireing agenst his preshus government will shurely set him off on anuther tirrade.

Ill get you an attornee down here he says like its allredy desided.

No you stay out of it I tell him aggen.

Stay out of it? Looks like Ive been dragged into it.

No ones dragging you into anything I feel like saying you jus want to interfeer but all I say is Im not going to hav anyone from down here. I want this one.

Well all rite then he says the threttening tone in my voise telling him to leev well enuff alone. Howevver if I kno Robert and his big bruther knos best ways he will not let the matter rest run strate to Fritz take it up with him try to find me a lokal man. I resolve to call Abt as soon as we are dun.

Well Lee he says I hope you kno wot you are doing with regards to this loyyer fella.

Dont you wurry about that I kno exackly wot Im doing.

OK then.

OK.

We stare at each other thru the glass we hav run out of words it is as simpel as that two bruthers who cood not be any more unallike. He wotches me appeers to be on the verge of aksing sumthing probly the qesshun on evryones lips but then thinks better of it meerly lets out a soft sigh gentley plases the handset bak in its cradel. I sit with the reseever still to my ear wotch him walk across the room his footsteps dont make a suond on the tiled flor becos of the glass between us it is like wotching a dreem. The gard opens the door it closes silently behine him.

I hang up my reseever tern to the gards standing beside the door.

I need to call my loyyer.

All rite we will see if we can make that hapen. Cuff him Bill.

They take me bak up to the 5th flor ware a pay fone is muonted on the wall neer the elevater.

He uncuffs me says Make your call.

Can I hav sum paper and a pen pleese?

He takes a notebook from his top pokket tares a page out hands me that and a pen.

Can I hav a litle privasy?

The two cops moove sevral feet away they will still heer evrything I say howevver with no other choise I lift the reseever.

Oprater I am looking for the nummer of a Mister John Abt of New York City.

One momment pleese. Sum stattic cums down the line. I hav two nummers for him here sir. They look like his home and work nummers. Wich wood you like?

I will take both pleese.

She reeds them out I jot them down.

Wood you like me to conneck you to one of them?

It is Saterday afternoon I figger he is more likly to be at home. Yes I say Call his home pleese.

Sertenly sir. Your name?

Lee Oswald.

There is a short pawse as she recognizes my name then she diles the nummer. Wen the call rings out she trys aggen then aks if I wood like to try his offiss. I agree she diles onse aggen there is statik a few cliks and whirs then the fone rings on the other end each unansered ring cawseing my hart to sink a litle further. Eventully the call disconnecks.

I deside to make one more call this time to a nummer I kno off by hart. I tell the oprater to call BL 3-1628 it rings jus onse befor been pikked up.

Hello says Rooth she suonds unserten perhaps afrade of who mite be calling.

Colleck call from Lee Oswald at the Dallas polise dept says the oprater Will you aksept the charges?

Oh. Well yes. Of corse.

You may proseed says the oprater.

This is Lee.

Well hi.

Lissen I need to aks you to do sumthing for me.

I -

I am trying to contak a loyyer in New York City but Im haveing trubble getting hold of him.

I see. Well Im not shure there is a lot I can do.

If I give you his home and work nummers can you try and contak him for me tonite? I am limted as to how offen I can call as you can imagin.

I spose –

Long distanse rates will be down tonite it shoodnt cost too much.

OK.

If you cant reech him tonite keep trying over the weekend. It is vry importent that I speke with him.

All rite she says altho I can tell by the suond of her voise that she is none too tikkled. I will do my best Lee she says half hartedly.

Thank you Rooth that is all I aks.

I hang up not wanting to get into a long conversashun abuot how am I doing how are they treeting me etc I hav been over that too menny times today alreddy.

I retern to my sell lie on my bunk for the neks huor. Flakeing paynt has left strange shapes on the seeling I see a bunny rabit sevral states of the unun also your fase Junie. I sift thru my predikament I do not like the way things are hedding. In less than twenty four huors I hav been charged with two merders yet I am still without legel repressentashun. I suspek there are nefarius purpusses at work that explanes why I can not get in

258

contack with Abt it is not jus becos he is spending the weekend upstate at his lake huose trowt fishing playing a qik eighteen holes there is sumthing more sinnister at play. Yet if the powers that be are trying to keep me from contakting my preffered repressentashun then that in itsself cood be good reeson to stay the corse not be tawked into haveing sum lokal yokel repressent me that is probly wot the authoritees want sum good old boy to do there bidding.

Jus as I ressolve to try harder to sekure the servisses of Mister Abt I heer footsteps in the hallway. A kee slides into the sell door it clangs open the gard cleers his throte.

Oswald. Visiter.

I swing my legs over the bunk stand up see Polise Cheef Curry hisself standing in the doorway with a bespectakled man about fourty yeers old. He towers over Curry cood be a Harlem globetroter excep he is wite. They step into my sell the stranger stooping to prevent strikeing his head on the steel bar atop the sell door.

This heres Mister H Loois Nikkels says Curry Mister Nikkels is presdent of the Dallas bar asosiashun. He wood like to hav a few minits of your time if that is all rite.

I run my fingers thru my hare straten my cloths as best I can. OK.

Ill leeve you two to it then says Curry vacateing the sell to wate outside with the gard.

Nikkels stands there nervusly I spose its not evry day one is in the cumpny of an accoosed presidenshul asassin.

Take a seet I say gestureing to the lower bunk I am always the grashus host ha. He does so hunching over to fit in between the top and botom bunks I sit ferther along there is but two or three feet betwene us.

Wots this all abuot? I aks.

Mister Oswald I am here to see if you hav a loyyer. His voise is deep his words vry delibrate the meerest hint of a lisp soffens his sentenses sum. He is one of those men who is more than acustummed to useing the power of there spokken word to convinse cajole otherwise get there way. I can tell it is a considdrable weppon I wunder if he has been aksed to use it on me. Unsure wether to trust him I ignor his qesshun go strate into wot has becum my standerd denyal.

Well I say I reelly dont kno wot this is all abuot. I hav been incarserated and kept incomoonicado.

Mister Oswald I hav cum up here to see wether you need a loyyer becos as I understand it you hav been charged with killing the pressident. He says this in such a way as to sugest that my innosense or gilt does not interrest him in the slitest.

I veheemently deny those charges.

Be that as it may you will still need a loyyer. Do you hav one? Not yet.

Do you want one?

Do you kno a man by the name of John Abt in New York City?

I dont beleeve I do.

I wood like Mister Abt to repressent me.

I see. Hav you tryed to contack him?

I hav this vry afternoon but so far hav been unsucessful.

I see.

My famly will continoo to try and reech him over the weekend.

Wot if it is not posible to reech him or aqire his servisses? Is there anyone else you wood like?

Do you kno any loyyers who are members of the American Civil Libertys Unoin?

Im not shure I do. I dont think so. Why?

I am a member of that organizashun and wood like sumone who is also a member to repressent me.

So those are your two prefrences? He takes off his glasses wipes them with his pokket hankercheef slides them bak on his nose refolds the hankercheef tuks it bak into his top pokket.

Yes sir. Mister Abt or sumone who is a memmer of the ACLU.

Faleing that? he aks.

Faleing that I spose sumone lokal if I can find a loyyer here who beleeves in anything I beleeve in and beleeves as I beleeve and beleeves in my innocense...

I struggel for the necks words there is sumthing about this Nickels fella perhaps his dissintrest in my gilt or otherwise that makes me want to spill the beens rite here and now. Howevver I cach myself it is not qite time for the grand reveel also he is not my loyyer and as such no client atornee privlege exists between us to proteck me shood he run off and tell Curry I hav confesst.

...beleeves in my innocense as much as he can I finnish I mite let him repressent me.

I see he says his gaze a serchlite illoominateing my innerds. I look down pretend to cleen my fingernales.

Wot I am intrested in knoing rite now he says is do you want the Dallas Bar Assosiashun to try to get you a loyyer?

No not now.

I see.

Releeved that he is not trying to convinse me to ditch Abt I deside to thro him a bone.

But you mite cum bak neks week I say And if I dont get sum of these other peeple to repressent me I mite aks you to find sumone.

Well now all I want to do is to make it cleer to you and to me wether or not you want me or the Dallas bar assosiashun to do anything about getting a loyyer rite now.

How menny times do I hav to say it I think to myself but I meerly state No.

Vry well he says standing up I will perhaps retern neks week to chek in and see that you hav adeqate representashun. If you do not we will see wot we can do.

I wood apreshiate that.

He turns to shake hands thinks better of it puts his hand in his pokket leeves the sell. He joyns Cheef Curry who has been wateing outside chatting to the gard. Curry mumbels sumthing about the press wateing as the two of them wonder off in the direcshun of the elevaters.

I bearly hav time to scrach myself befor the gards are onse aggen jiggeling the lok to my sell manhandeling me downstares to Fritzs offiss. The clok says a few minits past six as I take my usule seet opposit him the offiss is filled with the reglar attendees homiside detecktivs FBI Secret Serviss agents I eye them with disdane the feeling I observ is qite mutuel.

Good evening Mister Oswald says Fritz trying to pressent a veneer of good cheer but looking vry drawen indeed bags under his eyes the size of wheet saks his jowels suffring the affecks of gravvity. Still I myself hav not seen a mirrer sinse my kapture perhaps that is for the best judgeing by the state of those who suruond me.

Good evening Fritz says aggen I understand that you met with your famly this afternoon.

Thats rite.

I hope they are well all things considderd.

Oh they are jus fine I say Dont you wurry abuot them.

Did you manage to reech your loyyer this Abt fella?

Not yet I say But I will keep trying. Thank you for alowing me the use of a fone.

Of corse. That is your rite as you well kno.

I do indede.

Okey dokey lets get started then. Yesterday you tole me that you never owned a gun is that correck?

Of corse its correck.

OK he says I want to sho you sumthing.

He opens a plane brown envellope slides out a foto. I recognize it immediatly it is an enlarged sekshun of the foto your mama took of me in the bak yard at W Neely St with my rifel and pistul. Poseing for the foto had seemed like a fine idea at the time rekording myself for your benefit Junie also posterrity howevver I now see wot a hooge blunder it cood tern out to be.

How do you explane this? Fritz says the beginings of a smile on his lips.

Well thats not me! I say. So far I hav been happy to play nise for the most part it is now time to sho sum outrage at the predikament this innosent man finds hisself in.

But thats your fase rite there says Fritz.

Thats not my fase! I yell.

Then whos is it?

Well its not me. Sumone has superimpossed my fase on that body.

Oh so it is your fase then?

No its not even my fase. Its jus sumone that kinda looks like me.

Jus kinda looks like you he repetes the words suond holow even to me.

Thats not me. And the other part of the pitcher is not me at all.

Other part?

You kno. The arms and legs.

Hav you ever seen this pitcher befor?

Never.

Wot wood you say if I tole you it was recuvered from Mrs Pains garage?

I wood hav nuthing to say at all.

You still clame never to hav seen it befor?

Thats rite.

It has never been in your poseshun?

Thats rite.

Mister Oswald this reely makes vry litle sense.

Finely sumthing we can agree on.

Fritz reeches into the envalope aggen pulls out the orignal foto.

The enlargment I hav jus showen you was takken from this foto he says It was fuond in a serch of the Pains garage.

I hav never seen it befor.

How do you explane that this pitcher wich you say you hav never seen befor was fuond with your poseshons?

I dont kno how it got there.

Reely?

Reely. Anyone cood hav put it there.

I cast my eyes aruond the room the others stare bak defyantly they kno I am lyeing I care not one jot.

Howevver I say I do kno all about fotografy I hav dun a lot of it myself. Jus by looking at that smaller foto I can tell that the bigger one is an enlargment of it. They hav both obviusly been made by sumone unknowen to me.

Mister Oswald we made the enlargment.

See?

But we didnt make the orignal.

Sumone did.

Why wood they do that?

Serch me. You wood need to aks them.

Can you think of any way that sumone wood be able to superimpose your hed on that body?

Oh well now that wood be easy. They wood jus need a foto of my hed and sumone with a body like mine.

How wood they get a foto of your hed? he aks.

I leen bak in my chare reddy to hold forth releese a grate sermon on the fotografic arts. Well Capten Fritz I say how menny camras are there rite here in this bldg?

I hav no idea.

But youll agree there are menny?

Yes that is rite.

And youll agree that I hav had my foto takken menny times over the past day wile being transfered from my sell to your offise and bak aggen?

Yes Ill agree with that.

Not to menshun wile being takken to showups and the like.

Agreed.

All rite. So all sumone has to do is take one of the menny fotos of my fase and put it over the image of a body. It is all quite simpel reely.

I see.

I understand fotography reel well I tell him. If you gave me sum time I cood proove to you vry qikly that that is not my fase on that foto. It has been made by sumone else.

Im not shure I agree with you there Mister Oswald but we will hav our eksperts take a look at it.

Bah! Eksperts. They will only find wot you want them to find.

That is your opinun Mister Oswald but I can ashure you that evryone here is working hard to make sure you are treeted farely and justly.

Oh yes Im shure you are rite. Evryone wants to look after Lee Oswald.

That is correck.

Well I hav had qite enuff of this I say not wishing to discuss the foto ferther I dont think I want to anser any more qessshuns rite now.

If thats the way you feel why dont you go on bak to your sell and sit a spell to think things thru he says an air of viktory suruonding him that I hav not witnesed thus far.

The press bays ceeselessly for my atenshun as we pass thru there scrimage. I am weery of there game but consoll myself that there eegerness to heer my evry utterense cood play rite into my hands.

Dinner wates in my sell meetloaf you wood not feed to a stray dog rise pudding the skin hard as a drum I eat evry muothfull bilding strength to get me thru the nite.

Aruond 8pm I take a brake from labering over these wurds make anuther attemp to call Abt. A detektive with a most unusule monniker Poppelwell walks me to the pay fone I attemp to call Abt sevral times both at home and at work but to no avale. I can only hope Rooth is doing same.

I return to my sell onse aggen work on these historik notes.

At 9.30pm I am struk by an overwelming urge to heer your Mamas voise. Poppelwell aggen takes me to the pay fone the oprater connecks me to the Pain residense.

Hello Lee says Rooth.

Marina pleese I say eshewing any plesentrys all I can think abuot is heering your mamas voise also yours Junie altho it wood be gurgels not words cumming from your sweet muoth.

Lee she—

Marina pleese I say aggen.

She is not here Lee.

Wot do you meen she is not here?

She is not here. The polise or the secret serviss or sumone took her and the chillren and your mother to a hotel this afternoon.

I see I say the familar vale of anger dessending over my eyes Can you giv her a messege from me pleese.

Ill try my best says Rooth wich I kno is the trooth Rooth will do almost anything for other peeple. Im not shure wen I will see her or tawk to her aggen tho she says.

Well wen you do tell her that I want her bak with you.

All rite.

I want her to stay with you. I do not want her suruonded by the authoritees. They will fill her hed with all kinds of crazy thorts.

I understand Lee.

I hope you do Rooth. I also need to kno exackly ware she is as I may need her at any momment.

Understood she says her voise shakeing. My harsh wurds hav unerved her hopfuly my displessure will be relayed to your mama and she will act on it altho you never kno with Mama she can be vry hedstrong indede. In that sense we are two pees in a pod.

Thank you Rooth I say soffening my tone sum I will call aggen tomorow.

All rite Lee she says Good nite.

Good nite.

Sunday

Dawns erly lite leeks thru the prison windos my sell looks almost hevenly. I awate my transfer to the cuonty jale feeling vry allone my inabilty to reech Abt heer your Mamas voise reinforseing that a heeros path is not an eesy one.

Late last nite I was offishully advised that my transfer to the cuonty jale will take plase this morning. Today is my third day in this sell Hermans nummer three aggen cums to the fore a postive sine it is the rite momment to reveel all.

These riteings were a frantik rush agenst time Junie howevver I now kno I will acheeve my gole finish them befor the moove. Of corse I must divest myself of these pages befor then fortunatly I hav devised a cunning plan to acheeve same. As the gards leed me to the elevater to dessend to the bassment garage I will fane tripping on the lose tile the fat cop stumbeled on yesserday. I will tumbel to the floor slide fase down towards the elevaters with my hands cuffed to the frunt it shood not be difcult to extrikate the notebook hidden under my shert same as wen I smugled my historic diary out of Russia. I will slip it thru the narow gap between elevater and floor let it flutter down the shaft to the wateing dark belo. There it will remane amung candy rappers cigret butts and such until I hav reveeled to the world my reesons for the clensing. Folowing that I will tell the authoritees of its lokashun they will of corse be eeger to retreev this historik record use it as evidense agenst me then hopfuly they will pass it on to you Junie its riteful owner.

Howevver sekreting this diary for anuther time is but one part of a much more dramattik reveel I hav planned for today. As usule I hav outsmarted my kaptors worked out a way to announse my motivs befor they can silense me. I kno the press will be frenzyed wen I leeve the bilding evry newspaper raydio TV stashun in the world asembled in the bassment garage awateing my exit. I will insist on wareing my blak swetter to cuvver this durty tshirt look my Sunday best as I step into the floodlites live TV brawdcasting my evry move to the nashun as two detektivs one on my left arm one on my rite steer me towards a wateing sqad car Fritz leeding the way. A momment befor we reech the car I will pawse the cops to my left and rite look up wundering why I hav stoppt I wate for as long as it takes for silense to dessend befor ansering the qesshun that has been on the world lips sinse Friday tell evryone exackly wot happened in Deely Plaza that afternoon more importently why. Evryone will kno the undispootabel trooth I am a grate man who purformed a heeroic dede in serviss of mankind acheeved the imposible useing my wits and a cheep rifle as my only weppons nevver aggen will anyone qesshun the grateness of Lee Harvey Oswald.

The elevater bell chimes footsteps approche it is time to finnish these scribellings conseel them on my person if you hav red this far Junie I trust

Also by Simon Foster

THE LUKE BALES NOVELS

Wanderlust

Lazarus

Find out more at www.simonfosterauthor.com

About the Author

Simon Foster hails from Sydney, Australia, but has called New York home for many years. He holds a degree in writing and pays the bills by working as an ad man: a job that, whilst ranking just above car salesman in the credibility stakes, has helped him hone his writing skills and seen him walk the red carpet at the Emmys. Married with two daughters, he cycles, reads and visits the pub for relaxation.

To keep up with the latest on Simon's writing, subscribe at simonfosterauthor.com.

Please consider leaving a review of *The Diary of Lee Harvey Oswald* wherever you purchased the book. Thank you.